P9-CSC-753
Lost
Melody

LORI COPELAND

and VIRGINIA SMITH

ZONDERVAN.com/
AUTHORTRACKER
follow your favorite authors

ZONDERVAN

Lost Melody

This title is also available as a Zondervan ebook. Visit www.zondervan.com/ebooks.

This title is also available in a Zondervan audio edition. Visit www.zondervan.fm.

Requests for information should be addressed to:

Zondervan, *Grand Rapids, Michigan 49530*

Library of Congress Cataloging-in-Publication Data

Copeland, Lori.
Lost melody : a novel / Lori Copeland and Virginia Smith.
p. cm.
ISBN 978-0-310-28986-9 (softcover)
1. Women pianists—Fiction. I. Smith, Virginia, 1960- II. Title.
PS3553.O6336L67 2011
813'.54—dc22 2011022690

Any Internet addresses (websites, blogs, etc.) and telephone numbers in this book are offered as a resource. They are not intended in any way to be or imply an endorsement by Zondervan, nor does Zondervan vouch for the content of these sites and numbers for the life of this book.

Cover photography: Caleb Rexius
Interior design: Katherine Lloyd, The DESK

Printed in the United States of America

11 12 13 14 15 16 17 18 /DCI/ 21 20 19 18 17 16 15 14 13 12 11 10 9 8 7 6 5 4 3 2 1

Chapter 1

December 8

"Taxi, ma'am?"

Jill paused on the sidewalk just outside her hotel. Taxi or subway? A taxi would get her to Seventh Avenue early, with plenty of time to sign in and get her bearings before the workshop began. It would probably cost a ton, though. Everything in New York cost five times more than she'd budgeted for this trip. Besides, her legs itched for a walk. She needed to work off some of the excited energy that had kept her up most of the night.

Carnegie Hall, here I come!

She fastened the top button of her coat beneath her chin and smiled at the hotel doorman. "No, thank you. They told me at the front desk there's a subway station nearby."

The man pointed a gloved hand down the street. "Just around that corner. Can't miss it."

Jill hitched the leather strap of her music portfolio higher on her shoulder and took off at a brisk pace over concrete wet with melted snow. Clouds the color of the fat pigeons she'd seen strutting through Central Park yesterday threatened to gift the city with more snow before the morning ended. Of course she'd run out of her room without her hat. She shot an *I-dare-you-to-snow-on-my-parade* grin toward the sky.

Steam rose in thick ribbons from gutters to pollute her airspace with unpleasant underground odors, which she ignored. Yellow flashed in the corner of her eye and a taxicab sped past, spraying the sidewalk with dirty slush. A few heavy drops hit her left pant leg. She gasped and slid to a stop to examine the damage. Not bad, thank goodness. When she got to the Institute she'd run a wet paper towel over the black fabric, and they'd be good as new.

A completely un-Jill-like giggle tickled in her throat. Nothing could dampen her spirits today.

When she rounded the building on the corner, she spied the subway entrance halfway down the block. A handful of people, all of them bundled against the frigid weather, descended the concrete stairs. A couple of fat snowflakes floated in the air before her eyes and landed on her coat sleeve, instantly sucked into nonexistence by thirsty wool. Jill increased her pace, eager to get below ground before the snow began in earnest.

Down below, she purchased a MetroCard from an automated ticket machine and approached the cage-like turnstile behind a tall man in an overcoat. When she attempted to insert the card into the slot, the portfolio slid off her shoulder with a jerk and her fingers fumbled. The card slipped out of her grasp, danced like a jitterbug contestant on a phantom gust of air, and landed on the dirty floor inside the turnstile.

Jill gasped. "My card!"

The tall man turned and appraised her predicament in a second. "Allow me."

He retrieved the card and handed it across the thick metal

bar with the courtly flourish of a gentleman returning a lady's handkerchief. Kind, dark eyes caught Jill's and sparked with ... something. She found herself smiling, drawn by his charming, old-fashioned courtesy.

"Thank you." She took the card and inserted it into the slot. Who said New Yorkers weren't friendly? The turnstile rotated, allowing her entry. "For a second I thought I might have to crawl under."

He dipped his head in a hint of a bow. "My pleasure to come to the aid of a beautiful woman."

Heat threatened to rise into her cheeks at the compliment. His words were perfectly articulated, and spoken with the faint accent of one who had long ago adopted English as his primary language. Jill looked closer at him as they walked together down a set of stairs toward the subway platform. He was at least twenty years her senior, maybe twenty-five. Roughly the age Daddy would have been if he'd lived. His round face was graced with a deeply clefted chin, and silver-streaked dark hair swooped away from a part on the side of his head. He wore a blindingly white scarf twisted with an elegant flair at his throat. His hands — she always noticed hands — were slender and long-fingered, covered with soft, fawn-colored leather.

The roar of an approaching train echoed up the stairwell.

"You are catching the W line?" he asked.

"Yes, that's right."

"As am I." He quickened his pace. "I believe our train is arriving."

Jill glanced at the sign above her head and verified that the train was the one that would take her to Carnegie Hall's Weill Music Institute. She hurried to catch up, and arrived at the man's side as the train pulled to a stop. The compartment was nearly full of commuters. The doors opened, and only a few people exited. The rest compressed themselves to make room for those entering. Every seat was taken, so Jill filed as far inside as space allowed and grasped the overhead bar to brace for the forward motion, facing the stranger. The doors closed, and they began to move.

"I'm so glad we didn't miss this train. I don't want to be late today." She snapped her mouth shut. What was the matter with her, babbling like an idiot? She must be more nervous than she realized.

Well, if she was, then who could blame her? Today was probably the most important step she'd ever taken in her career. To study with masters—no, with *legends* of modern classical music—was a dream come true. This weeklong workshop would culminate in an evening that she'd dreamed of since she was seven years old and first placed her fingers on the silky keys of a piano. She would play Carnegie Hall.

Okay, just a recital, not a real performance. But it was an important step, and one day she *would* headline one of the famous Carnegie Hall concerts herself.

"You have an important meeting, yes?" He nodded toward the portfolio hanging from her shoulder.

"Sort of. I'm attending a music workshop this week."

A delighted smile lit his features. Even, white teeth appeared between the generous lips. "You are a pianist."

Jill's mouth dropped open. "How did you know?"

"I suspected the moment I saw you." He straightened to his full height, his chin tilted upward. "You carry yourself like an *artiste*."

She experienced a flash of pleasure. Back home, she was once accused of putting on airs, of walking down the street with her nose in the air as though she thought she was better than the other residents of Seaside Cove. Sort of like this man was doing right now.

His posture returned to normal, and his smile became conspiratorial. "Besides, I recognize the brand of your portfolio and surmised that it contains sheet music."

His laughter filled the compartment, and she joined in. Heads turned to glance at them, then people returned to their private contemplations of books or newspapers, or their study of the graffiti-covered concrete tunnel walls rushing by outside the windows. The train swayed, and a dark-haired child standing in front of her clutched his mother's hand. Jill tightened her grip on the overhead bar.

"What composer do you favor? Beethoven, perhaps, or Mozart? No, wait." A slender gloved finger rose to rest on his lips as he studied her. "Liszt. Definitely Liszt."

Delighted at the accuracy of his guess, Jill once again exclaimed, "How could you know that?"

Piercing dark eyes sparked with shared passion. "I see the love of the mystical in your eyes. Liszt's spiritual nature, his ever-searching musicality, would appeal to someone like you."

Jill's smile warmed with a sudden kinship. He was a musician too. Of course he was.

"My name's Jill." She released the bar to extend her hand.

He captured her fingers, pressed them with his. "Robert."

The screech of steel reached her ears in the split-second before she pitched forward. Something hit her hard from behind. She crashed into Robert, who tumbled backward. The cry of tortured metal drowned out the passengers' startled shrieks. Glass shattered. Bodies sprawled. The dark-haired boy bounced off of the ceiling, his arms and legs flailing. But the ceiling was where the wall should be. Then with a terrific crash, it wasn't there at all.

Screams.

Pain.

Darkness.

Jill woke minutes or hours later, she didn't know which. An agonizing pain in her left hip reduced her breath to tiny gulps. A tearful, high-pitched keen from close by filled her ears. For a moment she could hear nothing else, then other sounds gradually filtered through. A man's sobs. A woman's voice whispering the Lord's Prayer. Water trickling not far from her head.

She opened her eyes. A dim spot of light shone in the distance. Around her, darkness shrouded everything. Something lay across her chest, the weight crushing her, pinning her down. She tried to push it off.

Mistake. The movement sent shafts of agony slamming through her body. Stars danced in her vision, and she gasped in a hissing breath that expelled with a near-scream.

"Jill? You are alive." A voice near her head whispered something in another language, something incomprehensible. "Do you hear me?"

Something familiar about that voice. She tried to clear her head, to focus through the pain. Where was she? Who owned that voice? Memory returned in a rush, like a tide crashing onto the rocky shore back home. New York. The subway. The man who knew she loved to play Liszt.

"Robert." Her voice sounded raspy, faint. The weight across her body robbed her of breath. "There's something … on me.

Can't breathe. Can't see."

"On me too." A gentle pressure squeezed her right hand. Robert's fingers still grasped hers. "We are trapped together. Are you badly injured?"

"I ... don't know." The pain in her left hip was so severe she couldn't focus on anything else at first. Gradually another throbbing ache seeped through to her consciousness.

No.

A sob caught in her throat. "My left hand. I—I think it's injured."

No, God, please. Not my hand.

Robert understood immediately. "For a musician, music is breath. Life. An intimate form of worship non-musicians will never understand. Do not despair. God will not take that from you." His grip on Jill's fingers tightened.

She returned the pressure. "Are you okay, Robert? Are you injured?"

A pause. "Don't be concerned for me."

Something in his voice alarmed her. His hand squeezed hers once more, then loosened. The sound of shallow breathing near her ear was faint, nearly drowned out by the cries that filled the air all around them.

From far away, a man's voice echoed through the subway tunnel. "Hold on! Help is on the way." The thump of heavy boots on concrete. A beam of light flashed in the distance. Rescuers.

She ignored the pain and drew as deep a breath as the crushing weight on her chest allowed. "Help." Her voice sounded pitifully small. She tried again. "We're trapped. Help us. Please."

The effort sent pain exploding through her skull. Darkness closed in, and Jill knew no more.

Chapter 2

Thursday, November 24
Almost One Year Later

A ribbon of steam wisped upward and lingered for a final shadowy dance before the air cooled it into oblivion. Jill closed her eyes against the onslaught of an unwelcome memory.

Steam rising from gutters along the city street. A yellow taxicab speeding by.

"Another headache?"

At the sound of her grandmother's voice, the image dissolved. Jill fumbled in the box for a teabag and dropped it into her mug. She hadn't heard Nana come up the stairs, and the door that separated Jill's top floor apartment from the main house stood open, as it almost always did. One of the hazards of living with a relative — especially a nosey one — was a total lack of privacy.

"I'm fine." She pasted on a perky smile and didn't quite meet Nana's gaze.

"You're not fine. You haven't been since the accident." Shrewd eyes, heavily shaded with bright blue eye shadow, narrowed. "Do you want me to get your pain medicine?"

The kettle's insistent scream filled the cozy kitchen.

Grinding metal, screeching steel . . .

Jill snatched it off the burner. "I'll be okay. Really." She poured steaming water into her mug and held up the kettle in Nana's direction. "There's plenty left. Do you have time for a cup before you go?"

"No, I must be running along." She wrapped a Chinese silk scarf around her neck, her way of hiding evidence of the passing years. No growing old gracefully for Ruth Parkins. At seventy-nine she still dyed her hair the defiant, flaming red of her youth, ordered her underwear from the Victoria's Secret catalog, and declared to anyone who would listen that Father Time wouldn't take her out without a fight. "What time is your date tonight?"

"Greg will be here at seven. He made reservations for dinner in the city at eight."

"Oh, I'll be home long before seven." She extracted a pair of gloves from her coat pocket and pulled them on. "Are you sure you don't want to come with me? It will give you something to do, someplace to go."

Jill ignored the ill-concealed note of concern in the question and focused her attention on the mechanics of opening the sugar bowl, scooping out a spoonful, sprinkling it into the steaming tea. For a fleeting moment she considered accompanying Nana to her church knitting group. It *would* provide a distraction. But the minute Nana's cohorts laid eyes on her they'd rope her into volunteering for something. Probably put her in charge of organizing the music for the Christmas party. Jill's throat tightened. No. Not happening.

"Don't worry about me. I plan to go see Mom later this afternoon."

"That's good, dear. Take that poinsettia in my living room, would you? She would have loved that." Nana referred to Mom in the past tense, as though the thin, gaunt woman who awoke each morning in a skilled nursing center was gone. The stroke had taken her motor and speech skills, but inside her mother's haunted eyes Jill still saw the occasional flash of recognition.

"Well, I'm off. I'll see you tonight." Nana disappeared, leaving the scent of Estée Lauder Clean Linen in her wake.

Jill tracked her grandmother's progress by the sound of her footsteps down the narrow wooden stairs. Twelve, thirteen, fourteen … Her spoon kept time as she stirred her tea. The front door closed with a bang, and a heavy silence rose up the stairwell toward her. Like fog rolling in from the ocean, creeping toward the rocky finger of land where the lighthouse stood tall and brave, its light a visible warning that saved lives.

No warning. Women screaming. Bodies flying.

Jill's hand trembled so violently that hot water sloshed over the mug's edge, burning her fingers. She set the cup down and flapped her hand to cool the stinging pain. No brave lighthouse here. Just a mistake, an accident. A survivor who should have died with the others.

The nagging ache in her hip reminded her she had not walked away from the accident without injury. Six weeks in the hospital, even longer recuperation at home. Two surgeries on her left hand, and still the shattered cartilage on the thumb and forefinger had not healed properly. She would never dominate the keyboard as she once had, would never again play with the liquid grace of a gifted pianist.

She wiped the mug with a towel and carried it into the other room. The dark Christmas tree looked lonely with no ornaments and no packages beneath it. Nana had insisted on putting it up after they finished decorating the big one downstairs. Said it would put Jill in the holiday spirit. So far, it hadn't worked.

The tree downstairs had at least a dozen brightly wrapped packages beneath the bottom branches, all of them addressed to Jill in Nana's spidery script. Guilt stabbed at her. She should do some shopping before she visited Mom this afternoon. Make an effort to get into the Christmas spirit. Nana had hinted that she was nearly out of the peach-scented bath oil she liked, and Greg needed a new wool scarf and gloves. The guilt evaporated, replaced with lethargy that hung like heavy weights from her limbs. Join all those people that crowded the shopping malls this time of year? Not yet. Maybe tomorrow, or next week. She still had time before Christmas.

She opened the curtains in the big picture window in an effort to coax some light from the cloud-covered sky into the room, and stood for a moment looking out over the small town that had been her home as long as she could remember. Narrow streets. Rows of tightly clustered buildings. Wooden plank docks lined with moored boats that pitched with the motion of the dark water. In the distance, the lighthouse stood sentinel over the rocky shoreline. A ship's horn blasted, a huge tanker. She sipped tea and followed its progress as it sliced through the narrow channel on its way to Halifax Harbor a few miles away. On the docks below, people paused to watch the ship's passage. A few waved at the crew standing on the deck.

When the tanker had moved past the lighthouse, beyond the edges of Seaside Cove, the gawkers below continued going about their business. The oppressive silence returned. Jill positioned herself on the sofa facing the window, her back to the shrouded object in the corner. From beneath the padded cover, she heard the piano's call. It tugged at the edges of her mind, the lonely, desolate cry of a forsaken lover.

Kind, dark eyes smiling into hers. *What composer do you favor? Liszt. Definitely Liszt.*

What was with her today? Everything seemed to remind her of the accident. She needed to think about something else. With a savage gesture, Jill seized the remote control and jabbed the Power button. Thank goodness for the mind-numbing distraction of daytime television.

~

"Listen, Bradford, I hear what you're saying. I just don't know if this town can handle a whole flock of tourists." Mr. Allen, owner of the Midshipman's Inn, picked up the last of the cookies from the tray his wife had placed between them and ate half of it in a single bite.

Greg Bradford leaned toward the polished maple coffee table and set his china cup on the matching saucer. He remained on the edge of the chenille sofa, his arms resting on his knees, and held the older man's eyes. "It'll take some work, but I think it's a vital move. We have to take action to establish a solid tourist trade here in Seaside Cove. If we're going to survive, we need an influx of money in the town's economy. Outside money."

Mr. Allen puckered his lips and leaned against the chair back. "What do we have to offer tourists? We're just plain folks in these parts."

"We have the Atlantic Ocean, and charter fishing, and a lighthouse, and unique shops, and several great locally run restaurants." Greg opened his arms wide to indicate the Inn's tastefully decorated front room, complete with a bay window overlooking the harbor. "We have local charm, including your place here. The Midshipman's Inn is a terrific B&B, one of the best in Nova Scotia. It will play an important part in our new tourism program."

Interest sparked in the older man's eyes. "A friend of mine runs a B&B over in Peggy's Cove. His place is full every day of the summer. Raking in the money, he is."

"That's exactly what I mean." Greg folded his hands and rested them on his legs. "Seaside Cove has every bit as much to offer tourists as Peggy's Cove. There's no reason we shouldn't have as big a tourist industry as they do."

"Our wharf's looking a bit shabby, though. Have to spend some money fixing that up." Mr. Allen's eyes narrowed. "That's what Samuels is going on about. Says you'll drive the town to bankruptcy, and all the business owners with it."

Greg steeled his features against the grimace that threatened to appear at the mention of Richard Samuels, a current councilman on the Halifax Regional Council, and an outspoken opponent to Greg's tourism development plan. He picked up his cup and sipped lukewarm coffee, trying to give himself time to come up with the correct response. Samuels represented a small but powerful group of change-resistant residents who preferred to keep everything the same—always. Couldn't they see that the town needed to generate some revenue? The sidewalks were cracking, a quarter of the streetlights didn't work, and most of the public buildings were in need of repair.

"It will take some effort to get this place ready, by the town and by individuals, especially business owners." Greg caught and held Mr. Allen's eyes. "But I think the investment will pay off. If we can demonstrate that we have the infrastructure in place to handle an increase in tourism, then when I'm elected to Halifax Regional Council, we can lobby for additional governmental money. That's a critical element in my plan."

A thoughtful look crossed the man's features. "A couple of my rooms could use a bit of attention." He glanced toward the ceiling, above which lay several of the Inn's rooms. "And the building needs a fresh coat of paint to look her best. Been meaning to do that for some time now."

"The whole town could use a fresh coat of paint, my law office included." Greg grinned. "I've been thinking when the weather warms up we could have a couple of community clean-up days where everybody pitches in and helps."

Mr. Allen leaned back in his chair, studying Greg like he was contemplating a chess move. "So, what exactly is it you want from me, Bradford?"

"Your support," Greg replied without hesitation. "The election is six months away, and things are already heating up. In order to be elected as Seaside Cove's representative on the council, I need influential people like you to speak out for me. If the subject comes up, tell people you support the increased tourist trade program I'm proposing. And," he ducked his head, "if you're not doing anything Monday night, I'd sure appreciate you coming out to the town meeting and letting it be known that you support me as a candidate."

"In other words, you want me to go head-to-head with Samuels and his crew." A slow smile crept across the older man's lips. "Don't mind that a'tall."

Relief washed over Greg. With Mr. Allen in his camp, he had an important ally in the community of Seaside Cove. "Thank you, sir."

Mr. Allen got to his feet. "I suppose you'll be needing to do some fund-raising for this campaign of yours."

Apparently, the meeting was drawing to a close. Greg set his cup down and stood. "I'm spending as little as I can on the campaign, but mailers and postage and signs cost money." That was one part of campaigning he detested. Dad advised that he needed to get over his reluctance, be bold. But people in this town worked hard for their money, and he hated asking them to part with any of it.

"Thought so." Mr. Allen reached into the breast pocket of his shirt and pulled out a folded check. "Been planning to support you all along, Bradford. Just been waiting for you to ask."

Greg took the check, then clasped the man's hand in his. "Thank you. Your support means a lot to me."

Allen walked him toward the door. "How's that pretty girl of yours doing? She recovered from that accident?"

His coat hung on a rack near the front door. Greg shrugged into it before answering. "Jill's doing well. She's looking forward to Christmas this year, since she pretty much missed out on it last year."

Greg focused on fastening his buttons. At least, he *thought* Jill was looking forward to Christmas. She'd put up her tree, anyway. The accident still bothered her, which was understandable. It had been a terrible tragedy, one she was lucky to have survived. Almost a hundred people lost their lives in the subway crash, and she'd nearly been one of them.

Like it always did, the thought of how close he'd come to losing Jill hit him like a fist in the gut. Without Jill he might as well find a dark cave to live out his days in solitude. All his plans for the future, all his goals and dreams, included her.

He thanked Mr. Allen again and bid him good-bye. A cold breeze ruffled his hair with salt-scented fingers before he covered his head with his Stetson. When the front door of the Midshipman's Inn closed behind him, Greg followed the footpath to the small parking lot in the rear of the building, his thoughts on Jill. She hadn't been the same since the accident. Completely understandable. It had been a tragic, life-changing occurrence. But in recent months she was starting to look like her old self again. She'd gained back some of the weight she lost during her recovery, and every now and then he saw the old sparkle in her eyes. Maybe all those appointments with the therapist were helping. She didn't play the piano anymore, though, which bothered him. Shouldn't she want to play again? It had been so much a part of her life before. Not just the performances, but hours and hours of playing every day. Surely she missed that.

He arrived at his car and punched the button to unlock the door. As he slid behind the steering wheel, a smile stole over his lips. What Jill needed was something to look forward to, something to focus on. And he had just the thing.

Chapter 3

Centerside Nursing was lit with festive Christmas trees and fragrant evergreen. Jill found Mom parked in her favorite location, in front of the bay window in the sunroom. The nurses knew she favored the spot and rolled her out there every afternoon to watch the sun descend toward the horizon. No sun today, though, just heavy gray clouds. Jill set a large red poinsettia on the window shelf, and bent to kiss her.

"Hi, Mom."

Mom lifted her head, then dropped her chin back to her chest. Her left side curled, her lips fixed in a perpetual droop. Mom would be horrified if she were aware of her appearance. She'd once been a proud woman like her mother, Nana, but the stroke had stripped her of dignity.

Unbuttoning her coat, Jill slid out of the wool. "It's going to snow. Isn't that marvelous? You always loved snow."

Fat, puffy flakes landing on her coat sleeve ...

A smiling nurse appeared. "There you are, Ms. King. We wondered if you were going to make it today."

"I got involved in something and lost track of time." Jill avoided the woman's gaze. Judge Judy's docket this afternoon had been a doozy. "But Mom knows I wouldn't miss a Thursday."

The woman glanced at Mom. "Lorna's had a good day." Her voice rose, both in volume and pitch. "Haven't you, honey?"

Mom didn't acknowledge the question. Sometimes Jill imagined her mother raising her head and snapping, "I'm not deaf, and I'm not your honey." Of course, that was just Jill's own irritation coming through. Several of the staff members practically shouted when talking to Mom, as though the louder they spoke, the more likely Mom would understand the words. As far as the doctors could tell, the stroke had not affected her hearing, only her ability to speak coherently and her cognitive processes. Still, they were all kind and competent at Centerside, and Jill was grateful for the care they gave her mother.

She placed a hand on Mom's shoulder. The bones felt brittle beneath a thin cotton blouse and even thinner skin. "Did she eat?"

"A bit. I hope to tempt her with a bite or two of custard before she goes to sleep." She stepped toward the window and picked up the poinsettia. "How lovely. I'll just take this to her room. It will brighten the windowsill with a touch of the holidays."

"Thank you."

When the nurse left, Jill pulled a wing-back chair closer to the wheelchair and sat down before she began her customary one-sided chat. "I can't stay long today, Mom. Greg and I have a date tonight. He's taking me to dinner at 44 North, so I'll need to get dressed up. I thought I'd wear my burgundy dress with the black belt. Remember that one?"

She paused, but didn't expect a response. A glimmer of moisture appeared in the corner of Mom's mouth, and Jill wiped it away with an edge of the terrycloth bib that protected her mother's pretty pink blouse.

"Greg told me to tell you he's sorry he hasn't visited in a while. Between his law practice and the election, he's so busy he hardly has a free minute. But you'll definitely see him at Christmas."

Visits were so much easier with her boyfriend along to share the burden of conversation. Everything was easier with Greg around. His unending energy and boisterous enthusiasm had coaxed Jill back to life last year. After the accident he'd rushed to her bedside in New York, and spent more time there than in Seaside Cove during her hospital stay, even with a busy law practice to maintain and an upcoming election looming over his head. He was so patient with her recovery, even though he couldn't possibly understand the depth of her loss. How could he? Though he had a lovely singing voice, Greg didn't know a sonata from a waltz.

I see the love of the mystical in your eyes. Liszt's spiritual nature, his ever-searching musicality, would appeal to someone like you. The memories rose again.

Jill's throat tightened. She rose and paced to the window. The man's image was seared in her memory. Robert. She had not learned his last name. There hadn't been enough time before the crash. Before he died. He, and so many others. The ER doctor told her over and over how fortunate she was, the only survivor in that part of the train.

With an effort, she turned and gave her mother a bright smile that went unnoticed. "So, Mom, what do you want for Christmas? I haven't done any shopping yet, but I need to get started soon. It's only a month away. Would you like some new clothes? And what do you think about a housecoat for Nana? Hers is getting pretty ratty."

Jill prattled on, filling the silence in the dayroom with inconsequential chatter about Nana and Greg, and when she ran out of fresh news about them, the latest antics of the afternoon soap opera divas. Mom never moved, never raised her head. Sometimes when Jill visited, she interrupted the monologue with an unintelligible string of babble, her eyes urgent with a message that remained frustratingly incomprehensible. Not this evening. Today, like many other times, she seemed unaware of Jill's presence.

After she ran out of things to talk about, Jill fell silent. Outside, the sun had become a dim orange glow on the underbelly of low-hanging clouds. From somewhere in the depths of the nursing home, a phone rang twice and was answered.

"I dreamed about playing last night." Jill let the words fall quietly between them. They hung in the air, and left the relief of confession in their wake. "I could feel the keys beneath my fingers. Could hear the music. It was Liszt's *Sonata in B Minor*."

With a start, she realized her right index finger had moved with an unconscious gesture, tracing lightly over the ugly scar on her left hand. She jerked to her feet.

"I need to go, Mom. I want to be ready when Greg gets there." She forced a laugh. "Can't keep my best guy waiting, you know."

When her mother made no answer, Jill stooped to press a tender kiss on her forehead. "I love you, Mom. I'll see you tomorrow."

Jill followed Greg and the tuxedoed maitre d' through the dining room of 44 North, an upscale restaurant that boasted a spectacular panoramic view of Halifax Harbor through floor-to-ceiling windows. Outside, lights on the moored ships shone like stars floating on blue-black waters. Inside, white tablecloths, sparkling crystal, and gleaming silver created an elegant atmosphere. A well-dressed clientele spoke in soft voices that blended with the background music, a low blur broken only by the occasional clink of cutlery on china. The maitre d' led them to a table for two next to the window, then slid an upholstered chair out for her. Greg waited until she was settled to take his place on the other side of the table.

"This is beautiful," she told him, her gaze sweeping the room. "I've heard about this restaurant, but I've never been here."

"Me either." A smile shone in his eyes like the lights on one of the ships below. "Tonight's a special night, so I wanted to pick a special place."

Something in the way Greg looked at her sliced through the gloomy thoughts that never quite left her, like morning sunlight that cut through thick fog in the harbor. When he was around, Jill could put aside all the pain, the memories, the shattered dreams, and pretend that the accident had never happened. Or at least that it was over, that it had no power over her any longer.

She smiled, determined not to think about the accident tonight, and reached across the table to take his hand. "What's so special about tonight?"

"Oh, it's a celebration of sorts." A secret twitched at the corners of his mouth. "Carl Allen promised his support today. Even made a generous campaign donation."

"Greg, that's wonderful." She squeezed his fingers. "With him and Rowena Mitchell on your side, there's no way you can lose the election."

He laughed and released her hand to lean back in his chair. "I wouldn't go that far. There are still some pretty determined people who'd rather reelect Samuels. But at least it's starting to look like I might not get completely buried in this election."

Greg was unconscious of the impression he made on people, which was one of the things she loved about him. His open expression and unmistakable honesty, reinforced by clear eyes the color of the sea on a sunny summer day, created an instant appeal with everyone he met. Not just women, either, though his rugged, six-two build and thick, dark hair didn't hurt him any with the ladies.

"You're going to win." She picked up her water glass and held it toward him in a toast. "Here's to the Cove's new councilman."

He didn't lift his own glass. "I have a confession. That's not what's special about tonight."

Jill paused, her glass still in the air. "It isn't?"

"No." His voice trembled with barely concealed excitement. "I was going to do this over dessert, but I can't wait."

He fumbled in the inside pocket of his suit coat, his stare fixed on her face. The first inkling of his intention inched over Jill like rays of sunlight creeping into the morning sky. She set the water glass down on the table and straightened in her chair.

"Jill, you know I've loved you from the moment we met, when I was moving into my law office and you and Ruth welcomed me to the Cove with a loaf of warm apple bread."

Nana made it a point to act as a one-woman Welcome Wagon to anyone who moved into the community, and that day she had dragged Jill along with her. Jill had just come home from Ontario the day before, where she'd won the Chopin Piano Competition. The handsome young lawyer had made quite an impression on her, with his self-effacing manner and ready laugh. On Nana, too, who'd hatched a matchmaking scheme within ninety seconds of walking through his office door. Scheming wasn't necessary, though. Jill had accepted a date with Greg before the bread had a chance to cool completely.

Only four years ago, but it seemed like a lifetime. She'd had dreams then. Carnegie Hall was still a possibility then.

Numbness stole over her as Greg slid out of his chair. As though from a distance, she watched him drop down to one knee beside her, at the same time pulling a small box out of his coat.

"I will never accomplish anything worthwhile if you're not by my side. I can't imagine living without you. I want you to share my goals, be part of my successes. Part of my life. Jillian Elizabeth King, will you marry me?"

The hum of conversation in the restaurant grew quiet as the people at the surrounding tables paused to watch, indulgent smiles on every face. Greg opened the lid of the black velvet box. The diamond inside caught the light from the candle on the table and turned it into sparkles.

Share *his* goals? Be part of *his* successes?

A bitter thought slashed through the numbness. Why, yes. Of course. What else could she do? She had no more goals of her own.

No, that's not right. I love Greg. I want *to be his wife.*

Tears blurred her vision. If she wasn't entirely sure they were all tears of joy, well, at least most of them were.

She swallowed against a lump in her throat. Smiled. Drew breath.

"Yes." A sob came out with the word, and she tried again. "Yes, I'll marry you."

As Greg slipped the diamond onto her finger, the other diners and the waiters applauded.

Chapter 4

THE CLOUDS HELD ONTO THE promised snow during the ride home until the car crossed over MacDonald's Bridge and turned south on Eastern Passage Road. Jill watched snowflakes speckle the windshield in random patterns. Every few seconds the wipers swept them into oblivion like a giant Etch-a-Sketch clearing the slate for the next masterpiece. Jazz played softly through the radio speakers, and her ear automatically pinpointed the keyboard. The musician wasn't bad, but a little slow on the segue.

Greg's words penetrated her thoughts. "What do you think about a Christmas wedding?"

She'd never been one of those girls who spent hours planning her dream wedding. Practicing took all her time, and when her fingers weren't on the keys, she was studying the composers' lives, learning their personalities and the events that influenced their music. Last summer she'd attended a college friend's wedding, though, and it had been gorgeous, with tons of colorful flowers everywhere. She'd almost been able to picture herself up there at the altar, dressed in white and surrounded by pink blossoms. But a winter wedding would be beautiful, too.

"Our flowers could be red and white poinsettias." She aimed a smile sideways at Greg. "We'd better reserve the church soon, though. It's a busy place during the holidays, but if we pick our date now and get it on the schedule a year in advance, we should be safe."

Greg was silent for a moment, and then he spoke sheepishly. "Actually, I meant *this* Christmas."

She jerked her head toward him. "*This* Christmas? You mean, like, in a month?"

"Yeah. My brother and his family will be in for the holiday, so we could do it out at my parents' home in the orchard. Just a quiet ceremony. You know my sister-in-law is a nurse, so we'll have help caring for your mom, and Ruth would come, of course. I've already poked around and found out Reverend and Mrs. Hollister aren't going anywhere this year, and they were thrilled at my invitation to have Christmas dinner at the orchard." He glanced away from the road to catch her eye. "Unless you have your heart set on a big church wedding."

"No. It's not that. I just—" Jill grasped for words. He'd obviously put a lot of thought into this. But get married in a month?

Well, why not? It's not like she and Greg were strangers. They'd known and loved each other for four years.

"I've waited a long time for you, Jill." He reached across the console and picked up her hand, where it lay on her lap. His thumb brushed gently across the scar, on its way to touch the engagement ring on her third finger. "Your music always came first, and I understood that. But now it's finally time for us to come first."

Jill stared at their clasped hands. Is that how he felt, that he played second fiddle to her piano?

It's true. My music has always been my top priority.

But not anymore.

An ache of longing, of loss, throbbed in her chest. She'd lost one love in her life. God had taken it from her. She wouldn't lose Greg, too.

"A Christmas wedding sounds wonderful." She smiled and intertwined her fingers with his. "Nana is going to be thrilled."

~

"*This* Christmas?" Ruth grasped at the collar of her pink housecoat. "Impossible. It can't be done."

Greg laughed at her outraged expression and pulled Jill closer to his side. "What's there to do? A marriage license only takes five days."

The snow had started to fall in earnest, but hadn't yet begun to accumulate on the roads when they pulled into the Cove at ten thirty. Jill had invited him inside so they could deliver the good news to her grandmother together. Ruth insisted that she hadn't been sleeping, only reading in bed, but her fiery hair stood at spiky attention at the back of her skull, and her eyes had been half-lidded when she first entered the cozy living room.

Now, after hearing their news, they bulged like a bigeye tuna's.

"What's there to do?" The heated scorn in the look she turned on him could have popped corn kernels. "There are invitations to print, and decorations to arrange, and — " Her hands flapped in the air. "Oh, a million details to attend to."

"Nana, we're going to have a small family ceremony out at Greg's father's ranch. No need for invitations." Jill stepped away from his side to put an arm around her grandmother and lead her to the couch. "The house will already be decorated for Christmas, and it'll be gorgeous. Right, Greg?"

Greg watched in amusement as Ruth dropped onto the center cushion, her expression dazed. Jill perched beside her. A few strands of Jill's silky dark hair danced around her head with minds of their own, charged with static from the wool hat she'd removed moments before. Her ivory skin glowed in the soft light from the table lamp. She was the most beautiful woman Greg had ever known. He could hardly believe she would be his wife in a month.

"You know what everyone will say, don't you?" Ruth's eyebrows, practically nonexistent without the dark penciled lines that gave them emphasis during the day, arched high on her forehead. "They'll say you're pregnant."

Jill's face flamed, but Greg only laughed. He had considered the possibility. A small but extremely vocal segment of the Cove's population kept the gossip lines buzzing over something or other at all times. No doubt the juicy news of a rushed wedding would be the only topic of conversation for a long time.

"No one who knows us well will think that," he assured the ladies. "And the others can speculate all they want. What do we care?"

Concern drew lines across Jill's smooth forehead. "Greg, the gossip won't hurt your campaign, will it?"

"Not at all. Besides, the election is six months away. They'll see they were wrong long before then." He pulled his gloves out of his pocket. "I need to get going. I have another breakfast meeting at seven in the morning to talk about the campaign. Why people keep wanting to meet at such an uncivilized hour is beyond me." He pulled an elaborate grimace that made Jill smile and Ruth blast a horsey laugh.

The women rose together. Ruth crossed the room with outstretched arms and gathered him in a hug.

"Congratulations. I'm ecstatic, you know, even though you've just ruined my December." She awarded him a playful slap on the shoulder. "You might not get a Christmas present this year, young man. I'll be too busy planning a wedding to do anymore shopping."

Greg returned her hug, his gaze fixed on Jill. She looked like a vision standing in the middle of the room, so graceful and achingly beautiful, bathed in beams of warm yellow light. "I'm getting the best Christmas present in the world. I don't need anything else."

"You've got that right." Ruth released him and turned a proud look toward Jill. "You are getting the best."

A becoming blush stained Jill's cheeks. She walked with Greg into the entry hall. At the front door he turned and opened his arms. She stepped into them, and for a moment they stood, silent, while he breathed deeply of the clean, fresh scent that was uniquely hers.

"Are you as happy as I am?" he whispered into her ear.

"I'm very happy." His coat muffled her voice. "I know what Nana means, though. I'm just realizing how much there is to do between now and Christmas."

"The beauty of a private ceremony is you can do as little or as much planning as you want." He pulled back enough to place a tender kiss on her forehead. "It'll be good to see you enthusiastic about something again. Especially when that something is the beginning of our life together."

She leaned back, her eyes searching his. A tiny crease appeared to mar the skin between her eyebrows.

Greg traced the crease with his thumb. "What's wrong? You're not having second thoughts already, are you?"

The skin smoothed, and she shook her head. "Of course not. I love you, and I can't wait to become Mrs. Gregory Bradford."

Her arms rose to circle his neck and pull him forward. When their lips touched, her kiss chased away any doubt about her enthusiasm.

Snow swirled through the door on a blast of wind, and Jill pushed it shut behind Greg with a thud. She rubbed a shiver out of her arms as she returned to the front room. Nana was once again seated on the sofa. With a vein-lined hand she patted the cushion in an invitation to join her.

Jill dropped onto the cushion, kicked off her shoes, and grabbed a multi-colored afghan lying across the back to snuggle beneath.

Nana turned sideways until she was looking at Jill head-on. "All right, tell me the truth. Are you pregnant?"

"Nana!" Heat rushed into Jill's face. "I can't believe you'd ask that. I'm definitely not pregnant. Greg and I haven't ..." She dropped her gaze. "You know."

Nana nodded. "I didn't think so, but I know how these things can happen unexpectedly. Then why the rush to get married?"

Jill avoided her grandmother's piercing gaze by focusing her attention on the afghan across her lap. "There's no reason to wait, really. I love Greg. Neither of us cares about having a big wedding. Greg's brother and his family will already be here for Christmas, so they won't have to make a separate trip." She plucked at a loose stitch. "And to be honest, I think Greg is trying to push me back into the land of the living. You know, give me a reason to look ahead instead of behind."

She risked an upward glance. Nana studied her through narrowed eyes.

"That's not necessarily a bad thing. You haven't been yourself since the accident."

Jill could think of no reply for that colossal understatement.

Nana scooted closer, turned on the cushion so they were side by side, and pulled part of the afghan over her legs. She looped her arm through Jill's.

"You've been through a terrible ordeal, dear. You've lost your first passion, your music. There's no need to rush. You can take as much time to heal as you need."

Though Nana's words had been repeated many times before, at the mention of her music a familiar pain throbbed in Jill's chest. Pain she was tired of suffering. Would it never go away? Would she always feel such heart-wrenching grief every time she walked past her piano?

"No." She pulled Nana's arm tighter against her side. "I've taken enough time. Greg is right. It's time to move on, to move forward. I've even been thinking of— " She paused to draw a fortifying breath. "Of taking on a few students."

There. She'd said it. The thought had been hovering in the back of her mind like a child cowering in the wings of the theater, afraid to step into the spotlight of center stage.

Nana drew upright, surprise making her eyes as round as the life preservers the Cove kept placed strategically around the docks. "Piano students? Why, Jill, that's wonderful. You'll be blessing others with your gift again, just in a different way than before." She paused, and a look of concern shadowed her features. "But can you do it? Physically, I mean. I haven't heard you play in almost a year. Is your hand healed enough?"

Jill withdrew her left hand from beneath the afghan and held it in front of her face. The diamond glittered on her third finger, but it only drew attention to the angry scar that sliced across the skin from her wrist to the knuckle of her forefinger, with a Y-shaped fork toward her thumb. She splayed her fingers. Once she'd been able to span from C to D. Now, after two surgeries and a year of physical therapy, she could barely cover a full octave. Could she play? Probably well enough for most things, like church hymns and family sing-alongs. But "well enough" wasn't nearly enough for Jill.

Time to face facts. Her concert days were truly over. And without the drive to achieve perfection during a performance, the thought of playing anything brought a deeper pain than just the one in her hand.

"It's healed enough to give lessons." She hid it once again beneath the loosely crocheted wool.

Nana studied her for a long moment, then nodded. "All right then. We'll plan a wedding in a month." A sudden smile widened her mouth. "I have an idea. You can wear your mother's wedding dress. You're close to the size she was when she married your father. She would have loved seeing you married in that dress."

Jill returned the smile. "She *will* see me married in her dress. That's a terrific idea." She peeled back the afghan and stood, covering a yawn with her hand. "It's late. I'm going to bed."

"Good night, dear. I think I'll just jot down a few notes before I go to sleep." Nana stood and draped the afghan across the back of the sofa. "There's so much to do, we're bound to forget something if we don't take notes."

Jill laughed. "Get some sleep, Nana. We have a whole month."

When she left the room, Nana was rummaging in a drawer of her desk, mumbling about never being able to find a pen when she needed one. Jill climbed the wooden stairs that led to her apartment. Discomfort twinged in her injured hip with every upward step.

In the darkness of her kitchen, she paused for a moment. Should she make a cup of herbal tea to take to bed with her? No, the clock on the microwave read past eleven. Too late for tea. She crossed the living room, made a wide pass around the dark shape that used to occupy eight or ten hours of every day, and flipped the light on in her small bedroom. The bed dominated the available space, leaving barely enough room for a nightstand and chest of drawers along the far wall, opposite the closet.

Where would she and Greg live? Surely he wouldn't want her to move into his apartment, which wasn't much bigger than this one, only without the beautiful ocean view. But would he move in here and live upstairs from Nana? At the idea of moving out of her grandmother's house, a surprising wave of homesickness washed over Jill. She'd lived with Nana since she was fourteen years old, when the stroke had robbed her of her mother. Eleven years. At first she'd lived in the spare bedroom downstairs, but then she'd taken over the upstairs apartment when she came home from college. She guessed that if Greg preferred to live somewhere else, Nana could rent this place again.

A small sigh escaped Jill's lips. So many changes. At times the weight of them threatened to crush her like …

A weight across her body crushed her, pinned her down. She tried to push it off …

With a start, Jill shoved the memory away and jerked open the second drawer of her chest, which held her pajamas. Some changes were good. She and Greg would have a happy life together. The decision to offer piano lessons was also a good change. Giving lessons would help her move forward, help her do something with her time other than sit in front of the television set all day. Like Nana said, she'd be able to bless others with her gift. At least all those years of study wouldn't go completely to waste.

She ignored the tightness in her chest as she readied herself for bed and slid beneath the heavy quilt. When she turned off the light, strains of music flowed through her head, as they had done since she was a girl. Waltzes, concertos, sonatas. But tonight she refused to let the music she'd worked so hard to learn lull her to sleep. That kind of music was forever denied to her. With his final breaths, Robert had whispered that God would not take her music away from her, but that was only the wish of a dying man. One God hadn't seen fit to grant.

Why, God? Why did you let this happen to me?

A heavy silence met her unspoken question.

Fumbling blindly in the dark, Jill opened the drawer on her nightstand and felt inside for the bottle of sleeping pills. She hadn't taken one in months, but the doctor had prescribed them for nights like this, when her thoughts refused to be tamed.

A weight pressed on her chest . . .

Jill sat straight up in bed, heart thundering in her throat. She struggled to draw breath into uncooperative lungs. The sound of her gasping attempts filled the dark bedroom, like someone choking on a sip of water that had gone down the wrong way.

I'm having a panic attack. Can't breathe. I've got to relax.

She forced herself to focus on tactile details of her immediate surroundings — the soft mattress beneath her, the chill of the air in the room, the warmth of the quilt, the comforting scent of the salty Atlantic that permeated every room in the house. Before long her lungs relaxed and she was able to inhale deep, wonderful breaths of oxygen.

When her breathing returned to something that resembled normal, she slipped out of bed and stumbled through the dark apartment to the kitchen. A drink of water, that's what she needed. Something to soothe her raw, burning throat.

Green numbers glowed from the clock on the microwave.

Four twenty-three. She filled a glass with tap water and gulped it down, not even caring that it was lukewarm.

Was it normal to have a panic attack while sleeping? It had never happened before. What set it off?

She set her glass in the dish drainer and leaned against the counter. A dream. Yes, she remembered now. She'd had a dream, something about …

A disaster. Large-scale and devastating. A disaster in Seaside Cove. Her pulse picked up speed again.

It was just a dream. Forget it. No need to panic.

But she couldn't forget it. What kind of disaster? An earthquake, maybe? Or a fire? She squeezed her eyes shut and tried to recall the details. Tried, and failed. All that remained was a sense of urgency that suddenly gripped her like a fist, and a crazy idea that became more insistent with every passing moment. This was more than just a dream. She knew it.

She dreaded the thought, but she had to warn the people of Seaside Cove.

Chapter 5

Friday, November 25

"I don't know, Greg." Bob Carmichael stirred slow circles in his coffee, his free arm draped across the empty straight-backed chair beside him. "I hate to say it, but Samuels has a point. The Cove can't afford all these expensive renovations you're talking about."

Greg sopped up the last bite of egg with a corner of wheat toast and bit into it to give himself time to formulate his response. He and Bob had attended the same church since Greg first moved to town, and Greg had handled some minor legal affairs for him over the years. The news that Bob was leaning toward supporting Samuels's reelection bid had come as a surprise. He'd been counting on Bob's support.

The small dining room of The Wharf Café was almost deserted this morning. The owner and cook, Rowena Mitchell, worked the grill behind the counter by herself. The sizzle of bacon frying vied with a fifties' tune coming from a boom box tucked up on a high shelf beside an old-fashioned metal canister set. Rowena's off-key hum added a homey charm to the atmosphere inside the café. As Greg swallowed a gulp of coffee, she burst into a full, throaty chorus, waving the spatula above her head and winking broadly at a pair of weathered fishermen seated at the counter. They applauded, laughing, obviously infatuated with the flirty café owner, who was at least forty years their junior.

Greg pushed his empty plate aside and rested his forearms on the table. "I've gotta admit I'm surprised you'd take that attitude, Bob. Your business can only get better with an increase in the tourist trade. People love to fish, and your *Lucy* is the best-looking charter boat on the dock."

"You're right about that, but I'm not talking about my own business. We can't all just look out for ourselves, you know. We have to think about the town. The Cove doesn't have much money to spend on things like upgrading the docks and advertising for tourists." He pursed his lips, clearly uncomfortable to be in disagreement with Greg. "What if we spend a ton of money and no tourists come?"

"I hear what you're saying, and I appreciate the fact that you're civic-minded." Greg tossed the last uneaten crust of bread on his plate. "But the town is falling into disrepair. People are moving away, leaving the area, because there's not enough business to keep them here. If we keep going at the rate we've been going for the past ten years or so, we'll be in serious trouble." He leaned forward and held the man's eyes. "Besides, I just *know* we'll see an immediate response if we spread the word about what a great place we've got here. We're the best-kept secret in Nova Scotia. We've got to let the secret out or this town won't survive another couple of decades."

Bob didn't meet his eye, but his disagreement was plain on his face.

"Look, do me a favor." Greg pointed toward one of the page-size posters Rowena had tacked around the room advertising his upcoming event. "Come to the meeting Monday night. I'm going to lay my plan out in plain sight for everyone. Listen to what I have to say before you make a decision."

"I suppose I could do that."

The answer, grudgingly given, was at least better than a flat refusal.

"I appreciate that," Greg said. "I'll do my best to lay your fears to rest."

Rowena bustled over with a carafe to refill their cups. "I don't know what you're talking about over here, but you've got two of the sourest pusses I've seen in a long time. Anybody didn't know you, they'd think you're about ready to hop over the table and start pounding on each other."

Bob's scowl became a sheepish smile.

Greg wiped the serious look off his face and chuckled. "We're talking politics. Did you ever know anybody to smile over politics?" He put a hand over his coffee cup when she tried to pour more into it. He'd had enough coffee this morning to last him all day and halfway through the night.

"Ah, that explains it." She stacked Greg's empty plate on top of Bob's, but instead of picking them up, cocked her hip sideways and rested a hand on it to spear Greg with a speculative stare. "I heard a rumor about you this morning, darlin'. You want to refute it?"

"Depends on what you heard."

"I heard you proposed to Jill King, and she said yes."

Gossip traveled fast in the Cove, especially when it was news that Jill's grandmother wanted to spread around. How many people had Ruth called already this morning, at — he glanced at his watch — not even nine o'clock?

He didn't bother to stop the grin that took possession of his lips. "Well, that's one rumor I can confirm."

Across the table, Bob brightened. "You and Jill are getting married? Hey, that's great news."

"There goes the town's most eligible bachelor, hooked right out from under my nose." Rowena cut her eyes sideways at Greg and pulled a pretty pout. "I guess I've just been fishing with the wrong bait, huh?"

Bob laughed. "There's nothing wrong with your bait, Rowe. The right fish just hasn't swum close enough to get snagged yet." He nodded across the table at Greg. "Congratulations to you and Jill. I used to love hearing her play at church, and my wife listens to her CD at home all the time. She was quite a piano player before that subway crash. Closest thing the Cove has to a celebrity."

"And she's going to marry another celebrity." Rowena rubbed a hand across Greg's shoulder before picking up the dirty dishes. "Our next councilman is sitting right here."

Greg's lips twitched. "I don't know if councilman for Seaside Cove counts as being a celebrity."

"Besides, the election is still a ways off." Bob pulled out enough money to cover his breakfast and tossed it on the table.

Greg did the same, and rose when Bob did. "Thanks for taking the time to meet with me this morning."

The two shook hands. "Glad I did. All I can say is, I won't make up my mind until I've heard you out."

"Fair enough. I'll see you Monday night, then."

Bob raised a hand in farewell and headed out the door. Greg stared after him, his spirits flagging. He'd known when he started this campaign that he had an uphill battle ahead of him. Samuels, the incumbent, was a well-known local man, while Greg was a transplant to the Cove and not nearly as visible. He knew he would have to overcome the townspeople's natural distrust of outsiders, and especially of a newcomer to politics. But it had never occurred to him that he wouldn't have the support of those who knew him personally, who worshipped with him and Jill every Sunday morning.

"Don't you worry about Bob. He'll come around." Rowena set down the carafe to balance the coffee cups on top of the plates. "Besides, you'd better wipe that long, sad look off your face or people will think you're not happy about getting married. It's a happy day, right?"

The words lifted his spirits like a birthday balloon soaring into the sky. Rowena was right. The most beautiful woman in the world had said yes. They were getting married.

"You're right." He turned a grin on Rowena. "This is a happy day."

~

"This is a terrible day!"

Jill sprawled in the padded vinyl chair in her counselor's office, threw her head against the high back, and dropped her hands over the sides. As usual, Doreen Davenport's expression remained passive, her pink lipsticked mouth arranged into a pleasant, not-quite smile. She took her time crossing from the closed door to the neat desk, selecting a ballpoint pen from the crowded holder on the corner, and lowering herself into the chair beside Jill's.

"Now." She clicked the pen and leveled a calm gaze on Jill's face. "Why is this a terrible day?"

"Because I'm not fixed yet and I'm getting married." The last word came out in an unintended wail.

"First of all, the term *not fixed* presupposes that you're *broken*, and you're not. And second—" Nonchalance gave way to a wide grin. "You're getting married? That's wonderful news, Jill. Congratulations."

Jill lifted her head off the high chair back. "No, it's not. Last night it was wonderful news. Today it's a fiasco in the making. And you can say I'm not broken all you want, but I'm obviously not recovered yet. I'm not normal."

Doreen's smile twitched downward the merest fraction. "Why do you think you're not normal?"

The ludicrousness of the question silenced Jill for a moment. How could she even begin to answer? In fact, why did she have to, when the answer was so obvious? But this was the way sessions with Doreen went. She forced Jill to describe every emotion, every memory, in excruciating detail. Then she rarely voiced an opinion, merely nodded and murmured, "Hmmm," or prodded with frustratingly ambiguous questions like, "And how did that make you feel?"

But Jill had to admit the weekly sessions did help. Within the walls of this office she could vent her frustration, or mourn her loss, or literally scream at the unfairness of life, without fear of damaging someone's opinion of her or, worse, evoking their pity.

She folded her hands in her lap and inhaled a long, slow breath tinged with the faint aroma of lemon-scented furniture polish. "Normal twenty-five-year-olds have jobs. They go to work every day. They don't hover in their houses to avoid meeting people on the street who might ask, 'How are you doing, Jill?' or say, 'Such a terrible thing, that accident.'" The doctor's face blurred behind Jill's tears. "Greg's going to be a politician. He deserves a wife who can help him win elections, not one who runs from the public. Not one who can't even look at a piano without wanting to cry, or has dreams that give her panic attacks."

"Panic attacks?" The doctor crossed one leg over the other and bounced a high-heeled shoe in the air. "That's new, isn't it? You haven't mentioned a panic attack since a few months after the accident."

Jill rubbed her eyes with fingers that came away wet. "Last night was the first in a long time. I'm not even sure that's what it was. I had a really terrible dream, and when I woke up I couldn't shake this feeling of ..." She attempted a dismissive smile, but couldn't quite manage it. "Disaster. Like something terrible was going to happen."

Doreen clicked her pen open and closed. "It's *normal*," she smiled as she said the word, "to dream of a devastating event like the one you went through. You know that. You've dreamed before."

"Yes, but this was different." She paused, searching for a way to describe the intensity of the experience. "This one was far more vivid."

"Do you need something to help you sleep? I can have my secretary make an appointment for you with Dr. Bookman."

Dr. Bookman was the prescription-happy medical doctor Jill had seen off and on since the accident for medical checkups. Quick with the prescription pad, and the bedside manner of a hyperactive terrier.

"No, I still have the prescription I got after the accident. I took one last night, in fact." She scowled. "It didn't stop that dream from coming."

"Well, that might be a contributing factor. A common side effect of some sleeping pills is the occurrence of abnormal, vivid dreams, and you are approaching the anniversary of the event. That's always a traumatic time." She settled back in her chair. "What about the flashbacks you mentioned last week? Still having those?"

"I don't know if I'd call them flashbacks," Jill said quickly. "It's not like I'm reliving the accident or anything. They're just haunting memories, details of … that day. And of the people."

"Of Robert."

Jill looked at her hands. "It was just so strange, that instant affinity between us. Not romantic." She glanced up to assure herself that Doreen didn't misunderstand. The woman nodded, and she looked back down. "I've never met someone who could read me so thoroughly in such a short time."

"He died holding your hand." The doctor's voice was soft. "It's natural that you would feel close to someone with whom you've shared such an intimate moment."

"No, it was more than that. We had a kinship from the moment we met, even before the crash." Her throat tightened. "It was as if I'd known him forever. I think we might have been good friends if he had lived."

"And yet, you haven't made any attempt to find out more about him. Who he was. Where he lived. What he did for a living."

Jill didn't answer, just shook her head.

"Why do you suppose that is, Jill?"

A jolt of irritation jerked her upright in the seat. "I don't know." She ground out the words through clenched teeth.

"All right." Doreen's tone remained coolly dispassionate as she changed the subject. "You mentioned the fact that you don't have a job. Have you given any more thought to going back to school for an advanced degree, like we've discussed?"

Jill forced herself to relax again. There were still a couple of subjects she wasn't ready to face, and Robert was one of them. Thinking of him was too painful, too vivid a reminder of everything she'd lost. Admitting that made her feel like a failure. But at least she had some progress to report on the job front.

"Yes, I have, and I've decided not to for now. Until I know what I want to study, I need to start making some money." A humorless laugh heaved in her chest. The money she earned on the concert circuit before the accident hadn't run out yet, but it wouldn't last forever. "I'm going to give piano lessons. I decided last night."

Doreen's eyebrows rose. "That's a big step. Do you think you're ready for that?"

Jill turned the doctor's trick around on her. "Do *you* think I'm ready for that?"

The woman smiled an acknowledgement of Jill's use of her own technique. "If you do, then so do I." She sobered. "Here's an even more important question for you. Do you want to marry Greg? Do you love him?"

Finally, a question she could answer with certainty. She met the doctor's gaze straight on. "I love him more than anything. Yes, I want to marry him."

Doreen dipped her head in a nod. "If you want my opinion, I'd say last night was a big night for you. You got engaged, and you made a decision that you know will place you in a painful situation—back in front of a piano." She caught Jill's gaze and held it. "You're not broken, Jill. You've been wounded, but you're healing. Just keep the lines of communication open with Greg. Make sure he knows what you're feeling, what you're going through." She glanced at her watch and stood. "Perhaps you should try a different prescription to help you sleep."

Jill shook her head as she, too, stood. "No, thank you. No

more sleeping pills for me." She leaned over and scooped up her purse. "I'd rather not risk another disaster dream like last night."

"Well, if you change your mind, call me." Doreen replaced the pen in the holder and rounded her desk, a sign that the session was truly over. "I'll see you next week. Oh, and congratulations on the engagement."

"Thank you."

Jill left the room and nodded a silent farewell toward the receptionist in the small outer office. She felt better, her perspective restored. She did love Greg, and he loved her. It's not like she was trading her dream of being a world-class pianist in order to marry him. She'd envisioned herself married to Greg for years, and pictured their marriage as an overlay to her career, another layer in a satisfying life. The career may be gone, but that just left her with an altered version of the original picture. Their life together would be wonderful. And who knew? Maybe helping him with his campaign would be just what she needed to force herself out of the apartment and back into public view.

As for last night's terrible dream, no doubt the counselor was right. Yesterday had been a big day for her. A good day, but it was normal to experience some anxiety after making two life-changing decisions within a few hours of each other. No matter how much she loved Greg, marriage was a huge step and hers was going to happen in one month. That in itself was enough to send most brides cowering in a corner for a session of thumb sucking.

In some ways, the other decision felt bigger, more alarming. A custom-designed stress dispenser. Was she really ready to sit down in front of a piano again, even if it was only to teach? It felt like progress, a step in the right direction, and progress never came without a cost, right? Not that she had to jump into anything quickly. The end of June might be a good time to start, when school let out for the summer. She could take her time, work herself up to being ready to take on a student. No rush. After all, she really hadn't made a firm decision until the words tumbled out of her mouth while talking to Nana last night. Of course she'd feel anxious about it. Anyone would in her shoes.

So the dream had been merely a symptom of her subconscious stress over two major decisions. That, and a sleeping pill with side effects. Nothing more. Since the decisions were all made, and she wasn't going to take the pills anymore, she wouldn't have to worry about having any more weird dreams.

Then why couldn't she shake the unsettling feeling that the dream was only the beginning, and that the real nightmare was about to start?

Chapter 6

JILL'S HAND HAD BARELY TURNED the knob at home when the front door was jerked out of her grasp. Nana stood in the entry hall, her shiny red lips stretched into an exasperated grimace.

"*There* you are. Where have you been? Your appointment ended two hours ago, and you didn't answer your cell phone."

She reached outside to grasp Jill's coat sleeve, and in the next moment Jill found herself snatched over the threshold with a suddenness that nearly threw her off balance. The door shut behind her with a firm *thump.*

"I must have forgotten to turn my phone back on after my appointment, and then I went by Centerside to see Mom."

Jill had barely unfastened the last button of her coat when the garment was whisked off her shoulders and tossed haphazardly over an already-full coatrack.

"We've been waiting for an hour." Nana placed a hand on Jill's back and propelled her toward the living room.

Jill almost stumbled over the threshold. "We?"

The small room was filled to capacity with elderly ladies. Chairs from the kitchen table had been brought in and placed between the existing furniture to form a circle around the perimeter of the room. Every available seat was occupied, and somehow five ladies had managed to wedge themselves into the depths of the sofa. A mishmash of brightly colored clothing and various shades of gray hair blurred together in Jill's vision, while an alarming clash of perfumes threatened to send her nose into sensory overload. She barely had time to identify the mob as Nana's knitting group when a communal squeal arose from a dozen throats. In the next moment, they swarmed.

"You're getting married!"

"So happy for you."

"I remember your eighth birthday party like it was yesterday."

She was swept into a hug, then passed from one set of arms to another before being nearly squeezed breathless by Mrs. Montgomery, an enthusiastic eighty-year-old with the bosom of a stripper and the strength of a wrestler.

A clap of hands behind her cut through the excited babble. "All right, girls, we've got work to do."

At Nana's commanding voice, the chatter ceased and the ladies returned to their seats. Mrs. Montgomery gave Jill's arm a final pat before settling into one of the armchairs and picking up the cup and saucer from the floor beside it.

Jill turned to Nana. "Are you having a tea party?"

"No, dear. We don't have time for that. They're here to help us with the wedding."

Nods of assent around the room. Jill managed an awkward smile, then grabbed Nana's arm and pulled her toward the kitchen.

"But we told you last night we're having a private ceremony," she whispered. "Small. Just family. We don't plan to invite anyone from town."

"Oh, we don't expect to come, hon." Mrs. Tolliver twisted around on the sofa to give Jill an earnest glance. "We'll just help you work out the details beforehand. Then we'll watch the video at the reception."

"Video?" Jill widened her eyes. "Reception?"

Mrs. Fontaine spoke up from her chair near the fireplace. "We were thinking it would be nice to have a reception afterward, maybe in late January. You know, a celebration with your friends and church family."

"Now, Alice, we haven't made any decisions about the reception yet." Nana blinked blue-shadowed eyelids in a display of mild rebuke. "We have enough to handle with planning a decent wedding in exactly a month. And on Christmas, too."

"Oh, yes. Quite enough. I don't know how we'll manage to pull it all together in time." Mrs. Montgomery's eyes gleamed, obviously not the least bit intimidated by the daunting task.

Obviously, preparations for her own wedding had been plucked out of Jill's hands. She made one last attempt to wrest control from the tenacious troop of geriatric wedding planners.

"Nana, Greg and I really don't want an elaborate ceremony. Just a quiet exchange of vows in front of the Christmas tree. Maybe a few snapshots we can put into a photo album, but nothing extravagant, like a video."

"Extravagant? Nonsense." Mrs. Tolliver set her cup in the saucer with a determined *clink*. "You won't even know my nephew is in the room. He's an excellent videographer." She lifted her eyebrows and spoke to her neighbor on the sofa with obvious pride. "He used to work for a cruise ship doing vacation videos. People paid a lot of money for those videos."

Was she kidding? Take a man away from his family on Christmas to record a private wedding ceremony on an apple orchard ninety minutes away? Jill opened her mouth to voice another protest, but Nana grabbed her in a firm grip and turned her toward the bedroom.

"Let's get you into the dress. We need to get started on the alterations. You've a slimmer waist than Lorna when she married, and I'm sure we'll need to let out the bust."

They left the women scurrying for their sewing boxes. Judging by their energetic expressions, the alterations would be finished by the end of the day.

Her mother's wedding dress lay across Nana's bed. Jill stopped when she caught sight of it, and then inched slowly into the room. She'd forgotten how lovely the dress was. Creamy white satin fell in graceful folds from an empire waist, the bodice covered with subtle but elegant beadwork. She reached for the short train and caressed the silky fabric between her fingers. An image arose in her mind of the framed photograph on the dresser in Mom's room at Centerside. She'd been stunning in this dress, the smile on her youthful face radiant. Happy. So happy.

Would Jill be that happy on her own wedding day? If she could ever be truly happy again, surely it would be that day.

"Hurry up, now. Slip off those clothes." Nana flipped the dress over and began unfastening the pearl-shaped buttons. "Oh, before I forget to tell you, Eloise Cramer's granddaughter will be here tomorrow at ten, and then Alice's granddaughter at eleven."

Jill paused in the act of lifting her sweater over her shoulders. "Why?"

Nana blinked. "For their piano lessons."

The meaning of Nana's words sank in. She had two piano students coming in the morning. Anger flickered at the edges of her mind. Nana had arranged it without consulting her.

Jill let the sweater fall back in place. "Why did you do that?"

Her grandmother looked up from her work on the dress,

surprise widening her eyes. "Alice has been bragging about her granddaughter's talent for a long time, so I knew she'd jump at the chance for the girl to learn from you." She scowled. "I don't know a thing about Eloise's granddaughter, but she wasn't about to let Alice get away with saying *her* granddaughter was taking lessons from Jillian King." Concern replaced the scowl as Nana peered up at her. "You did say you wanted to give lessons, didn't you?"

Jill set her teeth together against the battling emotions that raged inside. Yes, she did say that, but there was a giant chasm between saying something and doing it, between making a decision and acting on it. She needed a few months to get used to the idea.

On the other hand, Jill knew Nana meant well. She wanted to be supportive, to help. Which was the reason she'd organized the planning posse in the living room. She didn't mean to meddle, really. Or if she did, it was only what she considered helpful meddling.

Jill swallowed a gulp of resentment. "Yes, I did say that, but I didn't intend to start tomorrow. I would prefer to arrange things on my own, that's all."

"I'm sorry, dear. I understand." Worry lines appeared in Nana's forehead. "You know I would never do anything to upset you. Alice and Eloise are both in the other room. I'll go right in there and tell them I spoke out of turn."

With an effort, Jill forced the knotted muscles in her shoulders to relax. "No, that's okay. It's done now. I—I appreciate your help."

Maybe this development was for the best. A kick in the pants by her well-meaning grandmother might be exactly what she needed. Now she'd be forced to cross the invisible barrier she'd erected around her piano.

With a forced smile to assure Nana she wasn't upset, she

allowed herself to be dressed. As the silky fabric slid down to settle against her hips, she realized she was hoping the fitting would take a long time—hours and hours. The longer she spent downstairs with the ladies, the less time she'd have upstairs where the piano waited for her, but that was merely a delay tactic that would ultimately serve no purpose at all. Before ten o'clock in the morning, she'd have to overcome her reluctance to touch the ivory keys.

Tonight, she'd have to play.

Chapter 7

Jill stood in the doorway between her kitchen and front room, her hand hovering over the wall switch. In the corner of the living room, the dark, winged shape of the piano waited. For nearly a year she'd managed to avoid approaching it — no easy task, since it dominated the room. If she allowed her imagination to run unfettered, she could feel the instrument's resentment as it hovered beneath the quilted cover.

Ridiculous. It's an object. It doesn't have feelings.

But all her life, the piano had been Jill's best friend. Oh, she had school friends, but why confide in another girl when she could pour her emotions out through the keyboard? The piano accepted. The piano understood. The piano responded with mournful canon when she felt sad, or joyous sonata when she felt glad. To her, the piano was the most *feeling* instrument ever created.

She hadn't touched it in a year. It was time.

At a flip of the light switch, the tract lighting she'd installed in the ceiling illuminated that corner of the room. From where she stood, Jill could see a thin layer of dust on the quilted cover. A twinge of guilt pricked her conscience. A Schimmel Konzert was an intricately crafted instrument, a work of art manufactured in

Germany, and far too expensive to be allowed to become a dust collector. At least she'd had the tuner here twice in the past year, so even though she had neglected it, the piano would be in good repair. And the cover had done its job in protecting the instrument.

For a moment, her feet refused to move. They felt heavy, stuck, as if she'd happened across a patch of sticky flypaper in the doorway. With an effort, she pried them up and dragged herself across the room.

Heart pounding against her ribs, she stood beside the hulking object and rested her right hand on the quilted cover. There. She'd touched it. She waited, giving her heartbeat time to return to normal.

I'm being silly. It's a piano, *for heaven's sake. It won't bite me.*

But no matter how much her mind understood that, her body reacted with a visceral tensing of every muscle, from her toes on up. For a full five minutes, Jill merely stood with her hand on the cover.

She heard Doreen's voice in her head. *Describe your feelings, Jill.*

Okay, use the tools she'd learned. What was she feeling? She closed her eyes and performed an inventory. Sadness. Anxiety. *Fear.* Yes, the overriding emotion was fear. Standing here beside the instrument that used to mean more to her than anything else reminded her of all she once hoped to attain. She flexed open her left hand, which hung at her side, until she felt the stretching pain she'd come to accept as normal in recent months. Those goals had been lost to her. Even though she could compensate for the smaller reach, the pain would impede her movements. She would never again play like she once did. She'd come to accept that.

But how much had she lost? That was the question that lay

at the base of her fear. What if she couldn't play at all? Could she live with never playing the piano again?

She opened her eyes. There was only one thing worse than never playing again, and that was living in fear. It had been almost a year since the accident. It was time to heal, to move on.

With slow, careful movements, she pulled back the quilted cover and exposed the graceful curves of the Schimmel. The glossy ebony finish gleamed in the soft tract lighting. She raised the lid and stepped back to admire the symmetry, the beauty of the instrument. This wasn't the same piano she'd used as a child. Nana could never have afforded a Schimmel. They'd owned an inexpensive upright until Jill started performing on the concert circuit during college. Then she had invested in this one.

Sitting on the padded piano bench felt like sliding into a favorite summer blouse after a long winter of heavy sweaters. She lifted the music rack and ran a finger across the smooth top edge. Her sheet music had all been stored in the attic, but she didn't need it. The notes from hundreds of pieces came into focus whenever she closed her eyes, and the intricate harmonies created by masters like Chopin, Beethoven, and of course Liszt, vibrated deep in her soul.

She rested her right hand on the keyboard. The ivory caressed her fingertips, smooth as the softest silk yet firm as marble. Her eyelids shut almost of their own accord as her thumb stroked middle C. The note rang out to fill the silent room with a pure, sweet tone that raced up Jill's arm, vibrated over her collarbone, spread through her ribs and, finally, crept into her heart with agonizing sweetness. A tear slipped between her eyelids and traced a path down her cheek. She ran up the scale, C to C, and her fingers flew over the keys as though they'd danced this dance only yesterday. They raced back down to middle C, then back up again, faster and faster, moving with joyful abandon through the familiar exercise that was seared into muscle memory from years of repetition.

Without conscious thought, she switched to a one-handed version of a simple tune she'd learned long ago. The chords of Beethoven's "Ode to Joy" flowed from fingertips that skipped across the keyboard's upper registers like a child on a sidewalk. The harmonies weren't complete, though. They needed the lower octaves. She raised her left hand.

In the moment before she touched the keys, she caught sight of the scar, red and vivid and ugly. Both hands jerked back as though the keyboard had grown thorns. The last notes she'd played hung heavy in the air.

I can't.

Tears clogged her throat as she slid off the bench and backed away from the piano. A harsh truth pummeled her brain. She couldn't risk knowing if she could play. Not yet.

Tomorrow's lessons were introductory sessions. She could spend the time getting to know her new students and introducing them to the basic keys and finger exercises. No need to play anything.

She rushed to the wall and flipped off the lights. The piano settled quietly into the darkness.

~

Flames, voracious and vicious, roared in the cold air, whipped into a fury by a morning breeze that drew its strength from the icy Atlantic. Screams joined with the fire in a deafening dissonance of sound. People dying. Suffering. Burning flesh, followed by freezing cold and a horrible squeezing of lungs.

No air. Can't breathe.

Jill sat up in bed, gasping. The roar of the fire deafened her. She covered her ears, pressing with her palms to block out the screams.

No. The room was silent. She was at home, in her own bed, her own quiet bedroom. No sound at all except her pulse pounding like an aboriginal war drum.

It's not real. I'm safe. I'm safe. I'm safe.

She repeated the mantra over and over, willing herself to believe it. But her thudding heart refused to take heed.

The people of Seaside Cove must be warned.

The idea again seeped into her consciousness as though from an outside source. It went deeper than thought, more like intuition, something that bypassed logic and resonated in her soul with a sense of urgency impossible to ignore.

"It's just a dream." She spoke aloud to drown out the tumult in her mind. "A stupid dream that happened because I tried to play the piano and couldn't. That's all it is."

But why was it the same dream as the night before? And why had it returned when she hadn't taken any sleeping pills?

And why couldn't she dismiss the thought — no, the insane notion — that she had to warn people about a coming disaster?

Chapter 8

Saturday, November 26

"Oh, Greg, I'm so happy. This will be the best Christmas ever." The enthusiasm in his mother's words bubbled through the phone line.

Greg laughed. "You say that every year, Mom." Standing behind his desk, he cocked his head sideways to wedge the receiver against his shoulder. His hands free, he flipped through a stack of law journals, searching for the issue containing an article on exclusivity in property law.

"Well, a wedding on Christmas Day will definitely make this year the best so far."

"I'm glad you feel that way." He couldn't help but smile. Mom could always be counted on to applaud any decision he made, and she had loved Jill from the first time he'd taken her home to meet his parents. "You're sure you won't mind having Reverend and Mrs. Hollister there for Christmas dinner?"

"Of course not. Here, your father wants to talk to you."

A shuffle sounded as the phone changed hands on the other end. Greg found the magazine issue he wanted and pulled it from the pile. He tossed it onto the corner of his desk, then straightened to attention as his father's voice came on the line.

"Congratulations, son. Jill's a fine young woman. She'll make a good wife for you."

Some of the tension left his spine at his father's words. He'd been a bit worried that Dad would chide him for not talking this decision over with him first. "Yes, sir, she will. And I hope I'll be a good husband for her."

"Timing's good, too. Marriage will be good for your career. People like their politicians to be married. Makes 'em more sympathetic, easier to identify with. It's a good move to get it done before the election."

Greg indulged in an eye roll that his father could not see. He didn't bother explaining that the timing of the wedding had nothing to do with the election. Dad wouldn't hear him anyway. That seat on the HRM city council meant the world to his proud and ambitious father.

Mom's voice sounded in the background. "Let me talk to him again, Harold." More rubbing noises, and then she asked, "Are you and Jill free to come for dinner on Wednesday night? I can just see the ceremony in my mind, with you two standing near the fireplace and a cozy fire burning on the hearth. I want her to see what I've done with the mantle decorations this year. She might not like all the greenery. If not, we'll need to hurry and figure out what we want to do instead."

"Mom, we don't want you going to a lot of trouble. We just want a simple family ceremony. No special decorations or anything."

Her voice became stern. "Gregory, don't be such a *man*. The most special day in a woman's life is her wedding day, so I want to do whatever I can to make it perfect for Jill. Just bring my future daughter-in-law for dinner on Wednesday night."

In other words, his presence wasn't necessary except as an escort to the bride-to-be, even in the eyes of his own mother. He didn't bother to filter the smile from his words. "Yes, ma'am. Whatever you say. I'll check with Jill and make sure Wednesday works for her."

"Good. See you at seven."

~

Kaylee Fontaine was a serious-faced child, with limp, pale hair that dangled from her skull like homemade spaghetti on an Italian chef's pasta rack. Red blotches from the cold winter wind stood out starkly on her pale cheeks and made her nose as bright as a clown's. The wide eyes she turned up to Jill, though, were a truly beautiful shade of blue-gray, framed by thick, curling lashes that would no doubt evoke envy in fashion models worldwide. Jill gave the girl a smile and extended her hand toward the woman standing on the front porch beside her.

"Hello. I'm Jill. You must be Mrs. Fontaine."

"Please, call me Becky. It's such a pleasure to meet you." She smiled as she took Jill's hand in her gloved one and pressed. "I can't tell you how thrilled Kaylee is to be taking lessons from the famous Jillian Elizabeth King. You're like her idol. She was so excited I don't think she was able to sleep at all last night."

Kaylee's gaze dropped to the floor, embarrassment expanding the red splotches on her cheeks. Her thin shoulders seemed to shrink in on themselves. Sympathy for the shy girl stirred in Jill.

"Please come inside." She took a backward step and gestured up the wooden stairs. "My apartment is upstairs."

Becky Fontaine hesitated. "Actually, I wasn't planning to stay for the lesson, if that's okay. My son is in the car, and I have to run him over to a birthday party. I'll be back before the thirty minutes are over, though." She turned a pleading expression on Jill. "Would that be okay?"

Actually, after the first piano lesson of the morning, Jill preferred not to have Becky hovering over her shoulder. Mariah Cramer's mother had refused to sit on the sofa, where Jill directed her, but paced behind the piano stool watching every move Jill and her daughter made. Mariah hadn't seemed to mind—she was probably used to having a helicopter mom—but Jill had been a bundle of nerves by the time the lesson was over. If this piano lesson thing continued, she might have to institute a rule about parents waiting downstairs in Nana's living room.

"That's no problem at all." Jill gave Kaylee a broad smile. "We'll be fine by ourselves, won't we?"

The child's head bobbed once, almost imperceptibly.

"Oh, good. Thank you." Becky stooped and planted a quick kiss on Kaylee's cheek. "Have fun, sweetie. Learn lots." She headed toward the car parked at the curb in front of the house. Jill caught a glimpse of a small, round face in the back seat.

Kaylee watched the car pull away, then faced Jill. Only her eyes moved as she looked up at her. She still hadn't said a word.

"Why don't we hang up your coat, and then we can get started?"

Jill closed the door behind the child, put her coat on the rack in the hallway, and led the way upstairs. When she entered the living room, Kaylee stopped in the doorway. Her eyes went round as she gazed at the piano.

"Wow. It's beautiful." Her voice, surprisingly low, was breathy with awe.

"Thank you." Jill couldn't help a swell of pride. She might be at odds with her piano at the moment, but it was still the most beautiful instrument she'd ever played. "Do you have a piano at home?"

The child nodded. "My grandma gave it to me last year. But it's old. Nothing like this one."

A rush of kinship warmed Jill. "My grandmother gave me my first piano, too."

Blue-gray eyes lifted to her face. "Really?"

Jill nodded. "It was pretty old, too, but I didn't care. I loved it anyway. I spent hours playing it." She seated herself on the bench and patted the cushioned seat beside her. "Ready to get started?"

Mariah had rushed for the piano the moment she spied it, but Kaylee approached slowly, almost reverently. The two looked to be close to the same age, but their temperaments were as different as girls could be. Kaylee slid onto the bench and sat rigid, her hands clasped in her lap.

"Have you ever taken music lessons?" Jill asked.

Kaylee shook her head.

"Do you know the notes on a piano?"

Again, the child shook her head. That suited Jill fine. Mariah had never taken a lesson either, which meant both her students would be at the same level. Much easier for her. They could use the same lesson book, and she would only have to prepare one lesson each week instead of two.

"All right, let's begin by learning the keys. The very first key on the keyboard is an A, just like in the regular alphabet. It's all the way down here on the left side."

Jill went through the same introductory comments she'd given to Mariah, only without parental interruption the lesson went much quicker. When she asked Kaylee to point out all the C's on the keyboard, the child did so quickly, without hesitation, but also with a soft touch of obvious reverence for the instrument that the other girl had not displayed. Jill found herself drawn to the shy girl, to her quiet manners and, especially, to her obvious deference for the piano. She also had a quick mind, and listened to everything Jill said with the attention of a cat focused on a bird's nest.

"That's really good, Kaylee," Jill told her when they'd covered the black keys and the concept of sharps and flats. "Now, I'd like to hear you play something. What do you play at home?"

When she'd asked Mariah to play, she'd been treated to a clanging but enthusiastic performance of "Chopsticks," followed by "Heart and Soul" pounded out with both index fingers.

Once again, Kaylee showed herself to be no Mariah. A look of absolute horror crept over the girl's features. She shrank from the keyboard, her fingers curled into fists and pressed against her collarbone. "But I don't know how."

"That's okay." Jill placed a comforting hand on her shoulder and squeezed. "You're here to learn how, and you will. I just want to hear what you can do. It doesn't have to be good."

The large eyes studied her, and gradually Kaylee's features relaxed. "Okay."

She extended her hands, and her childish fingers hovered for a moment over the keys. Then they lowered.

The piano awakened as music poured from beneath the raised lid like clear, fresh water bubbling over a rocky stream bed. Jill's jaw went slack during the first few, intimately familiar notes of *Für Elise*. The child, who'd never had a lesson, was playing Beethoven, and playing beautifully, with real feeling for the piece. Her dynamics were nearly flawless, her interpretation much the same as Jill would play herself. Her technique wasn't perfect, for sure. The tempo was a little off when she moved from the left-handed arpeggios into the relative major.

When she made a jarring mistake, blood suffused Kaylee's face and she jerked her hands off the keyboard. "See, I told you I couldn't do it."

For a long moment, Jill could only stare at the girl, incredulous. Had the child been lying when she said she'd never had a lesson? No, Jill saw no guile in Kaylee's face. And during the lesson it had been obvious that she didn't know a C from a D-sharp.

"How did you learn to play that piece?" she asked.

The child looked down at the hands in her lap. "From you."

"Me?"

She nodded. "Mama took me to hear your concert in Halifax when I was seven, and she bought me your CD. I listened to it over and over." Her thin shoulders lifted in a shrug. "Then I played it. But I can't get it right."

She played by ear. First she listened to a piece, and then she sat down and played it. No sheet music, no training, just an acute musical ear and a talent the likes of which Jill had never encountered.

An unexpected stab of jealousy knifed Jill in the stomach. She'd exhibited talent as a child, but nothing like this. Every song she played had been the result of hours of hard work at the keyboard. And this kid picked up Jill's CD, listened to it, and then played with a style and emotion many music majors never managed to attain.

Envy evaporated. How could she be jealous of a sweet child with an amazing talent? With work, Kaylee could be a great pianist. Her gift could take her all the way to …

All the way to Carnegie Hall.

Maybe Jill would never play Carnegie Hall herself. But wouldn't it be almost as good if a student of hers, her protégé, played while she watched from the wings?

She put an arm around Kaylee's shoulders and hugged her tightly. "I am so glad you wanted to take lessons from me. You have an incredible gift. We're going to have fun together."

Chapter 9

Sunday, November 27

The notes of the final hymn vibrated from the organ in the church sanctuary. Jill held her side of the hymnal and mumbled the words while Greg's melodious baritone rang in her ears. From the first time she'd heard him sing, sitting in this very church, she'd thought it was such a shame he never studied music. A voice like that could have taken him far on the performance circuit.

She clamped her teeth together in defiance of a yawn. She'd read an entire novel to postpone the moment when she had to close her eyes last night, though today she couldn't remember a thing about the story. Still, it had served its purpose. When she finally allowed herself to fall asleep around four a.m., she'd been so exhausted she didn't dream at all. But seven o'clock had come awfully early this morning.

The hymn ended, and after the minister's final words, the organist launched into the postlude, signaling the end of the service. Jill bent forward to grab her purse from beneath the pew in front of her, while Greg stepped into the aisle and waited for her to join him.

"There you are, Bradford. Could we have a word about this meeting of yours tomorrow night?" One of the church elders, Mitch Landry, plucked at Greg's sleeve.

"Of course." Greg gave her an apologetic grimace. "I'll just be a minute."

Jill nodded. "Take your time. You know it'll be at least half an hour before Nana is ready to leave."

Greg turned to give Mitch his full attention, and Jill scanned the choir loft to catch sight of Nana. Her gaze was drawn immediately to the fiery red head surrounded by a sea of gray. Nana stood out among her cronies like a stray dandelion in the middle of a manicured lawn. Her arms waved, hands churning the air around her as she spoke with all the dramatic flare of a stage actress. As Jill watched, her hands swept down her body toward the floor. Probably describing Mom's wedding dress, which meant news of the wedding had spread through the congregation. No surprise there.

Jill turned to pick up her bulletin from the cushioned pew, then straightened, catching sight of a man hurrying toward her. She bit back a groan. Paul Nester, minister of music, wore a purposeful expression that sent dread rippling through her. Before the accident he took every opportunity to pressure her into playing in church whenever her concert schedule allowed her to be in the Cove on a Sunday morning. The invitations stopped for a long time after the accident, but in recent months he'd dropped a few casual hints to let her know he hoped to schedule her on the special music calendar whenever she was ready to play again. Judging by the look on his face, he wasn't going to hint around this time.

She considered escape. Could she pretend she hadn't seen him? Slip into the aisle and lose herself in the crowd of chatting congregants? A second later, the opportunity fled. He made eye contact, held up a finger, and mouthed, "I want to talk to you."

Resigned, she waited until he sidestepped the length of the pew in which she stood, then forced a smile. "Hi, Paul."

"I heard your good news." His eyes flickered behind her back, where Greg stood talking with Mitch. "Congratulations on your engagement."

"Thank you."

"I also heard you've started giving piano lessons. Mrs. Fontaine and Mrs. Cramer told the choir this morning that you're teaching their granddaughters."

"That's true. We started yesterday, in fact."

"That's wonderful news. Does this mean you're playing the piano again?"

Here came the request. Jill started to shake her head, but he continued before she could even begin the gesture.

"Because if so, I have a slot in the Christmas program waiting for you." He cast a quick glance over his shoulder to see who was standing nearby, and went on in a lower voice. "The program is terrible. We need someone with talent. Your playing is such a blessing."

A blessing? The word struck her with the force of a slap. A blessing to whom? Certainly not to her, not anymore. God had taken away her blessing when he allowed that crash. When he crushed her hand beyond even the most skilled surgeon's ability to repair.

She swallowed back a bitter surge of acid and managed to choke, "I can't."

And even if I could, I wouldn't. If God had seen fit to take her gift from her, then why should she play for him? She would use her training to help students like Mariah and Kaylee, but that would be the extent of her giving musically to others. She would not play for anyone else, including God.

Paul's glance lowered to her left hand for a fraction of a second, which she realized she'd been flexing unconsciously, then flicked back up to her face. The sympathy she saw in his eyes twisted a knot in her chest.

He reached toward her, but did not touch her. "I'm so sorry. When I heard you were taking students, I guess I misunderstood."

She was saved from responding by Greg, who ended his conversation with Mitch and joined them.

"Well, that's good news." His grin swept them both. "He wanted to let me know he and the rest of the elder board will be attending the meeting tomorrow night as a group, as a public show of support."

"Hey, that *is* good news." Paul clapped him on the arm, relief at the interruption of their awkward conversation apparent in his exuberance. "I'm planning to be there too. Look forward to hearing what you have to say." He smiled another unspoken apology toward Jill, nodded farewell, and left.

"It's starting to look like the whole town is going to show up tomorrow night." Greg scooped up his Stetson from the pew and twisted his features into a grimace. "I hope they like my plan."

Jill turned her back on Paul Nester's retreating figure. At least that uncomfortable conversation was over with. Hopefully, she wouldn't be forced to have it again.

She made her way to the back of the sanctuary beside Greg. "You're not getting nervous, are you?"

"Nervous?" He shook his head. "Nah. I'm looking forward to laying everything out. If there are any real holes in my plan, I need someone to point them out so I can address them. Besides," He put an arm around her waist and hugged her close, "my number-one fan will be there. Who else matters?"

Jill almost stumbled. She'd said the same thing to him several times, just before she went onto the concert stage. Greg had traveled to as many of her performances as his schedule allowed, and always sat on the front row. His hands were always the first to start the applause after every piece.

We've changed places. I'm part of his *audience now.*

The discovery slowed her step with an unexpected wave of sadness. She'd become accustomed to the idea that she would no longer play on the concert circuit, but this was different. She'd stepped completely out of the spotlight. The rest of her life, she'd have a supporting role.

"Oh, by the way," Greg went on. "I forgot about a meeting I scheduled Wednesday at four, so I won't be able to pick you up until around five thirty."

She pulled herself away from her gloomy thoughts. "What's happening Wednesday night?"

He stopped and turned to face her. They'd almost reached the sanctuary doors, so the people behind them parted to go around them through the exit.

"We're going to my parents' house for dinner. Remember?"

Parents' house? Did she know this? Her face must have been blank, because Greg's expression grew concerned. "We talked about this last night. You said you were free Wednesday."

"I did?" Now that she thought about it, she did remember discussing dinner with his parents, though she couldn't recall that he mentioned a day. She'd been distracted during their phone conversation, only half-listening as she searched through Nana's bookcase for something to keep her awake so she wouldn't fall asleep and dream.

"Yes, you did." Greg peered at her closely. "Don't you remember?"

"Yes, I remember." She rubbed her eyes. "I'm sorry. I'm just tired today. Didn't sleep very well last night."

"If you'd rather not go, we don't have to. It's just that Mom wants to talk about the wedding decorations."

Great. Yet another wedding planner. As if she didn't have enough with Nana and her Dynamic Dozen.

Jill cleared her expression. "Greg, I want to go. You know I love your parents."

She did. Greg's mother was one of the sweetest women she'd ever met, and Jill loved spending time with her. His dad was a bit forceful, nothing like Jill's memory of her own mild-mannered father, but over the past four years Jill had come to admire him and his fierce devotion to his sons.

"Okay, good." The anxiety melted from his features.

Nana came up behind them. "I'm ready to go. And look what I have, Jill." Her arms were loaded down by an untidy stack of magazines, which she transferred to Jill. "They're bridal magazines. The girls gathered as many as they could find and marked pages for you to see. We've found some ideas for the flowers and the cake. You and I can go through them this afternoon, and report back when everyone comes over in the morning."

This afternoon? Jill hefted the heavy pile. It would probably take days to go through all these. She caught sight of Greg's grin over Nana's head. Was he laughing at her? If he thought he was sticking her with all the planning decisions, he'd better think again.

"I have a great idea," she told him. "You can come home with us and help us look through all these magazines. After all, this is *our* wedding, not just mine."

The grin faded, and his eyebrows drew together. "Me? I don't know anything about flowers."

"That's all right, dear." Nana patted his arm as she brushed past. "I'll teach you everything you need to know this afternoon."

"That's, uh, great. Thanks."

Jill bit back a chuckle at his discomfiture as she dumped the magazines into his arms. "Come along, dear." She gave him a sweet smile and followed her grandmother out of the church.

~

"What about that one, only with purple icing?" Greg tapped the picture of an elaborate, tiered wedding cake in one of the four magazines spread open on the coffee table in front of them. "That's my favorite color."

Jill twisted sideways on the sofa to fix him with an Are-you-out-of-your-mind stare. "A purple wedding cake?"

Beyond Jill, Ruth gave him the pitying look he'd come to recognize in the past hour as one women reserved for men who didn't have a clue. She stood, picked up her empty teacup, and headed for the kitchen without another word.

"What?" He lifted his hands in an innocent palms-up gesture. "You two said I could voice my opinion. I told you I wouldn't be any good at this."

Jill's eyes narrowed. "You're doing this on purpose. You think if you make ridiculous suggestions we'll get tired of hearing them, and we'll tell you to go home."

Busted. He ducked his head. "Well ..."

"Fine. Your heart's not in it, so you might as well go."

She gave him a shove. Was it a little too firm to be entirely playful? That wasn't like Jill. Greg examined her face for signs that she was upset with him. Her eyelids drooped, and a couple of dark smudges marred the smooth skin beneath her eyes. She'd mentioned at church that she hadn't slept well last night, and she looked like the lack of rest was catching up with her this afternoon.

Jill looked up and caught him watching her. A sheepish smile curved her lips. "Sorry. I didn't mean to snap. I guess I'm not my normal sweet self today, huh?"

"You look tired," he told her. "Maybe you should take a nap."

"No." Her quick response surprised him. She flipped the page of the magazine in her lap. "I'll be fine. I just want to get through all these before Nana's friends show up in the morning. They went to the trouble of finding them and marking their suggestions, and I don't want them to think I'm not grateful."

That was his Jill, too kind to hurt someone's feelings.

He settled deeper into the sofa cushion and looked at the magazine she held. "If you're going to suffer through another five dozen pictures of wedding cakes, I will too. What's next?"

The smile she turned toward him this time was tender. "You don't have to do that. I know you're concerned about your presentation tomorrow night, so I think you should go home and work on it. You've been tortured enough with wedding stuff."

Since that's exactly what he'd planned to do with this afternoon and evening before being drafted to look through wedding magazines, he leaned forward and placed a kiss on her brow. "Thank you for understanding. I love you, you know that?"

"I love you, too. You're going to be terrific tomorrow."

"And you are going to be a beautiful bride in just under four weeks." He stood and gathered up their teacups. "I'll take these to the kitchen and say good-bye to Ruth so she won't think I escaped without permission."

Jill smiled, nodded, and flipped another page. He examined her profile. She looked pale. As Greg headed for the kitchen, worry wormed its way into his thoughts. Her recovery after the accident had taken so long, and for a while they'd thought she might not make it. Maybe he'd been wrong to ask for such a quick wedding date. He really hadn't anticipated the planning would be very involved, but it looked as though he'd inadvertently created a stressful situation for her.

"Oh, thank you, Greg." Ruth took the cups from his hands when he entered the kitchen. "Would you like a refill?"

"Thanks, but I need to get going." When she gave him a sharp look, he rushed on with his excuse. "Jill said I could go home and work on my speech."

Her lips pursed as she considered, then gave a nod. "I suppose that's important too." She turned toward the sink with the dishes.

Greg stepped up beside her and pitched his voice low. "Is she doing okay? She seems pretty stressed today, and she mentioned she didn't sleep well. Do you know if that's just a one-time thing?"

Ruth glanced toward the open doorway. "Oh, I think so. She's just experiencing the normal pre-wedding jitters." He must have looked startled, because she rushed on. "Not about you, dear. Just about all the things that need to be done." Her expression grew stern. "Done in a very short time, I might add."

Of course, all those "things" weren't really necessary, if you asked him. And Jill didn't seem all that enthusiastic about having a wedding cake, or pictures, or anything like that either. It was Ruth who was pushing those "things."

He had to tread lightly there, though, since obviously Ruth cared a lot about them. "Well, maybe you could encourage her not to go overboard with the planning." He leaned a hip against the counter. "Remind her that one of the benefits we discussed about a family ceremony was not having to stress over the planning."

He couldn't tell if his subtle suggestion hit its mark or not. The only reaction he got as Ruth rinsed out the teacups was, "Hmmm."

He straightened. "Will I see you tomorrow night?"

"Absolutely." A broad smile stretched across her face. "My knitting circle is planning to get there early and sit up front."

"Good. Ask them to leave the rotten tomatoes at home, okay?" He grinned. "Save them for Samuels's next public appearance."

She laughed her hearty laugh, and fell in beside him as he headed toward the front door.

In the living room, he opened his mouth to say good-bye to Jill, but snapped it shut when he caught sight of her. She'd fallen asleep on the couch, the magazine still in her hand. Her head lolled backward against the rear cushion, her eyes closed, chest rising and falling evenly. Sleep smoothed out the lines he'd noticed earlier around her eyes, and her lips were soft and pliable. He resisted the urge to brush a good-bye kiss against them, lest he wake her. The sleep would do her good.

He mouthed a silent good-bye to Ruth and tiptoed from the room.

~

Crushing weight. Searing heat. Icy cold fingers reaching for her, pulling her down ...

Jill came fully awake with a gasp, screams from her dream still echoing in her mind. She was on her feet beside the sofa, and for a moment couldn't remember how she got there. The scattered magazines jarred her memory. The wedding. Flowers and cakes. She'd sent Greg home to work on his speech and then she'd done the one thing she had vowed not to do.

She fell asleep.

And the dream had returned.

Her chest heaved with a sob. What was wrong with her? It couldn't be stress from wedding planning. That wasn't stressful. In the past ten years she'd learned what real stress meant. The loss of her father, her mom's stroke, and finding solace in her music only to have it taken from her in the brutal accident last year. Having the only future you'd ever wanted ripped away from you, that was stressful. Having a doctor tell you another surgery would do no good, that you'd regained as much motion as you were ever going to have, that was stressful. Recurring thoughts of children flying through the air in front of your eyes and slamming into a window that was where the ceiling should have been, that was real stress. What was selecting bouquet flowers compared to that?

I'm losing my mind.

That was the only explanation for the recurring nightmare, and for the ever-increasing urge that someone wanted her to warn the people of Seaside Cove that they *must* leave. Evacuate their homes. Take their children, their loved ones, and head inland.

The feeling was so strong she found herself halfway across the room toward the front door before she realized what she was doing. With an effort, she stopped. What was she going to do, run into the street and scream at the top of her lungs?

Yes, that's exactly what her instincts told her to do.

That's crazy.

Which proved her point. She was losing her mind. The sight of Nana's cozy living room blurred behind a pool of tears. Poor Greg. He was engaged to a crazy person. He deserved so much better.

God, can't you make this dream go away? I don't want to be insane.

Could insanity be stopped? Reversed, even? Doreen would know. That's what she'd do. She'd call her counselor. A wild hope blossomed in her chest, but it felt alarmingly close to hysteria, so she clamped her teeth together before she made a noise that would attract Nana's attention from the other room.

Tonight was Sunday. Doreen would understand an emergency call on Sunday, but only if it was a true emergency. Did insanity count as a true emergency?

Jill bent her forefinger and bit down on her knuckle. No. She would *not* bother Doreen on Sunday evening. The dreams were getting more vivid, and the urge to warn the people of the Cove was growing stronger with each one. But it could wait until tomorrow. Nothing would happen tonight, she was certain of that.

Because now she knew when the disaster was going to happen. Now she had been given a date.

How crazy was that?

Chapter 10

Monday, November 28

Jill was waiting in the parking lot at seven-forty when a car pulled up in front of Doreen's office. From the passenger seat, the counselor's eyes connected with Jill's through the windshield and her eyebrows arched. Doreen had once mentioned that she chose to live in a small town so she wouldn't have to bother with owning a car. Jill switched off the engine and waited while Doreen gathered her belongings and stood. She bent to say something to the woman driving, then headed for the building carrying a briefcase, a purse, and a Starbucks cup already decorated with bright pink lip prints. The car left. Jill dropped her keys into her purse, shouldered the strap, and joined Doreen on the sidewalk.

"This is a surprise." The counselor walked up the short walkway, jangling keys in her hand. Her pumps crunched over gritty, blue salt the maintenance people had scattered over the concrete to melt a trace of snow that had fallen during the night. "Did we schedule an appointment this morning that I forgot to write down?"

"No." Jill clipped the word sharply. If she elaborated she

would cry, and she didn't want to cry in the parking lot where anyone in the Cove might drive by and see her.

Doreen shot her a keen glance, dipped her head in a brief nod, and unlocked the office's front door. She held the door open to allow Jill to enter the small reception area first. Jill stepped inside, stopped in the center of the room, and managed to wait until the lights flickered on overhead before losing her composure.

"Oh, D-*huh*- Doreen!" The words gushed out on a sob. She gulped some air. "I'm losing my mind."

"What?" Rarely did Doreen's professional mask slip, but this time surprise animated her features.

Jill jerked her head up and down. "I am, truly. Bonkers. Ready-for-the-nuthouse crazy. I'm having insane urges."

"Urges?" Concern carved lines in the skin above her eyebrows. "Have you considered hurting yourself?"

"No."

"Harming your grandmother, or Greg?"

The ludicrous suggestion shocked Jill momentarily out of her emotional outburst. "Of course not."

Doreen's face transformed into the calm mask Jill knew so well. "Let's talk in my office."

Jill followed her through the outer door, past the deserted receptionist's desk, and waited while she unlocked the inner office door. The instant Jill stepped inside the familiar room, the knotted muscles in her shoulders started to relax. This was a safe place. She could talk freely here, and together she and Doreen would figure out what was going on. She dropped into her regular chair.

Instead of taking her usual seat, Doreen stood in front of Jill and leaned against the desk. She did not, Jill noticed, pick up a pen or reach for her notepad. Did that mean this wasn't an official session? She folded her fingers and let her hands hang casually in front of her. "Tell me what's going on."

"It's that stupid dream. It keeps coming back, and it's not the sleeping pills. I haven't taken any more of those."

"Jill, we talked about this on Friday. Dreams aren't uncommon when someone has suffered a traumatic event, as you have."

"I know, but this one is making me want to ..." In her lap, the fingers of her right hand pressed against the scar on her left until pain shafted up her arm. "To do something."

"What does the dream tell you to do?"

Her throat burned like the Sahara in August. "Warn people about a disaster that's coming to Seaside Cove." She risked an upward glance and felt a ridiculous sense of relief when Doreen's expression remained impassive.

"What kind of disaster?"

"I wish I knew." Jill propelled herself out of the chair and paced to the center of the room, ignoring the twinge of pain in her injured hip the sudden movement caused. "It's all jumbled together. I see flames and water, feel hot and cold." She pressed her hands against her ears. "I hear people screaming."

"Like the screams on the subway?"

She shook her head. "No. These are different. Farther away or something." Her hands tightened into fists. "It's not the subway accident. This is something different, something worse. And I have to tell people, warn them to leave the Cove before next Tuesday."

Doreen's eyes widened almost imperceptibly. "You have a date?"

Miserable, Jill nodded. "Tuesday, December 6. Eight days from today."

For one moment, Doreen studied her face. Then she picked up a pen from the cup on the corner of her desk and slid into her chair. Relieved, Jill returned to her own seat. Now maybe they could get to the bottom of this.

The counselor clicked the pen. "How are the wedding plans coming along?"

"Nana has taken charge." Jill pulled a grimace. "She and her friends have all kinds of ideas."

"Hmm. And how did the piano lessons go on Saturday?"

"Fine. Great, in fact. One of the girls has a lot of natural talent." *No doubt where this line of questioning was going.* Jill leaned forward. "I know what you're thinking, but this dream isn't related to the wedding or my students."

"Are you certain of that?"

Jill hesitated. She wasn't certain of *anything* lately. Today, all she felt was exhaustion from sitting up all night, afraid to fall asleep again.

Doreen went on. "Perhaps this recurring dream is your subconscious mind's way of telling you that you're moving too quickly. There are still some traumatic experiences you have not faced about the subway accident, and maybe it's time to resolve them before you can truly put the event behind you and move forward."

"I've resolved everything," Jill insisted.

The counselor's eyebrows arched. "Even Robert?"

Jill's protest died on her lips. No, she hadn't resolved Robert's death. And she didn't want to. That was too harsh, too unfair. Too painful.

"Jill, what if you talked to Greg and requested to postpone the wedding for a few months?"

"No." She couldn't do that. Didn't want to do that. She loved Greg, and there was no reason to wait to begin their life together. "No, I want to get married on Christmas."

"Then what about putting the piano lessons on the back burner for a while? Just a few months, until the rush of the holidays and the wedding are over."

That's what she'd wanted to do from the beginning. If Nana hadn't pushed her into starting immediately, she wouldn't have begun for several months. And yet, could she call Kaylee and tell her to come back in six months? The shy girl's face flashed into focus, so excited and proud as Jill lavished praise on her. No, she couldn't disappoint the child that way.

"I don't want to do that either," she told Doreen.

A prolonged silence fell between them. Jill shifted her weight in the chair.

Finally, the counselor clicked the pen. "Jill, I don't think you're losing your mind."

Hope soared like a bird in springtime. "You don't?"

"No. But you are obviously under a tremendous amount of stress. That's completely understandable, given your past trauma and the recent changes in your life." She leaned forward, her arms resting on her thighs, and held Jill's gaze. "I'd like you to make an appointment with Dr. Bookman to talk about an anti-anxiety medication."

"Oh, that's a great idea." Jill didn't bother to filter the sarcasm out of her voice. "Pop a pill and *voila*! The dreams will disappear. Although I won't want to do anything except sit in a corner and tie knots in string or something, but at least I won't dream."

Doreen's laughter filled the room. "When did you become so dramatic? We're not talking about an antipsychotic medication. You won't have a sensation of being drugged. In fact, the only way you'll be able to tell you're taking anything at all is that you'll feel better able to cope, and you'll be able to get a good night's sleep. And let me repeat what I said a minute ago, in case you didn't hear me: You are not going insane. Anti-anxiety meds are just one part of a stress-reduction regime that can help you manage until your life calms down a bit. This doesn't have to be permanent."

Jill tried not to feel offended by Doreen's laughter. Didn't she realize how upsetting this dream thing was? How close Jill had come to running into the streets and making an idiot of herself like some sort of doomsday prophet?

Still, there was no doubt at all the stress was getting to Jill. Maybe Doreen was right. "What do you mean by a stress-reduction regime?"

"There are things you can do in combination with medication to help manage your stress level."

"You mean take up yoga or something?" That sounded more like something she could do. She'd done some yoga in college.

Doreen nodded. "Relaxation techniques are terrific. Rigorous exercise is also a great way to reduce stress. Whatever it takes, that's what I think you should do." The pen clicked closed and went back in the holder. "Now, I've got a client coming at eight, so I'm afraid we have to end this session."

Jill picked up her purse and followed the counselor to the door. Nothing had really been resolved, but oddly, she felt a tiny bit better. Maybe all she needed was to try those yoga techniques she'd learned years ago. Or join a gym, or something.

The counselor stopped in the doorway. "If you like, Nora can make that appointment with Dr. Bookman for you."

"Okay, thanks. And, uh," Jill gave her a sheepish smile, "sorry for the unscheduled visit."

Doreen shook her head, smiling. "Don't worry about it. I'm glad you came."

She disappeared into her office, and Jill made her way to the front door. The receptionist, now at her post behind the window, spoke quietly into a phone she held up to her ear. Jill fastened the last button on her coat and waited for the woman's conversation to end. Should she wait and ask her to call Dr. Bookman's office?

A moment later, Jill left the building. She was certainly capable of making her own appointment. In the meantime, she intended to try some of the other stress management techniques. Immediately.

When Jill entered her mother's room at Centerside, she stopped short. Mom lay in bed, still dressed in her nightgown and propped up on a pile of pillows, her eyes closed. Jill glanced at her watch. Ten minutes past eight. Mom's regular morning routine was for the nurses to get her up, bathed, dressed, and at the breakfast table by seven thirty. Why was she still in bed? Jill whirled and marched to the empty nurse's station at the end of the hall, where she stood, tapping her fingers on the high counter and waiting for someone to come.

A nurse's aide wheeled an elderly man out of his room nearby and headed down the wide hallway. Jill recognized her as one of the aides who helped take care of Mom.

"Excuse me."

The girl turned and, when she caught sight of Jill, smiled. "Good morning, Ms. King. You're here early today, aren't you?"

What was that supposed to mean? Did she need to call and make an appointment to visit her own mother? Or did they only get Mom out of bed at a decent time when they knew Jill was coming?

Calm down. That's not true, and I know it.

She dug at her burning eyes with a thumb and forefinger. Lack of sleep was muddling her thoughts.

She schooled her voice into a pleasant tone. "I was just wondering why my mother isn't out of bed yet."

The elderly man in the chair raised his head and extended his neck toward Jill. "Lazy!" His shout startled Jill so that she jumped backward. "No good lazy slob won't get a job."

Jill stared at the man, mouth dangling open.

The aide patted the man's shoulder. "Now, Mr. Jeffries, we're not talking about your son. We're talking about Lorna King. You know she doesn't have a job."

"Well, he ought to get out and find one, no matter what his mother says." Bushy gray brows dropped down over his rheumy eyes. "No excuse. I'm not supporting his lazy hide another day. I'm putting my foot down, I tell you." He raised his knee and stomped down on the wheelchair footrest with force.

The aide's shoulders lifted slightly in an apology. "Mrs. King didn't have a good night last night, so she was tired this morning."

"Is she sick?" Jill asked, concerned.

"She does have a slight cough." The girl's face cleared. "I'll ask the nurse to stop by her room and answer your questions." She wheeled Mr. Jeffries away.

Jill returned to her mother's room. Mom had not moved, but lay sleeping with her hands resting at her sides and her chest rising and falling with shallow breaths. The drawn side of her face wasn't nearly as noticeable in this position, and gravity smoothed away some of the wrinkles from the gaunt skin. She looked peaceful in sleep.

At least one of us is getting some sleep.

Jill dismissed the bitter thought and scooted a chair near

the bedside. The pleasant odor of lemons gave evidence that the room had recently been cleaned, and Mom's silvery hair showed signs of being brushed. Some of the tension left her muscles. Obviously Mom hadn't been ignored this morning.

A rustling noise behind her announced the presence of the nurse. Jill turned.

"Good morning." The woman smiled as she bustled around Jill to stand at the head of Mom's bed. "The night nurse said Lorna wasn't feeling well last night. Her temperature was slightly elevated, and she had a cough. Didn't you, honey?"

The last was directed at Mom in a near-shout that set Jill's teeth together. Mom's eyelids fluttered open.

"Is she sick?" Jill covered her mother's hand on the blanket with hers. The skin felt cool.

"Oh, I don't think so. Her vital signs are good this morning. The doctor is going to stop by when he does his rounds, but I doubt it's anything serious. Probably just a cold." Her voice rose again. "But every now and then we ought to be allowed to spend a few extra hours in bed, shouldn't we, honey? She was served her breakfast in bed just like a queen." The woman smiled at Jill. "She ate well, too. I don't think there's any reason to worry."

The nurse left the room, and Jill forced herself to relax. Mom's lids did not shut again. Her eyes moved in their sockets as her gaze circled the room, then came to rest on Jill. Not a hint of recognition, but at least Mom was looking at her. It was easier to carry on a conversation with her when she was in bed with her head back against a pile of pillows. At least they could make eye contact.

"I hope you're not coming down with anything," Jill told her. "I know how it is to get no sleep. I haven't been sleeping well myself lately."

An understatement of monumental proportions. A yawn took possession of her. Jill covered her mouth.

"Sorry. I didn't go to sleep at all last night, thank goodness. I know it's going to catch up with me sooner or later, but I just didn't want to risk it."

No reaction in the eyes fixed on her. In fact, a second later, the lids drooped, then closed. Jill leaned back in the chair. In some ways, visits with Mom were as good as therapy sessions with Doreen. She could pour out all her thoughts, and sometimes talking about them helped. Problems didn't seem quite so insurmountable when she articulated them, as though finding the right words to describe them reduced their power to something more easily managed.

"I've been having weird dreams, Mom." She glanced over her shoulder to make sure she wasn't overheard. "Well, just one dream, really. My counselor says it's from stress because of all the changes in my life lately. Or it might be from some unresolved issues left over from the accident."

Robert.

Jill braced herself against the pain that always accompanied thoughts of Robert. Was he somehow responsible for this dream? Not him personally, but what he represented?

And exactly what does he represent in my mind?

"We were friends." Her whisper crept into the silence of the room. "We only knew each other a few minutes, but we became friends. Like kindred spirits or something. He knew I was a musician, even what kind of music I liked." She brushed a finger over the diamond on her left hand. "Greg barely knows who Beethoven is."

The realization of the sentiment she'd just voiced struck her. She rushed on. "Not that there would ever have been anything romantic between us. It wasn't like that. It's just that ..." She bit down on her lip, stared at the sparkling stone. "Greg doesn't really know what I've lost. Robert knew. He told me God wouldn't take away my gift."

A bitter laugh welled up from somewhere deep in her chest. "Obviously, he was wrong about that. So I need to forget about him, put him out of my mind, and get on with my life. Maybe if I can do that, this stupid dream will go away."

Mom's eyelids fluttered open.

"I haven't told you about my dream, have I? I keep dreaming that some terrible disaster is going to happen in the Cove, and that I'm supposed to warn people. Problem is, I don't even know what this disaster is supposed to be, only the date. December 6."

Mom's gaze fixed on her face. Jill twisted her lips. "I know. Ridiculous, huh? Doreen says I should do whatever it takes to reduce the amount of stress in my life and the dream will go away. I'm sure she's right."

Mom's right hand, the one that retained limited movement after the stroke, flew up from the mattress and began waving in the air. "Eyuah, eyuah, aaahhhh." Her voice, so melodious and sweet in Jill's memory, croaked the harsh, low monotone that was the only sound she'd made in nine years. Jill had long since ceased trying to interpret the unintelligible noise. The doctors said the sound was merely vocalizing, as a baby who has no words does to express feelings. But even though Mom wasn't speaking words, the sound always meant she had something she wanted to convey.

"Mom, are you okay? Is something wrong?"

"Aaahhh, eyuah, aaahhh." The hand gyrated in the air above the bed.

Jill's heart sank. Most of the time Mom rested quietly, but these instances of wild, uncontrolled babble were happening more often lately. What did that mean? Was she developing Alzheimer's in addition to everything else?

"Eyuah, aaaahhh, eyuah, eyuah."

Jill rose from the chair and grabbed her mother's hand when the nurse hurried through the door.

"I don't know what's wrong." Her voice wavered as she held the hand close to her chest. "Is she in pain? Has her fever spiked?"

With cool professionalism, the woman placed a hand on Mom's forehead. "I don't think so, but I'll check her vitals in a second." She bent over the bed, placed her face six inches from Mom's, and shouted, "Lorna, do you need something?"

"Eyuah, aaaaahhhhh."

Jill ground her teeth in frustration, both at the nurse's shout and at her inability to understand her mother. "We were talking and she just started babbling. What does she want?"

The nurse straightened and fixed a sympathetic smile on Jill. "Honey, she does this sometimes. It doesn't mean a thing. Probably just her way of letting us know she's ready to get up." She turned and shouted into her patient's face. "Lorna, the doctor is in the building. He'll be here in a few minutes, and then I'll get the aide to come in here and help you get a bath and dress. It'll be just a minute, honey."

Amazingly, Mom's eyes focused on the nurse, and she calmed. Her hand relaxed in Jill's grip, and she fell silent.

"That's better." The nurse turned to Jill with a smile. "If you want to wait for the doctor, he'll be in here shortly." She patted Jill's arm and bustled out of the room.

Jill settled back in the chair. Doubt niggled at her mind like a worm winding its way through an apple. She hadn't said anything to set Mom off, had she? She searched the pale face resting comfortably once again on the pillows. Maybe the nurse was right, and Mom was simply letting them know the only way she could that she was ready to get out of bed.

Still, Jill would question the doctor closely. Maybe request that he perform whatever test they could to diagnose Alzheimer's. That would be icing on the cake, wouldn't it? Yet another stress factor. At this rate, she'd never be able to sleep again.

Chapter 11

NOISE AND AN ALMOST UNCOMFORTABLE warmth slapped at Greg when he stepped through the doorway and into The Wharf Café. He'd thought he would miss the lunch rush since it was nearly one o'clock, but every table was in use. He pulled the door closed behind him and unwound his scarf before shedding the heavy coat, his gaze sweeping the room for an empty table or at least a couple of friendly faces he could join. A few of the lunchtime regulars exchanged nods of greeting.

"Hey, there's our next councilman!" Rowena's cheerful voice rose over the top of her chattering patrons' heads. Behind the counter she stood, dressed in a thick white apron over jeans and a tightly fitted T-shirt, her cheeks rosy with a becoming flush from the heat of the grill.

Heads turned, and people smiled and called greetings to Greg.

"Come on over here, darlin'." Rowe beckoned with a long spatula. "This stool right here's got your name on it."

As he threaded his way through the café, people greeted him with smiles and nods. A man stood and thrust a hand toward him. Familiar face. Greg cast about in his mind for a name.

"Roy Newsome," the man supplied. "I'm looking forward to hearing about this plan of yours tonight."

Newsome. Lived on the outskirts of the Cove and worked for an insurance company or something in downtown Halifax. Greg had met him at a community picnic during the summer.

He grasped the man's hand and returned a firm handshake. "Thank you, Roy. I'm glad to hear you're coming. I hope you'll let me know what you think."

"I'll do it." The man returned to his lunch.

"Sit here, Greg." Rowena pointed toward an empty seat at the counter, near the grill.

As he slid onto the high stool, the girl who worked weekdays for Rowena plopped a glass of ice water in front of him. She started to pull out an order pad, but Rowena waved her away.

"I'll get this one." Dimples appeared in the flushed cheeks she turned toward Greg. "The chowder's good today. And I have a piece of warm gingerbread to follow it up."

"Sounds great. You know I love your chowder."

The dimples deepened. "I know. I made it special, because this is your big day."

When she turned toward the stew pot, he picked up the water and sipped. It felt good to get away from the office. The cozy atmosphere of the café provided exactly the distraction he needed to help him switch gears from a morning full of legal briefs to an afternoon of preparation for his presentation tonight.

She ladled a huge bowlful of creamy chowder and set it in front of him. Fragrant steam wisped upward. He closed his eyes and inhaled. "Mmmm. Smells wonderful, Rowe. Thanks."

"Anything for my favorite customer."

She gave him a saucy wink and returned to her position at the grill, which was situated directly in front of his stool so he had a good view of her profile as she worked. A pretty profile it was, too, and she used it to full advantage. The old fishermen who frequented the café hung out here for the view as much as for the gallons of coffee she poured them. Greg blew on a spoonful of chowder, then savored a bite of thick soup filled with chunks of haddock and lobster.

"So, are you all ready for tonight?" She expertly flipped a burger and mashed it flat with the spatula. Grease sizzled and popped on the hot grill.

"I think so." He scooped up another steaming spoonful and shot her a sheepish grin. "I've blocked off all afternoon to go over my presentation a couple of dozen times."

She chuckled, shaking her head. "You lawyer-types are so obsessive."

"Oh, I didn't learn that in law school. I inherited that quality from my mother."

She twisted sideways to look at him head-on. "I'd like to meet your mother. Will she be here tonight?"

" 'Fraid not. She and Dad don't leave the orchard much after dark in the wintertime. It's killing my dad not to be here, though." He heaved a laugh. "He requested that I have the meeting taped so we can go over it together later. I told him no way."

The burger done, she scooped it up and slid it onto a bun. When she'd dressed it with lettuce, pickles, and tomatoes, she handed the plate to the girl to deliver.

Wiping her hands on her apron, she tilted her head sideways. "I'd be happy to videotape it for you, if you like. I mean, I'm not a professional or anything, but I have one of those little handheld numbers. I can certainly sit on the front row and hold a camera steady."

Greg paused with the spoon halfway to his mouth. Visions of giant TV cameras on tripods scattered around the room, bright lights, and stage makeup had prompted him to dismiss his father's request. That would make him feel ridiculous, and Samuels would probably accuse him of trying to generate a bunch of fake hype or something. But a small, handheld home video camera on the front row would be unobtrusive. And watching the recording afterward would help him analyze his presentation skills, so he could improve the next time. Sort of like professional ball teams watched game clips.

"You don't think people would be intimidated by the presence of a camera? I want tonight to be all about getting people's honest reactions, and a free exchange of ideas."

Rowe's lips twisted and she rolled her eyes. "Trust me, honey. I've been talking this meeting of yours up for weeks now, and I've listened to what the folks who come in the café say. People are excited to hear about this plan of yours, and there's no danger a little handheld video camera is going to intimidate them out of giving you their honest reactions."

Greg set his spoon down and gave Rowe a long look. She really *had* been talking this up. The walls of the café were peppered with posters about tonight's meeting, and the café's owner had become one of his staunchest supporters in recent weeks. Rowe couldn't stand Samuels, and that didn't hurt Greg's cause any with the pretty café owner. Plus, The Wharf Café was exactly the kind of business that would reap the most benefit from increased tourist trade in the Cove, but he didn't think her support was entirely due to the possibility of personal gain. She seemed to genuinely like him.

"Thank you, Rowe. I haven't told you how much I appreciate all you've done. Your support means a lot to me."

She stepped forward and covered his hand with warm fingers. "I believe in you, Greg. You're exactly what I've been waiting for." She squeezed, and then released his hand. "For my business, I mean."

He grinned. "Don't suppose you'd be interested in a job as my campaign manager, would you?"

"Well, now, I just might." A flirty twinkle flashed in her eyes. "Depends on how you handle yourself tonight."

She disappeared through the swinging doors into the kitchen, and Greg picked up his spoon. The suggestion about becoming his campaign manager hadn't been serious, just lunchtime banter. But now that the idea had been voiced, he liked it. Everyone in the Cove loved bubbly, energetic Rowena, and he did need the help of someone who believed in his goals for the Cove, especially if tonight went well and he got enough public support for his plan. Jill would help with some of the details as the election drew close, but she certainly couldn't do it all, especially since she was just starting to show a few real signs of recovering from the accident.

People not only loved Rowena, they respected her. She was probably the youngest business owner in Seaside Cove, with twice the energy and five times the drive of any of the others. With money inherited after her parents' death several years ago, she'd bought a failing restaurant, and transformed the place into a thriving hub of activity in the community. In fact, what Rowe had done with the café was exactly what Greg hoped to do with the Cove, so she was the perfect person to partner with him. The more he considered the idea, the better it felt.

He scraped out the last bite of chowder, then picked up his glass as Rowena returned. "You know, Rowe, you really would make a great campaign manager. I think we'd work well together."

She set a huge piece of gingerbread in front of him and leaned a hip against the counter. "Oh, I'm sure we would." The dimples appeared. "I've thought that for a long time."

"So you'll do it?"

Her gaze went distant as she considered. Then she gave a slow nod. "I think I'd like that."

Greg grinned. "Excellent. With your help, this election will be a breeze."

"I don't know how much help I'll be, but I can tell you one thing. When I set my sights on something, I get it." She held his gaze while a slow smile curled the corners of her full lips.

The door opened behind him. Rowe's gaze wandered over his shoulder. Her eyes widened and the smile faded. She straightened and turned hurriedly back to the grill, leaving him with the impression she wasn't fond of whoever had just entered the café. Curious, Greg glanced over his shoulder toward the door.

~

Jill stepped inside the noisy café and scanned the room for Greg. She caught sight of him seated at the counter, talking with Rowena Mitchell. The café owner leaned over the counter toward him, her attractive features arranged into a flirty and disturbingly possessive expression. A sharp pang of jealousy stabbed at Jill. What was that woman doing flirting with *her* fiancé?

She'd never been overly fond of Rowena, though obviously Greg thought highly of her. So did everyone else in the Cove. And Jill had always grudgingly admired her spunk, her determination to overcome obstacles and make her restaurant successful. But there was a reason most of her customers were men. The woman flaunted her buxom build to full advantage, which hadn't made her many friends among the town's women.

Until this moment, Jill hadn't realized she'd set her sights on Greg. When did that happen?

The door whooshed closed behind her with a bang that

silenced the chatter in the restaurant. Every head turned her way.

"Hey, it's Jill." A big, burly figure rose from a nearby table to stand before her. "Good to see you out and about. You look great."

Jill tore her gaze from Rowena and focused on the man in front of her. Danny Ferguson. They'd gone to high school together. She found herself enveloped in a gentle hug, while other voices around the room called out greetings. When Danny released her, she was swept into another hug, and then another, as though she was a long-lost relative coming home for a family reunion. Gosh, had it been so long since she'd seen these people? Yes, probably. For the past year she'd spent most of her time huddled in her apartment, fighting memories and losing herself in soap operas. Obviously, she'd been missed.

The last set of arms to encircle her were Greg's. "This is a terrific surprise. We haven't had lunch together in a long time."

Before the accident, Jill met Greg for lunch several times a week, whenever her concert schedule allowed her to be in town. She'd forgotten. Her gaze met Rowena's. Obviously, the time had come to emerge from her self-imposed seclusion.

"I had to escape the clutches of the wedding planners, so I dropped by your office to see how the plans for tonight were going. Teresa told me you'd be here." Jill allowed him to lead her to the counter, and settled into the high-backed stool beside him.

When she'd returned from visiting Mom, Nana's knitting circle had been encamped in the living room. They'd consumed five pots of tea and three loaves of apple nut bread while they examined the magazine pages Jill had dog-eared. They shot down her flower preferences like so many clay pigeons, and ignored her when she mentioned that she didn't want a wedding cake at all. She'd slipped away when the conversation turned to newspaper announcements. Her eyes were so heavy she welcomed the ten-block walk along the harbor in the frigid air. Anything to keep her awake until after Greg's meeting tonight, when hopefully she'd be so exhausted she could sleep without dreaming.

Greg gave her a sympathetic smile. "You'll probably have to suffer through more of that from my mother Wednesday night. But look on the bright side. At least it will be over soon. Imagine if you had to put up with this for months."

"What can I get for you, Jill?" Rowena's question was couched in friendly tones, but she didn't quite meet Jill's eyes.

"Just some coffee, please." A jolt of caffeine might help. She rubbed her burning eyes.

Greg peered at her. "You look tired. Did you not sleep well again last night?"

She shook her head and stirred cream into the fragrant black liquid Rowena set in front of her. When his expression grew concerned, she flashed a quick smile. "I'll be all right. So, are you ready for tonight?" Deflection was a tactic at which she'd become expert in recent months.

"I still have to go over my talk a few times, but I think I'm ready." He sliced off a corner of the thick slab of gingerbread in front of him. "I have some good news. Rowe has agreed to become my campaign manager. Isn't that great?"

Jill cast a startled glance at the woman, who was suddenly busy scraping the grill with a metal spatula. *Great?* That's hardly the word Jill would use to describe the news. Her hand trembled as she set her spoon on the paper placemat and forced herself to speak pleasantly.

"That's wonderful. I'm sure she'll be a lot of help." With exaggerated care, she raised the coffee cup to her lips and gulped the hot liquid.

"Mmmm." Greg closed his eyes as he chewed the gingerbread

with obvious delight. He stabbed his fork toward the cake. "This is delicious. You should try a piece, Jill."

Rowena turned. "I'll be happy to get you one."

"Oh, don't bother. I'll just have a bite of Greg's."

Jill resorted to middle school tactics and placed a possessive hand on Greg's arm. She leaned toward him, her mouth open. He sliced off a bite and fed it to her, unaware that the gesture was being closely watched by the café owner. Jill saw her eyelids narrow a fraction, and knew the message had been delivered.

Unfortunately, Greg was right. It was the best gingerbread Jill had ever tasted.

~

The afternoon hours after she walked Greg safely away from the café and back to his office crept by like the last day of the school term. Jill returned home to find a note from Nana saying she'd gone to the church and wouldn't be home before tonight's meeting. In vain Jill surfed through the television channels for something to hold her interest. Her limbs felt as though someone had attached anchors to them, and by four o'clock she'd rubbed her eyes so much she looked like she'd been on a week-long crying jag. The fluffy throw pillows on her sofa beckoned. If only she could rest her head on them for just a few minutes.

No. She intended to stay awake until after the meeting. By then her brain would be as exhausted as her body, and maybe she would sleep without dreaming. In the meantime, she had to do something to occupy herself for the next three hours.

Her gaze went to her silent piano, no longer shrouded but still ignored. Before the accident she'd lost herself in music more times than she could count. The minute her fingers touched the keys, she'd be transported into another world, the intricate world a brilliant composer had labored for months or sometimes years to create. Emotions would rise, crest, and fall like a stormy sea, and hours would slip away unnoticed.

But that was before. Now, her left hand wouldn't be able to handle the intricacies of any piece that mattered. She couldn't bear to perform ineptly, to ruin a masterpiece that she'd previously played with the grace and ability the composer intended.

I have to play sometime before next Saturday. A piano teacher has to touch the whole keyboard, not just the upper registers. Kaylee and Mariah need someone to demonstrate the proper techniques, not just describe them.

She clenched the fingers on her left hand into a fist. Today was only Monday. She had five more days to worry about that.

In the meantime, she could dig out her old music books and glance through them. When she was a girl, she'd filled the pages with painstaking notes about her lessons, notes which would no doubt come in handy as a teacher.

Since Jill's apartment occupied the top floor of the house, the entrance to the storage area of the attic was covered with an access panel in her kitchen wall. She slid open the panel and stooped nearly double to enter the cold, dark space. The musty odor of old insulation tickled her nose, and dust danced in the beam of her flashlight. A plywood floor had been laid across the wooden rafters, not quite all the way to the sloping walls. Dozens of boxes had been stacked three deep, each labeled with Nana's careful script.

The plywood creaked as Jill crept among the boxes, looking for the one in which she'd packed away her old music books. She found it near the back, beneath an ancient box labeled LORNA'S THINGS. The masking tape along the seams of the upper box was cracked and stiff with age. When she shoved the heavy box out of her way, it fell to the floor and the tape broke on impact.

"Great."

She knelt, turned the box upright, and inspected the seam. Later she'd bring a roll of tape in here and do a repair job. For now, she'd just push it off to one side. She began to shove things back inside. An empty picture frame. A heavy glass paperweight. A couple of old cassette tapes. She glanced at the covers. Kansas and Journey. Mom had always liked classic rock. An old paperback novel, *The Thorn Birds.* Jill shined the flashlight on the back cover to read the description. The story sounded good, and it was thick enough to keep her entertained for hours.

She set the book aside and scooped up a pair of envelopes held together with an oversized paper clip. The top was a letter addressed to Mom. When she caught sight of the return address, Jill's heart lurched. *Lieutenant Michael King,* HMCS Huron. Daddy had served in the Canadian Navy before he and Mom married. He'd been a cook on a ship, and Jill had a dim memory of him setting a plate of scrambled eggs covered in ketchup in front of her when she was tiny and saying, "That's exactly the way the skipper liked them." The memory brought a smile to her face. Mom must have kept a couple of his letters. Jill flipped to the second envelope, and recognized the same handwriting. Maybe Mom would enjoy hearing the letters again. Jill set them on top of the paperback and finished scooping the rest of the stuff back into the box.

She found her old music books exactly where she'd left them and flipped through the pages of the oldest ones. A glance at her own childish scrawl made her smile. Yes, these were going to be helpful. After sorting through the ones she wanted, she repacked the rest and left the attic.

~

Flames crept along a thick rope, blackening it to char. Voices reached her, oddly distant and yet distinguishable. The high-pitched question of a child. A woman's patient explanation. Conversational tones, without a trace of the urgency that held Jill's breath in her chest like a fist shoved down her throat.

Why were they just standing there talking? They had to leave! She had to warn them.

The pounding of her heart echoed throughout her skull and drowned out their voices.

The dream again.

I'm not here. I'm on the sofa in my living room. I can even feel the cushion beneath my cheek. God, please. Help me wake up.

The burning rope disappeared, followed by a series of images parading before her eyes almost too quickly to see. A child flying through the air. A line of people, covered with blood. The face of a wristwatch. A jagged boulder. Newspaper headlines, all the letters blurred except the date — December 6.

Jill's eyes flew open. The fabric of the sofa beneath her face was wet with tears. She struggled to raise herself upright, her vision blurry, her brain groggy with a dream hangover. Music books lay scattered across the coffee table, and one sprawled open on the floor beside the sofa. She'd been reading that one when she fell asleep.

Her moan echoed in the room. She'd tried so hard not to sleep. Which was stupid, because nobody could go without sleep forever. No matter how hard she tried, sleep would eventually catch up with her, and the dream would come. It seemed nothing could stop it, except ...

The silence around her grew heavy with certainty. She knew

how to stop the dream. She had to warn the people of Seaside Cove to leave town in the early morning hours of December 6. When she'd done that, the dream wouldn't return.

This is ridiculous. How do I know that?

No answer came, just an escalating conviction that she had to act, and act quickly. Only then would the dream set her free. If she didn't act, it would drive her truly crazy.

She forced herself off the couch and stumbled into the bathroom to splash her face with cold water. Doreen said to do whatever it took to get rid of her stress. Okay, if she had to make herself look like a lunatic to rid herself of the dream, she was ready to do that. But how could she get a message to everyone in the Cove? Rent a billboard? Take out an ad in the paper? Cold water filled her cupped hands, and she bent over the basin. Maybe she could print a notice and pass it out all over town, like a politician during an election.

In the act of lowering her face into the pooled water, she froze. Greg's meeting. Half the town would be there. Everyone was interested in his plans, because the future of Seaside Cove concerned them all. But if her dream came true, Seaside Cove might not have a future.

I've got to talk to Greg.

She dashed out of the bathroom toward the kitchen, and rummaged in her purse for her cell phone. The display was dark. Oh, yes. She'd turned it off this morning when she went into Doreen's office, like she always did before a counseling appointment. She punched the button to turn the phone on, and while it powered up, glanced at the clock on the microwave. Her stomach plummeted as the numbers registered on her sleep-fogged brain. Seven twenty-one.

She'd missed the first half of Greg's meeting. If she didn't hurry, she would miss the whole thing.

Chapter 12

GREG PRESSED THE BUTTON TO advance to the next slide. The screen on the stage lit up with the colorful chart he'd worked so hard on.

He spoke into the microphone. "Several of the Nova Scotia communities who have developed targeted tourism programs were happy to share their numbers from last year with me. As you can see, the green bars here represent each town's total budget, and the red sections indicate the percentage of that budget allocated to their tourism programs." He pressed the button again and more bars appeared on the chart. "Now, take a look at their tourism revenue. The correlation is obvious. The higher the budget allocation, the higher the return."

He scanned the faces in the crowded school gymnasium and saw the understanding he'd hoped for. A few wore skeptical expressions, but many heads nodded. The hum of whispers bounced off the elementary school's polished wooden floor as people whispered a comment to their neighbors. In the center of the front row, Rowena sat with her video camera trained on him.

Hers wasn't the only one, either. He saw several cameras in the crowd, and he'd lost count of the number of flashes as people snapped pictures. Best of all was the presence of a reporter from the local newspaper standing against the rolled-up bleachers to the right, who stopped scribbling on his notebook only long enough to take pictures with an elaborate-looking camera. He'd hoped *The Cove Journal* would cover the event.

He still couldn't believe the turnout for tonight's meeting. He'd expected several dozen, maybe, though the handful of folks who'd showed up to help him get the gym ready had insisted on unfolding a hundred chairs in rows facing the stage. Turns out they'd underestimated the crowd by at least half. They'd ended up grabbing more child-sized chairs from the classrooms, and still, standing spectators lined the rear walls of the gym. From his seat in the middle of the fifth row, Samuels's heavy glower stood out among the smiles like a mustard stain on a white shirt.

But where was Jill? Greg's gaze switched to the two empty chairs on the front row, beside the ladies from church who'd showed up to support him, as Ruth promised. Worry gnawed in his stomach. Jill knew how important tonight was to him. She wouldn't miss unless something was wrong. Had something happened to her mother? Or, God forbid, to Jill herself? He'd tried repeatedly to call her before the meeting began, but her phone went straight to voicemail. The rational side of his mind told him that she had probably taken his suggestion of an afternoon nap and overslept. She'd looked so tired at lunch he could easily believe that.

Ruth, also worried, had left to go check on her a few minutes after seven. Greg delayed the meeting as long as he could, but people began to grow restless. When he could stall no longer, he'd reluctantly begun without her.

I hope everything's okay.

Greg returned to the podium and set down the computer's remote control. The chart was his last slide.

He addressed his audience with his closing statements. "I think Seaside Cove has every bit as much to offer as any of these other communities. When we start spreading the word about our town, I am confident that we will realize the same financial results."

A movement at the back of the gymnasium drew his gaze. Relief swept through him at the sight of Jill and Ruth stepping through the door. Jill's head swiveled as she looked around the room, her expression a bit dazed. Ruth touched her arm, then pointed toward the front row and their empty chairs. They began making their way around the left side of the room.

Relieved, Greg flashed her a smile, then turned it on the crowd. "But we have some prep work to do before we can handle an influx of tourists." He held Samuels's gaze for an instant. "And yes, we're going to have to spend some money. Not only that, but we're going to have to roll up our sleeves and get our hands dirty, and I'm not talking about just the business owners. Seaside Cove is a community, and we'll all enjoy the benefits of a healthy tourist trade. If we work together, we can make this happen."

Rowena set her camera in her lap and clapped her hands, her grin wide. The church ladies joined in energetically, and then applause thundered throughout the gymnasium. A bit overwhelmed, Greg made eye contact with as many of his audience as he could, smiling his thanks. This reaction was better than he'd dared hope. After a few seconds, he held up his hand and the sound quieted.

"That's all I have to say tonight, folks. Now I want to hear from you. What do you think? What questions do you have?"

More hands than he expected shot into the air. He'd planned to pass the microphone down the rows, but that would take forever. Better take a town-hall-meeting approach.

"Tell you what. If you have a question, would you mind coming up here so you can speak into the microphone? That way we can all hear."

He drew a line with his hand around one side of the chairs, and a line began to form there. The first person to take the microphone was a woman he didn't recognize.

She held it tentatively, obviously uncomfortable speaking in front of a crowd. "I was just wondering what places you think should be fixed up first." She thrust the microphone back at him like a kid playing a game of Hot Potato.

Greg bit back a grin as she scurried back to her seat. That was exactly the kind of question he hoped he'd get. It meant they were already thinking in terms of putting the plan in place.

"That's a great question," he said, smiling in her direction. "If the residents of the Cove decide my idea has merit, I think we all need to have some input into decisions like that. Maybe we'll put together a planning committee. But personally, I think repairing the docks should be at the top of the list, with repainting the lighthouse a close second. Those are going to be among the biggest draws for tourism."

A smattering of applause answered his suggestions, but he didn't give it time to catch. The line of people with questions snaked around the spectators and almost to the back of the gymnasium. At this rate they'd be here all night, but it was important to make sure everyone had time to voice their opinions.

During the next hour, Greg did his best to answer every question, to give every opinion his full consideration. He was dimly aware of the reporter circling to the other side of the room in front of the long line and snapping a picture of him. People started to filter out of the gymnasium around eight thirty. He didn't see when Samuels left. One minute he was there, his glare heavy as a cement truck, and the next time Greg looked, he was gone.

Finally, the line dwindled to a handful of people. With a start, Greg realized the last person in line was Jill. What was she doing? Was she planning to make a public statement of support for his plan? He gave her a questioning smile, which she did not return. Instead, her lips formed a tight white line, and she stared at him through solemn, red-rimmed eyes. She looked tired. Unwell, even. Was she ill?

~

Her nerves stretched tighter than an overtuned piano string, Jill didn't hear a single question asked by the people in front of her. Every step took her closer to the microphone, closer to the moment of her announcement. She scanned the audience. At least half of the people had already left.

Good. Fewer to see me make a fool of myself.

Not that the number of spectators would make much of a difference. Word would spread through the Cove quickly. How could it not? Her gaze strayed to the newspaper reporter leaning against the bleachers. He'd put away his notepad, but the camera still hung from a wide strap around his neck.

She glanced down the front row. Most of Nana's knitting circle was still here, their hands busy knitting socks for orphans. They'd taken their job of supporting Greg seriously, and though they couldn't applaud without interrupting their sock production, they tapped the gymnasium floor loudly with their shoes at every opportunity. On the end of the row, Nana's gaze locked with hers. Jill looked away. She'd just stumbled through the front door, still buttoning her coat, when Nana's car pulled up in front of the house. From her worried expression now, she must know

Jill was about to do something alarming. Nana would likely have her committed after tonight.

Only one person stood between her and Greg now. Nausea roiled in her stomach. Would he be upset with her? She knew he would. But that no longer mattered. Nothing mattered, except plowing through the ordeal of making a public spectacle of herself. Afterward, when she'd had about twelve hours of uninterrupted sleep and the pressing urgency of her warning was gone, she could deal with the aftermath. Greg loved her. He would understand. She'd *make* him understand.

But what if the dream didn't leave? What if she acted like a lunatic in front of the whole town and it did no good?

It has to. If not, I'll check into a mental ward myself.

The person in front of her complimented Greg on his plan and made a public statement of support, then turned and handed the microphone to her. Her stomach lurched when her fingers closed around the warm casing, and her throat spasmed shut. The handle shook with such violence she had trouble holding it still in front of her mouth. Directly behind Greg, Rowena Mitchell's camera lens pointed in her direction.

Greg stepped in front of her, concerned creases etched in his forehead. He spoke in a low voice that only she could hear. "Jill, is everything okay?"

"Yes. I mean no." She stepped sideways to look out over the heads of the seventy or so people left in the gymnasium. That was a trick she'd learned from one of her professors in college. To ease the pressure of stage fright, you were supposed to look at the tops of people's heads instead of their faces. Jill had never needed to worry about stage fright since she'd been supremely confident in front of a crowd for as long as she could remember. Until now.

She cleared her throat. "I support everything Greg said, and I think his plan is vital for the future of Seaside Cove. I hope you'll vote for him to represent you on the council." She swallowed, and held Greg's eyes in a mute apology before continuing. "But that's not what I want to say. I want — no, I *have* to tell you something that's going to sound really crazy. I've been having these dreams. Well, only one dream, but I've had it several times in the last few days."

With a dry tongue, she tried unsuccessfully to wet her lips. Instead, she filled her lungs and spoke in a rush.

"Seaside Cove is in danger, and unless we evacuate the town next Tuesday morning before ten o'clock, something terrible will happen."

There. She'd done it. She thrust the microphone back into Greg's hands and headed for her chair on the end of the first row without waiting to see his reaction. Though her gaze was fixed on the floor as she hurried past, she couldn't help but notice that the nimble fingers of every member of Nana's knitting circle had gone still, and their mouths gaped open like a neat row of ice fishing holes on a frozen lake. Nana's jaw yawned wide enough to pull a whale through.

"Uh." Greg's voice filled the silence as Jill collapsed onto her folding chair. She risked a glance at him and cringed at the uncertainty of his expression. "Well, I guess if there are no more questions — "

"No, wait." Someone from the back of the gym interrupted. "She can't say that and walk away."

"Yeah," shouted someone else. "What do you mean by 'something terrible'?"

Several voices mumbled in agreement. Jill didn't turn her head to face them, but she did speak loudly enough to be heard by everyone except perhaps those in the back of the room. "I don't know what's going to happen. Only that it's going to be devastating."

"Devastating? You mean like a hurricane or an earthquake?"

The catastrophe in her dream didn't feel like a natural disaster. "No, nothing like that."

"What then?"

She opened her mouth to say she didn't know, but Nana placed a hand on her arm and shook her head almost imperceptibly.

Greg's voice boomed over the speakers. "Folks, Jill hasn't been feeling well lately. She's tired, like we all are. It's been a long meeting, and I appre— "

A chorus of shouts interrupted him.

"Wait a minute."

"Tired? Crazy's more like it."

"Hold on. Let her tell us about that dream."

Chairs scraped across the floor as people got to their feet. Out of the corner of her eye, a movement drew Jill's attention. The reporter from *The Cove Journal* had stepped to the front of the gymnasium and was pointing his camera at her. Jill slumped down in the metal chair.

"Oh, come on," someone called from right behind her head. "Do you think we're fools? This is a publicity stunt, right?"

Jill shook her head at the same time Greg answered, "No, this is not a publicity stunt." A touch of anger gave his denial extra volume. Anger at her? She squeezed her eyes shut. Probably.

"There's only a couple of fools in this room tonight," someone else shouted, "and it ain't us."

The comment was met with laughter that made Jill cringe. In the next instant, she found her chair surrounded and questions thrown at her faster than she could keep up. Someone tugged at her arm, and then several hands were touching her. Not roughly, but she sank lower in the chair and covered her eyes to block out the sight of their scornful faces.

"Hey, isn't she that piano player?" someone asked. "The one who got hurt last year?"

"Yeah, that's her. Maybe she isn't, you know, *right*."

"Ssssshhh! Don't be rude."

A camera clicked, then another one, and bursts of light flashed in the darkness behind her eyelids. A hand grabbed her arm in a gentle but insistent grip.

"That's enough." Greg's voice sounded directly in front of her. She opened her eyes to see several people step back in the face of his stern stare. He stooped over until his nose hovered inches from hers, and his expression softened as his grip on her arm squeezed. Jill looked up into eyes full of tenderness. "I'm taking you home now, okay?"

A wave of gratitude filled her eyes with tears. Unable to squeeze a sound through her tight throat, Jill nodded.

Chapter 13

Greg guided Jill into Ruth's house with a protective arm around her waist and closed the kitchen door behind them. An alarming air of frailty hovered around her, evident in her bowed head and slumped shoulders. She moved like a ninety-year-old. In all the months since the accident, he'd never seen her like this. The realization frightened him. Something was terribly wrong, that much was obvious.

They crossed the main floor and ascended the stairs to Jill's apartment. When he would have taken her to the bedroom to tuck her in, she stopped him.

"Do you mind if we talk for a minute before you leave?" She didn't raise her head high enough to meet his eye, but nodded toward the couch.

"Of course."

He led her there, settled her on one end, and then slid onto the cushion next to her. Still, she didn't look at his face, but stared at her hands. With her right hand, she twisted the diamond around her left ring finger in an unconscious gesture that sparked a flicker of discomfort in him. Was she going to pull the ring off and return it? A trace of lingering irritation at the way she'd taken over his meeting evaporated with the thought.

"Greg, I'm sorry about tonight. I know how important this meeting was to you, and I ruined it."

"I wouldn't say you *ruined* it." He forced a quick laugh. "You certainly gave them something to talk about, though."

She acknowledged the understatement with an upward twitch of her lips, but kept her gaze fixed on her fidgeting hands. "I know I should have talked to you first, let you know what I was going to do. But I fell asleep, and by the time I woke up the meeting was already underway. And I have to warn them, Greg. I have to."

She did look up then, and held his gaze. Her eyes, though red-rimmed, were clear. Sincere. And full of a determination he hadn't seen in over a year.

He leaned back and laid an arm across the top cushion behind her. "Tell me about this dream."

For a moment, he thought she wouldn't answer. But then her chest inflated with a deep breath, and she started speaking.

"The details aren't clear. I know there's a fire, but I'm not sure how it starts. I can smell the smoke, and then everything gets really cold. And there are people." Her eyes closed. "People hurt. Screaming and bleeding and ... dead." When she opened her eyes, they held an intensity that darkened the brown almost to black. "And then I know I have to warn them, as many as possible. They have to get out of town on December 6."

"Is it an accident of some sort?"

She hesitated, then nodded. "Yes, I think so."

Now it was his turn to look down. That this dream was related to the subway crash last year seemed obvious. "Like, maybe, a ... subway accident?"

With force she propelled herself off the couch and across the room to stand in front of the window. "Do you think I haven't thought of that? It's not the same, Greg. For one thing, the Cove doesn't have a subway."

"I know, but— "

She stopped him with a raised hand. "No. This dream is not about the accident. I'm sure of that. It's something else, something totally different. And I had to warn people. I had to." Her eyes begged him to understand, to believe her.

He wanted to. She seemed so convinced, so certain. But to believe her claim that through a dream she'd been given special knowledge of a disaster that was going to happen in the sleepy little community of Seaside Cove was, well, unbelievable. The more likely explanation was that Jill was suffering from post-traumatic stress disorder or something similar. That would be natural, given the trauma she'd experienced last year. PTSD took awhile to show up sometimes, didn't it?

Her hands dropped to hang at her sides. "You don't believe me."

"I want to. Really. But it just sounds ..." He didn't finish the sentence. He didn't have to.

"Crazy." Her shoulders slumped. "I know. I've probably gone off my rocker."

"Now, don't talk that way." He crossed to her side and put a hand on each of her shoulders. "You're just tired and stressed out with wedding plans and the Christmas season and everything." He led her back to the couch.

"That's what Doreen said," she admitted. "She thinks the dream is stress-induced."

She'd talked to her therapist about this dream? Good.

"What did she suggest you do about it?"

"She told me to get rid of my stress, whatever it takes." A shadowy smile curved her lips, the first of the evening. "That's what I was doing tonight. I thought if I warned people, like the dream was urging me to do, then it would go away. Leave me alone." Her head tilted back and she looked fully into his face. "I really am sorry I railroaded your meeting. Have I completely destroyed your campaign?"

Greg wasn't sure how he felt about that right now. He'd been pretty angry with Jill at the time, until the crowd surrounded her and pounded her with questions. Then his protective instincts had kicked in. Still, it would take him awhile to process the impact of tonight, and figure out how to recover. He did know, though, how he felt about Jill. He loved her. Whatever she was going through, they'd deal with it together.

"Well, your timing could have been better." He wrapped an arm around her and pulled her close. "But I'll regroup. We'll figure it out tomorrow, after everyone's had a good night's sleep."

She snuggled into his side. "I can't tell you how much I'm looking forward to that."

He leaned his cheek against the top of her head. *Yeah. Well, at least one of them might get some sleep tonight.*

~

For the first time in days, Jill wasn't afraid to go to sleep. Of course, now that she wanted it, sleep eluded her like a stray pup running from the dog catcher.

She'd started to feel drowsy on the sofa, snuggled up close to Greg, her head on his chest, ear pressed against his shirt so tightly she felt the vibration of his lungs when he started to sing a soft lullaby in the melodious voice she loved. One day he would sing their babies to sleep with that song. Tonight, though, there were no babies to lull, only Jill. And for some reason, now that she desperately *wanted* to sleep, her mind was as alert as if she'd chugged caffeine all day. After a few minutes, she kissed him good night and retired to the bedroom to snuggle beneath the soft, thick quilt. That only woke her up even more.

It didn't help that Greg refused to leave until Nana returned home, as though he feared the minute he left her alone she'd form a noose out of her bed linens and do herself in. His concern was touching, but after a few minutes became slightly irritating. She could hear his steady pacing right outside her bedroom. Every so often the sound of his footsteps would pause just outside the door. She pictured him resting his ear against the wood, listening. The image set her teeth against each other. He was taking this protective thing a bit too far. She wasn't suicidal, if that's what he was concerned about.

He's just worried about me.

She sat up and punched her flattened pillow with a fist. Yeah, well, he should be. If she didn't get some sleep soon, she would do something crazy.

Laughter snorted through her nose. Like anything could be crazier than standing up in a public meeting and announcing that the town had to be evacuated because of a dream. She threw herself backward on the mattress and shoved the pillow over her face with both hands. If Greg heard her laughing, he'd call for a straitjacket for sure.

A familiar noise reached her. Nana's heels on the staircase. No doubt the sewing circle ladies had lingered after the meeting to rehash all the juicy details. Greg's footsteps receded toward the kitchen, and she heard the mumble of low voices as he and Nana conferred. More footsteps on the stairs, this time Greg's heavy tread descending. The relief shift had arrived, and he was going home.

Jill rose up in bed, switched on the lamp on her nightstand, and arranged her pillows behind her. When the door cracked open and Nana peeked in, she was sitting comfortably with her hands folded on top of the thick quilt.

"Greg said you were sleeping."

Jill shook her head. "Who can sleep with all that worrying and pacing going on right outside the door?"

Nana opened the door wider and stepped into the room. "You can hardly blame him."

A sigh escaped Jill's lips. "I know. Instead of worried, he should be furious with me."

She scooched sideways and patted the mattress beside her. Nana hesitated only a second before accepting her invitation. She lowered herself to the bed, kicked off her pumps, and twisted around until her legs were parallel to Jill's. Jill removed one of her pillows and plumped it behind Nana, who settled back into it. The sweet scent of her perfume seeped into the air, bringing with it a wave of comfort. The smell of childhood, of nighttime prayers, tight hugs and lipstick-kiss prints on her cheek.

"So. Tell me about this dream."

"There's not much to tell, really." Jill described the disjointed images and associated feelings, and tried to convey the sense of urgency that increased with every recurrence of the dream. "I had to do something. I couldn't ignore the warning anymore."

"You could have talked to me about it."

"You're right. I should have." Jill plucked at an imaginary thread on the quilt. "I didn't really plan to do that tonight. It just happened."

Nana's eyes narrowed. "You mean you couldn't help yourself?"

Jill didn't answer at first. Could she have stopped herself from standing up in front of the town spouting doom like some deranged fanatic? Yes, of course she could have. It hadn't been an irresistible compulsion, like she was possessed or anything. It had been a conscious — albeit desperate — decision.

"I wanted to stop the dream from coming back." Her words were slow. "I figured one way to do that would be to get it out of my system. But there was another reason." She caught her lower lip between her teeth and held it there.

"And that was?" Nana prompted.

She twisted sideways in the bed to look her grandmother full-on. "What if it's real? If some disaster really does happen in Seaside Cove next week and I didn't warn people, I'd never be able to live with myself."

Nana searched Jill's face. After a moment, she nodded. "You did the right thing."

"I did?"

She nodded. "Given your position, I'd have done the same thing." A grin twisted her lips. "Of course, I'm a fossilized old Fruit Loop myself, so that's probably not a comforting thought."

Laughter bubbled up from deep inside Jill. "If you're a Fruit Loop, I guess I'm a Honey Nut Cheerio, huh?"

"We *are* related, after all." The grin melted away, replaced by concern. "Are you better now that you've delivered your warning?" A note of worry crept into her tone. Worry, or maybe skepticism?

"I think so." Jill closed her eyes and took an inventory of her feelings. The anxious urgency that had become her nearly constant companion the past few days was gone. In its place was a hot, sticky embarrassment when she remembered the shock on Greg's face tonight, the scornful expressions of her fellow Cove residents. Mostly, though, she felt the soft and insistent nudge of slumber pressing her down to her mattress. Finally. "Right now

I'm too tired to know what I'm feeling. All I want to do is sleep for a million years."

"I'll leave you alone then. We'll talk more tomorrow."

Nana rose from the mattress. When Jill slid down beneath the quilt, she grasped the edges and pulled the covers up beneath Jill's chin, then tucked the sides firmly around the outline of her body like she used to years ago. With cool fingers she brushed the hair off of Jill's forehead and planted a soft kiss there.

Jill searched the face that hovered over hers. "You don't believe my dream is true, do you, Nana?"

Tenderness softened her features. "I don't know what I believe. I'll have to pray about that, just as I'm sure you will. But I know I love you."

She reached for the light switch, and darkness descended on the room. With a satisfied sigh, Jill nestled farther beneath the covers and, for the first time in days, welcomed sleep's embrace.

Chapter 14

Tuesday, November 29

Greg approached the door of the counseling office and tried the handle. Locked. He glanced at his watch. Just past seven thirty in the morning. What time did they open? He hovered on the concrete stoop, trying to see through the gauzy curtains that covered the narrow window beside the door. He could wait around until eight, but he had a meeting with a client at nine.

He'd just about decided to leave and call later when a car pulled into the parking lot. The woman in the passenger seat eyed him curiously through the windshield. Doreen Davenport. Jill had introduced them a couple of times. He tucked the newspaper he carried beneath his arm and shoved his hands in his coat pocket to wait for her to exit the car.

She did, her gaze fixed on him. She approached carrying a briefcase in one hand and a cardboard coffee cup in the other. The car pulled out of the parking lot.

"Hello." She spoke when she was halfway down the sidewalk. "Can I help you with something?"

"You're Doreen Davenport, aren't you?"

"That's right." She set down the briefcase and thrust a hand toward him. "How are you this morning, Mr. Bradford?"

Ah. She knew who he was. Good. That would save time.

He shook the hand, then picked up her briefcase for her while she unlocked the door. "Not too good, actually. Sorry to show up unannounced, but I was hoping I could talk to you about Jill."

The door opened, and he followed her inside the dark office. "I do have a minute, but I'm afraid I can't discuss Jill with you." She gave him a smile of thanks as she took her briefcase from him. "Confidentiality. I'm sure as an attorney you understand that."

"But I'm her fiancé."

The smile became apologetic. "I know, but she hasn't signed a release form that would allow me to discuss her condition with you."

Greg set his teeth together. He knew the counselor was right. "Okay. I'm going to ask her if she's willing to do that as soon as possible. In the meantime, maybe we could talk in general terms. If you've read the morning paper, I'm sure you'll understand my concern."

Her head cocked upward, her expression curious. "I usually read the paper here, after I get to the office. Has something happened?"

In answer, Greg unfolded the newspaper. The story wasn't the top headline, but it did take up the bottom right quarter of the front page. At the top of the article was a picture of Jill seated on the front row at last night's meeting, slumped down in a metal folding chair with a hand shielding her eyes. A half-dozen or so people towered over her, their expressions ranging from angry to outraged. In bold letters, the headline read, "Local Woman Predicts End of the World."

"Oh, dear."

Doreen took the newspaper from him and turned to go through a door into an office, reading as she walked. Greg followed her.

"She didn't really predict the end of the world," he pointed out as she rounded her desk, still reading. "That headline is obviously an attempt to sensationalize the story and sell more newspapers."

She lowered herself in her chair and indicated with a wave that Greg should sit in one of the guest chairs in front of the desk. He sank into it, but perched on the edge, watching her eyes move as she read the article. When she finished, she set the paper down on the clean desktop and met his gaze.

"Was the rest of the article accurate?"

Greg nodded. "Afraid so, though that reporter manages to make it sound like I think Jill's ready for the loony bin without ever saying so." Greg's fist clenched as he remembered the section that had set his teeth together when he read it this morning. *Mr. Bradford offered this excuse for Ms. King's outrageous claim: "She hasn't felt well lately."*

"Has Jill read this?" Doreen gestured at the newspaper.

"No. I called her grandmother as soon as I saw it, and she said Jill was still sleeping peacefully. We agreed to let her sleep as long as she can."

Doreen nodded. "That's good."

"But then what?" Greg ran a hand through his hair. "She told me you said this dream was probably because of stress, and if she wanted it to go away she had to get rid of the stress." He tapped a finger on the paper. "This is a pretty extreme way to get rid of stress. Was it your suggestion?"

"Absolutely not." Doreen leaned back in her chair, her long-fingered hands folded in her lap. "She must have decided on her own that the way to get rid of her stress was to follow through with what the dream was urging her to do."

"Well, she's not thinking straight." Greg launched himself off the chair. "Maybe next time you could suggest a bubble bath, or a massage. Something other than an announcement in a public meeting."

"Maybe you could suggest those things."

The woman's face remained completely impassive, which in comparison made Greg feel like a raving maniac. He circled the chair in which he'd been sitting, stood behind it with his hands grasping the back, and schooled his voice to match her calm tone. A question had plagued him all night, one he had to ask even though he was afraid of the answer. "Am I the cause of Jill's stress? Does she not want to marry me?"

For one moment, he thought the counselor might actually answer him. Her expression grew soft, and she looked at him as though evaluating whether or not to take a chance on talking to him. When she put her hands flat on the desk and pushed her chair backward to stand, Greg knew she wasn't going to answer.

"Mr. Bradford, I am going to tell you the same thing I told Jill." She came around the side of the desk. "You need to talk to each other. If you want to schedule an appointment together, I'll be happy to speak with both of you. But that's all I can say at this time."

Defeated, Greg's shoulders slumped forward. "I understand."

Doreen placed a hand on his arm and gave him a kind smile. "Look on the bright side. If her grandmother said Jill was sleeping peacefully, maybe her strategy worked. Maybe she got the dream out of her system, and this will be the end of it."

"I sure hope so."

When he picked up the newspaper and his glance fell once

again on the headline, he couldn't help the sinking feeling that this thing wasn't over yet.

~

Jill woke a few times, once during the night to stumble through the darkness to the bathroom, and then again hours later when a ship passing the Cove on its way to Halifax Harbor blew its horn. The third time she pried her eyelids open enough to see sunlight streaming through her bedroom window, pulled a pillow on top of her head, and went back to sleep.

Consciousness returned to her hours later, when someone slammed the front door downstairs in Nana's house. She welcomed the day slowly, giving herself time to enjoy the drowsy feel of sleep creeping away, replaced by a growing wakefulness. The sheet felt soft and luxurious beneath her as she stretched and then curled up on her side, hugging her pillow. Her eyes drifted open and she caught sight of the alarm clock on the nightstand.

She shot straight up in bed. One o'clock? She'd slept for fifteen hours.

A smile tugged the corners of her mouth upward. Fifteen hours of dreamless sleep. Ah! What a blessing, one she would never take for granted again.

Indistinct voices drifted upward through the wooden floor. Nana had company. Probably another meeting of the overenthusiastic wedding planning committee. With a grin, Jill realized she was looking forward to hearing the ladies' latest outrageous suggestions. Pink and blue daisies for a Christmas wedding? Well, why not?

As she dressed, she recalled Greg's tender care last night. He would have been within his rights to ask for his ring back after she turned his meeting into a fiasco. Heat burned her cheeks at the memory. Nobody would blame him, especially her. Yet he'd brought her home, listened to her crazy-sounding explanation, calmed her, even sang to her. Was there another man in the entire world as understanding? She doubted it.

Maybe now she could put this dream behind her. Last night would become nothing more than a bad memory, a funny story for her and Greg to laugh over together in the years to come. Starting today they could move forward with their wedding, and with the start of their new life. Forget the whole disaster thing.

Except …

A sudden realization froze her hand in the act of running a brush through her hair. Except she couldn't forget it. The dream had not returned, thank goodness. But if she thought about it, she could still feel a certainty of the impending disaster, and a sense of urgency to warn others.

It's not over yet. Not until December 6 has come and gone.

She sank onto the edge of the bed, fighting a sudden rush of tears.

This is so unfair! Why me, God? Can't you make this go away?

Certainly he could. So why hadn't he? Did that mean he didn't want to rescue her from this nightmarish situation? Maybe he was even responsible for the whole thing. He'd taken her music away from her, and still expected her to sacrifice everything else.

It was too much to ask.

Maybe she should leave town for a week and come back next Wednesday, on December 7. Sure, she'd take a little ribbing when she returned and nothing had happened on December 6, but she could handle that.

As long as nothing really did happen.

She practically jumped off the bed and crossed the room to

stare out the window. The sun shone today, turning the water green-blue in the shallow sections of the channel closest to the shore. A wave crashed up onto the jagged rocks near the lighthouse and painted a bright rainbow in the air with salty spray. In the opposite direction lay the town. The familiar buildings of Seaside Cove lined Harbor Street, forming a man-made barrier that faced the Atlantic. This was her town, her home. Its residents were her extended family, even if they did think she was crazy.

With a shudder, she let the curtain drop back into place. No, she wouldn't leave town. If something did happen, she didn't want to be the lone survivor. Not again.

Dumb, Jill, dumb. Nothing is going to happen. This is a result of stress, that's all. Get over it.

But how? She'd done what she was supposed to do, made a fool of herself and delivered the ridiculous warning. Why had the cloud of doom not left along with the dream?

What if she just ignored it? She'd done her duty. If people chose not to listen, her conscience was clear. She blinked a couple of times, banishing the tears that prickled in the back of her eyes. There were plenty of other things for her to concentrate on these days. A wedding. Christmas. Her students. Maybe if she ignored the feeling, it would go away. The cloud would lift and go hover over somebody else's head. Today that felt entirely possible. With a good night's sleep behind her, she could be strong and keep her mouth shut. As long as the dream didn't return and she could rest at night, this feeling of impending disaster would fade.

That's what she'd do. Ignore it. Surely she could do that for one more week. And then, on December 7, things could get back to normal for Jill and for Seaside Cove.

I hope.

Her decision made, she felt a tiny bit better as she finished dressing. In her kitchen, she downed a full glass of water to quench a throat parched from fifteen hours without liquid, and decided against making a pot of tea. Nana probably had tea downstairs, and maybe some more of that apple bread she'd served yesterday. Jill's stomach rumbled as she made her way down the stairs toward Nana's kitchen.

Halfway down the staircase an odd odor reached her. She wrinkled her nose. Definitely not apple bread. Cleaning products, maybe? The sound of ladies' voices alerted her to the presence of a group of Nana's cohorts, but maybe they weren't the wedding planners. Maybe they were a cleaning crew or something.

The sight that greeted her downstairs halted her progress toward the kitchen. She stood in the hallway to stare, mouth gaping, at the chaos in the living room.

The coffee table had been pushed aside and the sofa shoved back against the wall. Two large cardboard boxes had been stacked in front of the fireplace. The rug in the center of the room was covered with a white bedsheet. Arranged around the sheet, three elderly ladies perched on the sofa and chairs, and another stood with her back to Jill. Everyone's attention was focused on Nana, on her hands and knees on the sheet, a paintbrush in one hand.

"There." She balanced her brush carefully on the rim of a can of black paint, and surveyed her handiwork with a satisfied nod. "I think that will work just fine."

"It looks better than I thought it would," agreed Mrs. Montgomery.

"What's going on?" Jill asked from the doorway.

Five heads turned her way.

"Our Sleeping Beauty is finally awake." Nana struggled to rise to her feet, and Jill rushed forward to give her a hand up. "We'd decided to wait until two before waking you."

"We've been checking on you though, honey." Mrs. Cramer patted her arm and smiled. "You were sleeping very soundly."

"Snoring," put in Mrs. Tolliver.

"She was drooling when I checked," announced Mrs. Montgomery from her perch on the sofa. She glanced at Mrs. Fontaine seated next to her. "Before we leave we should change those pillowcases for her."

Jill's cheeks warmed.

"Do you feel better, honey?" Nana's anxious face peered up into hers.

She nodded, then waved a hand around the room. "What's all this?"

"It's for your campaign." Mrs. Tolliver jerked a single nod, as though that explained everything.

Jill frowned. What in the world was the woman talking about? "You mean Greg's campaign?"

Nana dismissed that with a flick of shiny red fingernails. "We have months before the election. No, dear, we mean your campaign. We've decided to help you spread the word."

She stooped to retrieve her handiwork, and Jill saw she'd been painting a sign. Hand lettering in neat bold print announced: EVACUATE SEASIDE COVE ON DECEMBER 6.

Jill's jaw went slack. They were going to put up yard signs?

"What — " Too many questions crowded her mind. She closed her mouth, shook her head, and tried again. "I don't understand."

"We've been talking about it all morning," Nana said, "and we decided if you say something terrible is going to happen in the Cove on December 6, we believe you."

"And we want to help." Mrs. Tolliver's watery blue gaze held Jill's.

"Help?" Jill's voice squeaked.

Nana nodded. "Myrtle's grandson used to be in real estate so he had all these signs."

"He *pretended* to be in real estate." Mrs. Montgomery's wrinkled lips pursed with sour disapproval. "Never sold a single house. Gave it up and moved to Alaska to sell used dogsleds, or some ridiculous story." Her gray eyebrows arched and she said in an aside to Mrs. Tolliver. "I think he's living in sin with a disreputable Eskimo woman, but nobody will admit it."

Nana gave her a commiserating look and continued. "Anyway, he had about a hundred signs stored in Myrtle's garage, and we were just trying to see if we could cover them with poster board and use them."

"I paid for them. Might as well get some use out of them." Mrs. Montgomery's grumble earned her a sympathetic pat on the arm from Mrs. Tolliver.

"We've got other ideas for spreading the word, too." Mrs. Cramer held up a spiral notebook filled with writing. "We've got to cover every avenue possible, so no one can say they weren't warned."

Momentarily speechless, Jill stared in turn at each of the six elderly ladies, and received encouraging smiles and nods of support. So much for ignoring the feeling in hopes it would go away.

"But why?" she finally managed to squeak. "I must have sounded like a lunatic last night, jumping up and ruining Greg's meeting like that." She turned on Nana. "When you tucked me in bed, you said you didn't believe in my dream."

Nana wagged a finger. "I never said any such thing. After you fell asleep I had time to consider everything you said, and to pray about it."

"We've all prayed about it." Mrs. Tolliver's voice dropped into mysterious tones. "You know what the Bible says, don't you?

It says in the last days *our young people will dream dreams.*"

"It doesn't either." Mrs. Montgomery's mouth became a hard line of disapproval. "If you're going to quote the Bible, Edna, at least get it right. It's the old men who are supposed to dream dreams. The young people are supposed to prophesy and see visions."

Mrs. Tolliver's nose tilted and she gave an offended sniff. "Prophesies, dreams, they're all related. Anyway, that's what Jill did last night. Prophesy. And it also talks about disasters like earthquakes and pestilences and so on." She leaned eagerly toward Jill. "What kind of disaster is it going to be, honey?"

An expectant hush fell upon the women. Their eyes fixed on Jill, glittering in anticipation of the gruesome details. Jill didn't know what to say. Part of her felt flattered that someone had actually listened to her, that they didn't think she was crazy. Another part of her thought, with the fiendishly zealous expressions they wore, none of these ladies looked particularly sane themselves at the moment.

"I—I really don't know." Jill folded her arms across her middle. "I'm pretty sure there's a fire. And heat, followed by freezing cold. And people screaming." She shuddered, the screams loud inside her head. "That's all I know." Their stares became disappointed. "I'm sorry. I wish I knew more."

"No pestilence?" asked Mrs. Cramer hopefully.

Jill only vaguely knew what a pestilence was, so the only answer she could give was an apologetic shrug.

Nana slapped her hands together. "Well, the fire is something. Maybe it's going to be like the fire that destroyed Chicago, or San Francisco. Regardless, people have got to be warned, and we're going to help you do it."

Jill looked around the room, touched in spite of herself. First, these ladies dove enthusiastically into making her wedding day special, and now this. They believed in her, in her dream, and wanted to stand with her, no matter how crazy it made them look.

But only part of the wedding committee was here.

"Where is the rest of your knitting circle?" She asked. "Mrs. Lewis and the others?"

Nana busied herself with fanning the wet paint on her sign and didn't meet Jill's gaze.

"Skeptics." Mrs. Tolliver dismissed them with a flick of her fingers. "They'll be sorry."

So, her dream had divided the knitting circle. Somehow she doubted theirs would be the only group in the Cove to split before this was over.

"But what if I'm wrong?" Jill's voice broke on the last word. "What if I really am just stressed out because of last year's accident and the wedding and — everything?"

Nana stepped forward to pull her into a hug. "If you're wrong, then we'll all have egg on our faces next Tuesday when nothing happens. Won't be the first time I've played the fool in this town." Nana released her and ran a hand briskly over Jill's arm, ending with a pat. "Being considered eccentric isn't so bad. You get used to it."

The ladies all nodded and fixed her with wide smiles, as though welcoming her into their private club. A club Jill was pretty sure she didn't want to join, no matter how much she loved the redheaded leader. Somehow she didn't think Greg would view an eccentric fiancée as an asset to his political future.

Greg. Now that she'd finally gotten some sleep she could think more clearly, and she needed to talk to someone levelheaded. Someone not — she looked around the room from one eager, wrinkled face to another — eccentric. She needed to talk to Greg.

"I've got to make a phone call." She edged backward toward the entry hall.

"You don't want to help us paint signs?" Mrs. Montgomery waved to indicate the boxes near the fireplace. "We have plenty."

"Unfortunately, I have some errands I need to run." She gave a halfhearted laugh. "I slept half the day away, you know?"

"You go ahead, Jill." Nana waved her off with an absent smile as she stooped and picked up her paintbrush. "We'll get a few done before our meeting with the minister."

That halted Jill's retreat. Surely they weren't going to try to enlist the aid of the minister in their sign-painting campaign. "The minister?"

"Oh, yes." Mrs. Cramer stopped in the act of removing another yard sign from the box to explain. "Someone has put obscene pictures on the bulletin board in the Fellowship Hall, and we want them removed."

"Pinups of teenage girls." Mrs. Montgomery's voice dropped and took on a tone of outrage. "In *bathing suits.*"

"We tried reasoning with the youth director, but he insists there's nothing inappropriate in pictures of the youth group's swimming party." Mrs. Tolliver's eyes gleamed with purpose. "We'll see what Reverend Hollister has to say about that."

With a thought of sympathy for poor Reverend Hollister, Jill escaped up the stairs to her apartment.

Chapter 15

JILL'S PANTRY WAS SUFFERING FROM a state of neglect, but she didn't want to return downstairs and risk having a paintbrush shoved in her hand. She grabbed a half-full bag of Doritos and a tub of pimento cheese to dip them in, and took them into her living room with her cell phone.

Greg's secretary, Teresa, answered the office phone and informed Jill that Greg was in a meeting with a client. Was it Jill's imagination, or was there a touch of disdain that hadn't been in the coolly professional voice yesterday? She couldn't be sure, but she didn't think she'd ever heard Teresa sound quite so condescending. Jill left a message for him to call when he was free, and hung up.

She was still staring at the cell phone thoughtfully when it rang. A vaguely familiar number with no associated name in her contacts.

"Hello?"

"Jill? This is Doreen Davenport."

Surprised, Jill didn't at first respond. In all the months she'd been meeting weekly with the therapist, Doreen had never called her. Not once. It didn't take a genius to figure out the reason for this call.

"I guess you heard about the meeting last night, huh?"

"Oh, yes. That's quite an article. You made the front page, even."

The front page? Between sleeping past noon and then watching Nana and the ladies plan a communication campaign, Jill hadn't had a chance to read the newspaper. "I haven't seen it yet. Does it make me sound like a lunatic?"

"Well." Doreen paused, then went on in the tone of someone searching for the appropriate words. "Apparently, the reporter who wrote the article wasn't convinced about the validity of your dream."

"Terrific." Jill slumped down on the sofa cushion and propped her feet, knees bent, on the edge of the coffee table.

"Listen, I was calling to find out if you've made that appointment with Dr. Bookman."

She winced. This had definitely never happened before, Doreen feeling the need to push her into the shrink's office. "I haven't had a chance to do that yet. But I did try to relieve some of my stress, like we discussed. That's what last night's announcement was about."

"I figured as much. Did it work?"

"Sort of. I got a great night's sleep and didn't have a single dream." She thought of the troop of geriatric sign painters at the bottom of the stairs. "But the feeling that I need to warn people about a coming disaster is still there. Just not quite as urgent as it was before."

"Why don't I have my receptionist set up the appointment with Dr. Bookman for you? I really do think it's best if you talk to him. When Greg was here this morning, he seemed to think — "

Jill shot upright on the cushion. "Greg came to see you?"

"Well, yes." She seemed embarrassed. "I assumed he would

tell you, because he mentioned asking you to sign a release form."

So he could get a report on her progress after every appointment? Check her sanity level, maybe? *Sooo* not happening. "What did he want?"

"He was very concerned about you. He was afraid the stress from the upcoming wedding might have clouded your judgment."

"He thinks I'm nuts." Jill's voice was flat. He'd been so understanding last night, so concerned. He'd sung to her, watched over her. Hovered outside her door. Turns out she'd been right last night after all. Greg thought she was mentally unstable.

"He didn't say that."

"But he thinks it," Jill insisted. "Otherwise, why would he go to my therapist behind my back?"

Doreen didn't answer, and in the ensuing silence, Jill heard her own words replay in the pinched tone she'd used. She sounded paranoid. Like a crazy person.

She inhaled a deep breath through her nose and forced herself to let it out fully before replying. "I'm sorry. I know he's worried. He has every right to be. I just wish he'd discussed this with me instead of you."

"That's exactly what I told him. In fact, I offered to do a joint session with the two of you. You can bring him with you on Friday, if you like. In the meantime, my receptionist will set up an appointment with Dr. Bookman and call you. Sound good?"

Did Doreen honestly think she couldn't make a simple phone call for an appointment? No, she was worried Jill wouldn't make the appointment at all.

What if she said no, just to be obstinate? But getting obstinate with a therapist when her sanity was already in question might not be the wisest course of action.

She forced herself to answer evenly, even pleasantly. "Thank you. I appreciate that."

"Good." Doreen sounded relieved. "If you need to talk before your appointment on Friday, please call me. Otherwise, I'll see you then. And Jill? Bubble baths are great stress reducers. Maybe you should try that."

Jill promised to give bubble baths a try and pressed the button to end the call.

Where did Nana put that newspaper? Downstairs, probably. She shoved a loaded Dorito into her mouth and settled in on the couch, waiting for the sound of chatting voices downstairs to stop. She'd gone through nearly the whole bag when silence from the main part of the house told her the ladies had left, so the coast was clear. Nana stacked her newspapers on the screened porch behind the kitchen when she finished reading them, so that's probably where this morning's edition was. On the way past Nana's front room she glanced inside, and saw that the ladies had painted four more signs before leaving to torment Reverend Hollister.

She found the paper and spread it on the kitchen table. After one look at the picture, she almost couldn't make herself read the article. It was like one of those purposefully unflattering snapshots of famous celebrities on the cover of gossip magazines in the grocery store checkout aisle. And that headline. The "End of the World"? That made her sound like a kook.

Still, what else could she expect? She *did* sound like a kook. Her stomach grew more and more uneasy with the Doritos and pimento cheese as she read the account. The reporter had dug up a few details from her career, and though he never said the accident that ended it had thrown her mentally off balance, the implication was hard to miss. The only good part was that Greg didn't come off as badly as she feared. The reporter obviously didn't know about their engagement, thank goodness.

There was almost no mention of Greg's plan. Did the journalist not include anything about that? She flipped a couple of pages. Ah, there. Way back on page four, sandwiched between a report of the police responding to multiple car eggings and a lengthy notice on the planned replacement of the Cove's recycling bins. The story did a good job of recapping Greg's meeting and outlining the main points of his proposed tourism plan, but he probably wouldn't be happy about it. Her performance had taken top billing over his proposal.

Perhaps she should get Greg some bubble bath as an early Christmas present.

The ringing of the doorbell sounded from the front hallway. Jill left the paper on the table to head for the front door. Two blurry figures stood beyond the frosted decorative glass. Probably selling vacuum cleaners or something. She wiped orange Dorito cheese from her fingers on the seat of her jeans and opened the door to find an unfamiliar couple standing on the front porch.

"That's her!" The woman's finger waved in Jill's face. "She's the one."

Uh-oh. Jill's grip on the door knob tightened.

The man's head cocked sideways as he studied Jill through narrowed eyes, clearly skeptical.

"You're Jillian King, aren't you?" The woman didn't wait for an answer, but rushed on, slightly out of breath. "I heard you play the piano once when we lived in Montreal."

Tension rushed out of Jill's muscles. A music fan. She smiled into the woman's flushed face. In all the years she played on the concert circuit, she'd never had a fan show up at her front door. "Yes, that's right. I'm Jillian King."

"We moved to Seaside Cove a few months ago, and I heard you lived here. I recognized you at the meeting last night." The woman leaned forward, her eyes wide. "Tell my husband about your dream."

Jill's mouth dried. Her words stumbled over a tongue gone suddenly awkward in the face of the man's scowl. "I, uh, had this dream about — well, it's hard to describe really — it's more like a feeling than anything."

"And there's going to be a terrible disaster on December 6, right?" The woman was so excited she rose on her toes like a child. "The whole town is going to die in a horrible earthquake."

Jill shook her head. "Wait a minute. I didn't say anyth — "

The woman brushed away her words with a hand in the air. "Or maybe it was a hurricane. Whatever. Jillian said we have to leave before December 6 or we're all going to die." Her gaze fixed on something over Jill's shoulder, and her eyes went round as life preservers. "Lance, would you look at that?"

Before Jill could stop her, she brushed into the house. Stunned, Jill turned to watch as she ran into the living room, seized one of the freshly painted signs, and held it up in front of her, eyes shining like she'd found a treasure at a half-price sale at Sears. "It's true! I knew it was true!"

"Gina, get out of there." Lance's voice boomed into the house. He seemed to swell to bear-sized proportions as he glared down at Jill. "You had to get her started, didn't you?"

"Can I have this one?" The woman turned a pleading expression Jill's way. "I'll put it in my yard, where lots of people will see it. Okay?"

"S-sure, I guess so."

"Thank you!" She rushed through the open door and held the sign out for her husband's inspection. "Jillian King painted this."

Jill didn't dare correct the woman or she might come back inside. Instead, she pushed the door closed, twisted the deadbolt, and collapsed against the thick wood. The woman's excited tones grew distant as she and her husband retreated down the sidewalk.

First Nana's knitting group had taken up her cause, and now a complete stranger. What had she started? And more importantly, where would it end?

~

The time was nearly four o'clock when Jill entered her mother's room at Centerside Nursing. Greg hadn't yet returned her call, and Jill hesitated to call again. She told herself that she didn't want to bother Greg during what must be a busy day, and that her reluctance had nothing to do with avoiding the stiffness in Teresa's voice again.

The soft strains of classical piano music filled Mom's room. Jill recognized the piece instantly, and shut her eyes against a stab of pain. The nurses liked to play Jill's CD on the portable stereo in Mom's room, because they said it soothed her when she was restless.

The wheelchair faced the window, but Mom's head drooped forward, her eyes closed and her body pressed against the restraint belt that kept her safely in the chair. If she'd been restless earlier, apparently the music had done its job. Jill pressed a button on the stereo, and when the music stopped, her mother's eyes fluttered open.

"Hi, Mom." She bent to press a kiss on the slack cheek. "Sorry I'm late. I overslept."

She laid her coat across the colorful quilt that covered the hospital bed and scooted the guest chair to her mother's side. Dull eyes followed her progress but failed to focus on her when she settled onto the cushioned seat.

A noise behind her drew her attention. She turned to find the nurse standing in the doorway.

"I heard the music stop, and I was coming to turn it back on." The woman's glance slid to the CD player, and did not return to Jill.

"She was napping when I came in, so I turned it off." Jill smoothed a fold out of the bib around her mother's neck. "Has she had a good day?"

"Yes." Her voice sounded odd, stilted. "A fine day."

Instead of bustling into the room as usual, the nurse hovered in the doorway. Jill studied the normally friendly woman. Her fingers flexed nervously at her sides, and then as if she realized her fidgeting had been noticed, she folded her arms across her chest.

"Is her cough better?" Jill asked.

"Oh, yes. Fine. We haven't heard her cough at all."

Their eyes finally connected. An antiseptic smile flashed onto the nurse's face, and then disappeared just as quickly.

She's seen the newspaper article.

Jill's neck grew hot and sticky beneath the collar of her sweater. The nursing home staff probably all thought she was nuts. Judging by the concerned glance the nurse kept flicking toward Mom, they might even be worried about leaving their charge alone with her. The thought sent heat flooding into her face.

"I'm relieved." Jill turned her back on the woman and settled in the chair again. She reached over and grabbed her mother's hand. "We're just going to visit for a little while. I'll turn the music back on when I leave."

"All right."

Jill did not turn around, but watched the nurse's figure in her peripheral vision. She hovered in the doorway for a moment, but finally left. The squeak of her white nurse's shoes on the polished floor faded. Jill's lungs deflated with an audible *whoosh*. What were they afraid of, that she'd hurt her own mother? How incredibly insulting. And humiliating, too.

With an effort, she forced a smile for Mom.

"I have a treat for you." Jill pulled the two envelopes from her purse and held them out for Mom's inspection. "I was going through some stuff in the attic yesterday, and I found these letters to you from Daddy. I thought you might like to hear them."

No reaction on the slack features.

Jill opened one of the envelopes and slid out three pages, each covered front and back with even, cramped writing. "This first one is dated March 27, 1982. That's a year before you were married, when Daddy was stationed on the destroyer, right?"

She glanced up. Mom's eyelids blinked in slow motion, as if she might nod off again in a second. Jill had hoped the letters would spark a flame of recognition or something, but she wasn't even sure her mother knew what a letter was anymore. Or even who she was. With a sigh, Jill began to read.

Dear Lorna,

Today the post finally caught up with us, and brought five letters from you! I told myself I'd space them out and enjoy one every few days, but I couldn't do it. I devoured them one right after another. I miss you so much. You can't know how holding a piece of paper you've touched comforts me. You'll think I'm a romantic fool when I tell you I press my lips to the seam where you sealed the envelope, and dream of the day when I can kiss you in person.

Jill gave Mom a tender smile. "He certainly was romantic, wasn't he? I hope he doesn't say anything you don't want your daughter reading." She chuckled and continued.

You said you were afraid your letters would bore me since you describe trivial things like shopping with your mother and going to the dock with your father. You have no idea how much pleasure reading those details gives me. In my mind I picture you picking through a bushel of apples to find the perfect ones for a pie, or standing on the rocks near the lighthouse, gazing seaward toward me. I wish I had something equally interesting to describe for you, but life at sea is rather monotonous.

Something strange has happened the last few nights, though. I've had the most disturbing dream—

Jill's voice stumbled over the last word. The hair along her forearms prickled to attention as she reread the sentence, and then continued.

I've had the most disturbing dream the past two nights, though I can't remember exactly what happens. But when I wake, I feel the strongest impulse to tell one of the helicopter pilots that he shouldn't fly next week. Isn't that ridiculous? Imagine me, a nobody from the galley, telling a pilot not to fly. They'd laugh me off the ship. It's a nuisance not being able to get a full night's sleep, though. I hope the dream goes away soon.

One of the midshipmen got a package from his wife today, and she sent …

Jill fell silent as she skimmed the rest of the letter, searching for some other mention of her father's dream. There was nothing, only a description of the book his friend had received and more romantic protestations of his undying love for "my beautiful Lorna." Jill's eyes were drawn back to that one short paragraph, and she read it again.

Realization penetrated her brain like a bullet. Her father had dreamed, too.

Fingers trembling, she put the first letter back inside its envelope and slid out the second. This one was much shorter. The writing covered only one side of a single page. The date at the top read March 31, four days after the previous one.

Dear Lorna,

My hand is shaking so badly as I write that you probably won't be able to read my words. I don't know if I'll have the nerve to send this letter, but I must get my thoughts down or they're going to explode inside me. Something terrible has happened, and it's my fault.

Remember the dream I told you about last week? I haven't mentioned it in my last two letters because I didn't want you to think I was losing my mind, but it kept coming back. Every time, I was left with an overwhelming desire to tell Captain Hiller not to fly his helicopter. Oh, how I wish

I had! This morning Hiller was in command of a standard training mission on one of the Sea King choppers. The bridge hasn't given us the details, but according to scuttlebutt Hiller had a stroke or heart attack or something, and the aircraft crashed. The whole crew was killed — the copilot, the navigator, the weapons system officer, and Hiller himself.

Four men are dead because of me, Lorna. I knew something was going to happen. Why didn't I warn them? So what if everyone thought I was a fool? Hiller might have listened to me, and then I wouldn't have these deaths on my conscience. How will I ever live with the guilt?

Jill's fingers were so cold she could no longer feel the paper she grasped. The pain in her father's words clawed at her throat and squeezed, choking the breath out of her. She leaned forward and buried her face in her hands. She didn't want to feel the same guilt, to bear the burden her father had suffered.

When she looked up, she found her mother's gaze fixed on her. All signs of drowsiness were gone. In its place, a spark of awareness sharpened the normally dull eyes.

"You knew." Jill's whisper held a touch of awe. "Yesterday when I told you about my dream, you remembered that Daddy had dreams too, didn't you?"

"Eyuah, eyuah, eyuah." Mom's right hand shot upward from her lap to wave sporadically above her head. "Eyuah, aaaahhhh."

Her nonsense shout filled the room and echoed down the hallway.

"Mom, calm down." Jill leaped to her feet and grabbed at the wildly gesticulating hand.

"Eyuah, eyuah, aaaaahhhhh."

The nurse ran into the room, followed by an aide in pink scrubs. "What's going on?"

"She's trying to tell me something." Jill dropped to her knees in front of the wheelchair and clasped the frail hand between both of hers. "We were reading an old letter from my father, and she got excited." She didn't dare mention her father's dream, or the nursing home staff would think her insane for sure. "What is it, Mom? What are you trying to say?"

Tears filled Mom's eyes. "Eyuah, eyuah." The unintelligible words came out in a sad whisper that twisted Jill's heart in her chest.

"I think Lorna needs to finish her nap. That way she'll be fresh and alert for supper. Isn't that right, honey?"

The nurse's high-pitched voice grated against Jill's nerves. She ignored the woman and instead searched her mother's face for the spark of intellect that had been there a moment before. Had she imagined it? Mom's cloudy eyes did not focus on her, but stared off into the distance as though at something visible only to her. Her lips moved, but no sound came.

"She does usually sleep before supper," the aide said from the doorway.

The nurse patted Mom's shoulder. "We'll just help her into bed and put her music back on. That always soothes her." She spared a brief not-quite-smile for Jill. "Maybe when you come back tomorrow she'll feel more like visiting."

Swallowing against a painful lump in her throat, Jill nodded. She gathered her father's letters, kissed Mom's cheek, and got her coat from the bed.

Her tears held off until she left the nursing home.

Chapter 16

The wind hurled snow into Greg's face with the force of a BB gun during the short run from the driveway to Jill and Ruth's front porch. Tuesday night dinners at Ruth's table had become a tradition in the year since Jill's accident. He twisted the knob and shoved, eager to put a barrier between him and the weather. The handle didn't budge. Unusual, because Ruth normally left her door unlocked when she knew he was coming. He rang the bell, and when a particularly fierce gust of wind slapped with stinging force at the back of his neck, hunched his shoulders and knocked with a gloved fist.

Ruth opened the door. "Come on in. Goodness, it's getting nasty out there."

"Tell me about it." A welcoming warmth enveloped him when he entered the house. He shrugged out of his coat and hung it on the stand while Ruth shut the door and twisted the deadbolt. "What's up with the lock?"

"We've had some visitors this afternoon, and a few of them have gotten a little pushy." Her lips drew a disapproving line as she bustled past him. She pointed toward the living room. "Jill's in there. I'll get you something hot to drink."

"Thanks." She disappeared into the kitchen. Just inside the living room, he stopped short. "What's all this?"

Jill sat cross-legged in the middle of the floor, a paintbrush in her hand. Black paint splattered her jeans and the white sheet beneath her, and a smear stained one cheek. For one moment he saw nothing except the smile she turned up at him — a little sheepish, but full of the impish humor that had surfaced so rarely in the year since the accident. Warmth seeped into his heart. If she'd keep smiling at him like that, he could stand here all day.

Then he noticed the partially painted sign in front of her. Black letters on a white background proclaimed in words that slanted downhill, EVACUATE SEASIDE COVE. Completed signs leaned against the furniture and the walls, and covered much of the empty floor space. The dire warning was repeated dozens of times: Evacuate the Cove by ten o'clock in the morning on December 6.

A chill froze his spine like an ice cube down his shirt.

She rose from her position on the floor with a grimace, and favored her injured hip when she crossed the three steps to the doorway to plant a kiss on his cheek. "We're making yard signs."

"I see." Safe response, though untrue. He didn't see. Not at all.

"I know what you're thinking."

If she did, that would make one of them. His thoughts were a blur inside his own brain.

She pulled him into the room and led him to the couch. "You're thinking I'm three eggs short of a dozen." Her clear gaze held his. "I'm not crazy, Greg. And I can prove it."

From her jeans pocket she withdrew two envelopes and handed them to him. Then, with a smile, she gave him a gentle backward push onto the couch. He obediently sat on the cushion, while she returned to the floor and her unfinished sign.

He examined the top envelope. "Letters from your father to your mother?"

She dipped her paintbrush in the can and nodded. "Read them."

He did. At the mention of her father's dream, the prickle of spider legs crept across the back of his neck. He glanced up at Jill, and she gave him a serene smile and nodded toward the second letter, then returned to her painting.

Ruth bustled into the room as he opened the second letter. "Here you go. My special hot cocoa, guaranteed to put the zing back in your zipper."

"Thanks, Ruth." He took the steaming mug from her and sipped. Delicious, as usual. Sweet and ultra-chocolaty, with a touch of vanilla and cinnamon.

Within a few words, the second letter drew his attention away from the drink. Michael King had experienced a prescient dream, very much like his daughter. The guilt lay heavy in the words Jill's father had penned, and it slapped at him as he digested the somber message they carried.

He looked up from the letter to find Jill watching, her paintbrush poised over the sign and an anxious expression on her face. "You see now why I can't sit by and do nothing, don't you?"

"I wouldn't call last night *doing nothing.* Have you seen the newspaper today?" He tried to filter the frustration out of his voice, but apparently failed because she winced.

"I've apologized for ruining your meeting. I really am sorry."

"That's not what I meant. I'm saying you warned people already. Don't you think that's enough? Why is all this necessary?" His wave took in the paint and signs.

Ruth bent over a sign in the corner, testing the paint with a finger. She straightened and looked at him. "That's probably my fault. The girls and I were trying to think of ways to help, and this seemed like an easy and inexpensive way to get the word out."

"The signs are reusable," Jill added. "When this is over, we'll repaint them for your campaign."

Her grin drew a reluctant answering smile from him. She looked more relaxed, more at peace, than he'd seen her in days, like she'd come to terms with whatever had been tormenting her. Wasn't that a good thing, even though her actions weren't ... well, normal? Uneasiness kept his thoughts in turmoil as he refolded the letter and slipped it back in the envelope.

He just didn't buy it. The idea that Jill, or anyone for that matter, could foretell a disaster was too big a stretch. And what about these letters? Evidently Jill's father had experienced something that affected him deeply, but they knew nothing about the circumstances surrounding an accident that happened more than twenty-five years ago. Even if that proved to be a valid incident, it had no bearing on Jill's dream. Admittedly, Greg was no expert on prophetic dreams, but the idea that the ability to predict the future could be an inherited trait seemed pretty farfetched to him. Whereas mental instability ...

He thrust the thought away and set the envelopes on the end table. A thought had occurred to him during a long court session this morning.

"You say this disaster is going to happen on December 6." He cleared his throat. "You realize what that date is, don't you?"

Quizzical lines appeared between her eyebrows.

"It's not only two days after the anniversary of your accident, Jill. It's also the anniversary of the Halifax Explosion." He spoke gently. In 1917 a tremendous explosion in Halifax Harbor crippled the city and destroyed businesses and homes. Sixteen hundred people were killed in the worst disaster Nova Scotia had ever experienced.

Jill's face went white. Clearly, she hadn't remembered the date's historical significance.

"Maybe you've been subconsciously aware of that," he said softly, "and if you add to it the stress you've been under lately ..." He lifted his shoulders.

For a moment, a struggle took place on Jill's face. Then her expression cleared. "What about my father's dream? It came true. You read his letters."

Ruth crossed to the center of the room and stood beside Jill, her eyes boring into Greg's with unvoiced disapproval.

Greg ignored her. "Maybe you knew about your father's dream too." Jill shook her head and opened her mouth to respond, but he held up a hand to forestall her. "Again, subconsciously. Maybe he told you about that incident when you were little, or you heard your parents discussing it. You put the two together, along with everything else you've been through, and came up with a dream."

Doubt clouded her eyes, and Greg hated himself for being the cause of the return of that haunted look. But somebody had to be the voice of reason here. Obviously, that wasn't going to be Ruth, who took her role as supportive grandmother too seriously.

Ruth planted her hands on her hips. "I never heard Michael mention the dream, or Lorna either." The set of her jaw dared him to contradict her.

With slow movements, Jill set the brush on the open paint can lid, picked up a splattered rag, and scrubbed at a drop of paint on her wrist. "I know it's asking a lot, Greg, but I really hoped you, of all people, would believe me."

The disappointment in her voice pierced him like a dart. An answering stab of anger threatened. First, she commandeered his meeting without regard to the effects of her actions on his career, and then she expected him to buy this crazy idea that she'd somehow inherited the ability to predict disasters through her dreams?

He drew in a slow breath and didn't bother to hide his frustration. What did she want from him? Blind acceptance of this crazy idea?

He ignored Ruth's stern glare and leaned forward, his hands on his knees, to hold Jill's gaze with his. "Jill, you've been through a lot in the past year. It's understandable that there would be some lingering …" He grappled for a word, " … effects from the accident."

Her eyes widened. "So you think my dream is a result of post-traumatic stress from the accident?"

So she'd thought of that too. Relieved, he nodded. "It would be completely understandable, given what you went through. It's partly my fault too. I thought our engagement would help you quit obsessing about the past and look ahead, but all I did was add more stress to your life."

Her eyebrows inched upward. "Obsessing about the past?" Her voice held more chill than the wind that blew against the front window.

Uh-oh. Poor word choice.

In a completely uncharacteristic move, Ruth slipped out of the room without a word, leaving them alone.

Greg made an attempt to control his rising temper. "Okay, obsessing isn't what I mean. Of course you'd be upset after losing your whole career. It's understandable that you'd be depressed about that. All I'm saying is I was trying to help you get it out of your system and move on."

"Get it out of my *system*?"

If her eyes were flamethrowers, he'd be burnt toast. Greg leaned back against the rear cushion as if slammed there by an invisible force. What'd he say?

Her mouth a hard line, she picked up the paintbrush, placed the lid on the can, and smacked it with such force that he jumped.

"If you think music is something I'll *get over*, then you don't know anything about me."

"What?" He shook his head. "That's not what I meant. It's just that — "

She stopped in the act of rising to her knees, paintbrush and can in one hand and the finished sign in the other. Any words he might have spoken evaporated from his brain in the face of her piercing stare.

A flame of anger flickered to life and smoldered along the edges of his thoughts. He wasn't in the wrong here. She was putting words in his mouth.

He forced a calm, reasonable tone. "Look, you're obviously upset. Let's talk about this another time, when we can discuss it rationally."

The moment the word left his mouth, he knew it was a mistake.

Her spine stiffened, and breath sucked into her lungs in a hiss. "So now I'm irrational?"

There was only one thing he could do. As his father was fond of quoting, *He who turns and runs away lives to fight another day*. A wise man knew when to retreat.

With an iron control on his own rising temper, Greg stood. "I just remembered some work I need to get done before a meeting in the morning." The statement didn't really feel like a lie, because they both recognized it for the lame excuse it was. "I'll pick you up tomorrow at five thirty to go to my parents' house."

"Fine."

She followed him to the door and maintained a chilly silence while he donned his coat. Stepping through the door into the frigid wind was almost a relief. The door shut behind him before he could turn for a final good-bye. He heard the deadbolt click, and tried not to imagine it slid home with more force than necessary.

Hunching his shoulders against the wind, he hurried down the porch steps. He hadn't been free for dinner on a Tuesday night in months. Tuesdays were meatloaf nights at the café. Not his favorite, but he'd rather eat meatloaf served with a generous helping of Rowena's friendly smile than continue the verbal sparring match with Jill. Stubborn woman.

Anger buzzing in her ears, Jill twisted the deadbolt and turned to find her grandmother watching her from the kitchen doorway.

"Greg's not staying for supper?" Nana maintained a carefully bland expression while she wiped her hands on a tea towel.

"No, he's not." Her voice came out louder than she intended, and she smiled a quick apology. "He remembered some work he had to do tonight."

"I see."

By the sympathy in the eyes that watched her, Jill knew Nana did, indeed, see what had happened. She'd probably heard their raised voices from the other room. Correction. Jill's raised voice. Greg had maintained a trial lawyer's composure throughout the entire encounter, which had served to inflame Jill to the point that she lost her temper. *Irrational*, he'd called her.

No, he didn't. He said we needed to have a rational discussion. And he was right. I wasn't acting rationally.

Time for a feelings inventory. Anger and frustration, but the overriding emotion she felt was …

Her anger evaporated like a drop of water on a hot griddle. Disappointment. She'd picked a fight with Greg because she was disappointed that he didn't believe in her dream.

She sagged against the door, her shoulders drooping. "Oh, Nana, I wanted him to believe me."

Nana hurried down the hall and gathered Jill in a hug. "I know. I'm sorry."

Jill breathed in the familiar scent of Estée Lauder. Tears prickled in her eyes. "I can't blame him. It sounds crazy." She raised her head and sniffled. "I guess I just hoped he'd support me even if he doesn't believe me."

"That's a reasonable expectation." Loyalty and sympathy in equal measures shone in Nana's eyes. "I think tomorrow I'll go have a talk with him."

An image flashed into Jill's mind of Nana marching into Greg's office with the ferocity of a lion, complete with a mane of red hair. Teresa, fierce protector of Greg's schedule, would be no match for Nana. The idea made Jill's lips twitch in spite of the heaviness in her heart.

She straightened. "Please don't. This is something I need to do myself. If I can't convince Greg that I'm not insane, how in the world can I expect anyone else in the Cove to believe me?"

A proud smile curved Nana's lips. "That's my girl." She patted Jill's arm. "Go finish cleaning the paintbrushes. Supper will be ready in a few minutes."

Jill headed for the living room. She really ought to call Greg and ask him to come back, but the idea of facing more of his disbelief tonight was overwhelming. She'd apologize tomorrow, on the drive to his parents' house.

Chapter 17

Wednesday, November 30

Long stretches of awkward silence dominated the ninety-minute drive to the orchard. Jill watched through the passenger window as the sun set over kilometers of undulating ridges and fertile valleys. When Greg had arrived to pick her up, she'd apologized for snapping, but his skepticism hung between them like morning fog hovering over the harbor.

When they passed the last small village before the turnoff to Bradford Orchards, he broke a silence that had brooded for the past thirty minutes.

"I just don't see why you have to keep pushing." He kept his eyes fixed ahead, where twin beams from the car's headlights carved through the darkness that had fully descended outside. "You've delivered your warning. You even got a front page article in the newspaper."

Jill winced at the unmistakable frustration in his voice. Guilt stabbed at her, but she refused to accept it. It wasn't her fault the newspaper buried the story of his tourism plan.

"Only a handful of people are taking my dream seriously. That article made me sound like a lunatic."

"And planting a bunch of yard signs all over the Cove doesn't?"

She clenched her jaws to keep from firing back a response. The last thing she wanted to do was fight with Greg again.

After a short silence, he spoke in a calm tone. "Look, I'm trying to understand your viewpoint. I know those letters from your father struck a chord. But it's like Rowe said last night — "

Jill's head whipped toward him. "You talked to Rowena Mitchell about me?"

"Well, uh." Words stumbled uncertainly out of his mouth. "She asked why I looked upset. I happened to mention we'd had a disagreement. She offered a sympathetic ear, that's all."

Fury buzzed in her brain as the scene unfolded in her imagination. He made up an excuse to escape his crazy fiancée and ran straight into the arms of that oh-so-sympathetic flirt. "I'll just bet she did."

A large sign situated on the side of the road announced the entrance to Bradford Orchards. The car slowed as they approached the turnoff.

"What's that supposed to mean?" Greg asked as he guided the car onto the long, narrow driveway that carved the orchard into two sections.

Jill studied his face. When the car straightened, he looked away from the road, directly into her eyes. She saw no secrets there, no sign of hidden feelings for the pretty café owner. Was it possible Greg hadn't picked up on the blatant flirting? Her sudden rush of jealousy calmed to a manageable level.

"I don't appreciate you going to Rowena for advice about me. She's after you, Greg. She's going to try to make me look bad."

"What?" The surprise on his face could not be feigned. He shook his head. "No. You're way off base."

"She flirts outrageously with you."

"She flirts with everybody." He dismissed that with a shrug. "It's her personality. She doesn't mean anything by it."

He faced forward as the car approached the house. Jill watched his profile while he shifted into Park and turned off the ignition. The car's engine fell silent. He appeared entirely unaware of Rowena's designs, which served to douse the remnants of her jealousy. That didn't change the fact that he'd left Jill's house last night and ran straight to Rowena to talk about it, but at least he wasn't harboring feelings for the woman.

She wasn't through discussing Rowena with him, not by a long shot, but now wasn't the time. The curtains in the front room parted, and Greg's mother peered out. A nervous tickle erupted in Jill's stomach. The time had come to answer the question that had worried her all day. Had news of her performance at Greg's meeting last night reached his parents?

~

It had.

Faye was as warm and friendly as always, and put Jill to work carrying steaming dishes from the kitchen to the dining room the minute they arrived. Jill found it easy to relax in her company, her worries slipping away as her future mother-in-law kept a pleasant chatter flowing throughout the meal. Across from Jill, Greg joined in the conversation and, at his mother's urging, described his marriage proposal in the restaurant. Harold, whom Jill had never found to be overly chatty, sat at the head of the table and devoured the delicious roast beef in near silence. He answered his wife's occasional questions with single-word answers.

His silence became worrisome as the meal progressed. He usually talked more than this. And why wouldn't he make eye contact with her? With rising discomfort, Jill picked at the last half of her dinner, her insides churning into knots while Greg and his mother discussed the latest escapades of the grandchildren in California.

When the supper dishes had been cleared and they each had a thick slice of warm apple pie in front of them, Greg's father broke his moody silence.

"So, would someone like to tell me just what in the dickens went on at that meeting Monday night?"

The food turned to cement in Jill's stomach. From the disapproving glance he threw in her direction, she had no doubts he wasn't asking for a simple recap of Greg's presentation.

"Harold." Faye's voice, though low, held a weighty warning.

"Don't *Harold* me. If she's going to be our daughter-in-law, I refuse to tiptoe around her." He glared across the table at his wife, but softened his gaze considerably before he turned toward Jill. "I read the article on the Internet. Were you having some sort of delusional episode or something?"

Heat flared into Jill's face.

"Dad, Jill's not delusional." Greg caught her eye across the table. If his smile was tentative, at least he'd jumped to her defense.

She set her fork down and faced Harold. "The article outlined the essentials. What it didn't mention is the fact that the dream kept returning, over and over, and every time I knew I had to warn people." Her gaze flickered to Greg's for an instant. "I admit my timing was atrocious, but I had to do something."

She raised her chin defiantly. "When my father was alive, he had dreams like this, too."

Harold stabbed at his pie and speared a gooey apple. "I don't care what your father did. We don't act like this in the Bradford family."

Jill's spine stiffened. Was he saying she wasn't good enough to be a Bradford?

Greg opened his mouth, but before he could speak his mother stood. Her chair legs scooted across the hardwood floor with a jarring scrape.

"Jill, let's you and I go look at the living room, shall we? I want to talk to you about the decorations for the wedding. We'll finish our pie later."

An overwhelming desire to escape seized Jill. She stood almost as abruptly as Faye, and followed her out of the room.

~

Greg tried to catch Jill's eye as she left the dining room, but her stony stare did not turn his way. Red splotches covered the smooth skin of her neck, and her face glowed like an ember. As soon as they were out of earshot, he turned to his father.

"That was unnecessary, Dad."

Dad looked momentarily startled. Greg was not in the habit of scolding his father. Nevertheless, he refused to look away from the stern stare aimed his way. That stare had never failed to evoke instant obedience when he was a boy.

After a couple of seconds, Dad's forehead dipped once. "I could have approached the subject more diplomatically. Your mother warned me not to cause a ruckus. I'll apologize to Jill. But I'm concerned about the damage this has done to your campaign."

The idea had certainly occurred to Greg during the long hours of the past two nights. He pushed the half-eaten pie away and leaned back in his chair. "The meeting went well up until that point. I've had a lot of positive feedback, and gained some important supporters. I think I handled myself okay."

"I'm sure you did, but Seaside Cove is a small town. Everybody knows you two are a couple. There's sure to be some fallout if your fiancée is running around screaming that the sky is falling." His gaze became piercing. "Remember what's at stake here."

Greg didn't need the reminder. His future was at stake, all the plans he and Dad had talked about for most of his life. This election to the Halifax Regional Council was the first step in a political career that could potentially take him all the way to Ottawa.

He forced a calm smile. "If damage has been done, it's done. The only thing I can do about it now is move forward."

And try to keep Jill and Ruth from plastering yard signs all over town.

Dad leaned toward Greg and lowered his voice. "Son, are you sure she's mentally stable?"

The same thought had occurred to Greg Monday night, but he would not admit that to his father. He forced a laugh. "Yes, Dad, I'm sure. Recovering from that accident last year has taken a toll. And she's been under a tremendous amount of stress recently."

Dad shot a glance in the direction of the living room. "But if her father had similar delusions" — he held up a hand to forestall Greg's correction — "I mean dreams, then maybe you should think twice about having children with her."

The comment produced a genuine laugh from Greg. "That's ridiculous. All anyone has to do is talk with her to see she's perfectly sane. She feels strongly about this dream thing."

His father straightened in the chair, his eyes narrowed. "You almost sound like you believe she's had some sort of prophetic vision."

Now it was Greg's turn to lower his voice. "No, I don't. I think there's a logical explanation, like long-buried memories that are resurfacing and post-traumatic stress from her accident. But the important thing is that Jill believes it. She's acting out of a genuine desire to save people, because she couldn't save anyone last year."

As he articulated the reason, it made even more sense. That's exactly what was going on here. Jill was the most loving, soft-hearted person in the world, which was one of the attributes that attracted him to her four years ago. He'd been looking at this all wrong, thinking she was acting out of character. In fact, it was her loving nature that lay at the root of the whole thing.

"Hmmm." Unconvinced, Dad's lips pressed together into a tight line. "Well, whatever is happening, it's got to stop before she does any more damage to your campaign. Nobody's going to vote for a man who's married to a raving lunatic." He leaned forward again and held Greg's gaze. "You've got to get this under control, son. Get a grip on it."

He knew his father was right, but the memory of all those yard signs covering every square inch of Ruth's living room made him squirm in his seat. Before long they would be all over town. He'd already tried to reason with Jill, and look what happened. What more could he do to convince her to abandon this crazy scheme?

Next Wednesday couldn't come soon enough. When Tuesday came and went without a disaster, maybe they could put this mess behind them and get things back to normal.

"Now, if you aren't fond of the candles, we can certainly get rid of them. In fact, we can redo the whole thing." Faye stepped back from the fireplace and tapped her fingertips on her lips as she examined the mantle. "Pink poinsettias might add a touch of wedding color."

Jill made an effort to forget her irritation with Harold and focus on the lovely Christmas decorations that covered the living room. An eight-foot tree dominated one corner, swathed from tip to trunk in gauzy gold and brilliant red. A mountain of gold and white-wrapped packages piled beneath pushed against the lowest branches. Every surface around the room bore evidence of Faye's love for elegant Christmas decorations, from tiered crystal tea-light holders to an exquisitely carved ivory nativity set. But the fireplace dominated the room, the mantle resplendent with bushy garland, gold and red candles, and tiny white lights that twinkled like stars at midnight.

"I love it." Jill turned in a slow circle, taking in the entire room. "It's perfect just the way it is."

Creases appeared in Faye's brow. "You're not just saying that? Don't worry about hurting my feelings. I want this day to be special for you."

"No, really. It's gorgeous. I can see myself walking through there in Mom's wedding dress, carrying a bouquet of red roses." She pointed toward the arched entry from the hallway, around which draped more garland studded with clusters of red berries. "Don't change a thing."

A smile illuminated Faye's face. "I'm so glad. But before you make up your mind, I want to show you a picture of the giant wreath we sometimes hang above the fireplace." She bustled over to the settee that had been pushed against a wall to make room for the tree, and picked up a thick scrapbook. "We have it stored in the attic, but I usually only get it down every other year. It's so big it tends to overshadow the tree, but it is lovely above the mantle. Take a look at it."

Jill seated herself close to Faye so the open scrapbook lay across both their laps. Christmas stickers decorated the pages, and each picture had been bordered with brightly colored embellishments. She inspected the wreath in the photo Faye pointed out. It was beautifully ornate, but gigantic. It would definitely become the centerpiece of any room in which it hung.

"No, I think I prefer the decorations you have up now." Jill smiled at her. "You certainly have a gift for decorating."

A becoming blush colored her cheeks. "Oh, no. It's just something I enjoy, especially at Christmas."

Jill looked at the other pictures on the page. Family shots, mostly of Ryan and Dawn, the children of Greg's brother who lived in California. She'd met them for the first time two years ago. They looked older in this photo, which meant it was probably taken last year, while she'd been in the hospital in New York. She turned a page backward. There stood Greg beside his brother Ted. Greg had left her side only long enough to spend a day with his family and take care of a few things for his clients.

She touched a finger to his face. His smile looked painted on, his expression strained. "He looks so tired."

"Oh, he was. He was very worried about you." Faye placed an arm around her shoulders and squeezed. "We all were."

Jill flipped backward through a few more pages. The children opening gifts, seated at a loaded dinner table, grinning at the camera in crisp new pajamas. Greg was only in a small number of them.

She turned another few pages, then received a start. "That's me."

"Yes. This is my Christmas scrapbook, and that section is

from two years ago. Remember? You joined us for dinner Christmas Eve."

The Jill in the photo looked like a different woman than the one who peered at her from her mirror every morning. Much, much younger, for one thing. The past two years had taken more of a toll than she realized. She looked closer and decided the younger Jill looked happier, too. Well, that was to be expected. That Jill had a hip that didn't ache, a whole hand, and a promising career as a concert pianist.

"Just look at that." A tender smiled curved Faye's lips, her eyes on the photo. "He loves you so much."

It was true. The picture depicted Jill and Greg standing on the front porch, bundled in jackets with gloved hands clasped, smiling into one another's faces. No strain marred the love apparent in Greg's face as he gazed at Jill. And her own eyes practically glowed with joy as she looked up at him. If she remembered correctly, he kissed her right after his mother snapped this shot.

"You know," Faye spoke slowly, giving each word the weight of wisdom, "two people who love each other that much can overcome anything." She glanced up at Jill. "Don't you think so?"

Jill couldn't tear her eyes away from the picture. They looked so happy.

"I hope so," she whispered.

The first part of the drive back to Seaside Cove was almost as silent as the outbound trip. Snow had started to fall from the dark sky. Scanning the roads for treacherous icy patches required all of Greg's attention, but he watched Jill out of the corner of his eye. Her thoughts were focused somewhere far away. Heat blowing from the vents kept the interior of the car toasty, while outside the wipers put forth a valiant effort to keep the windshield clear with a noisy *slap, slap, slap*.

He cleared his throat. "I'm sorry about my father. He didn't mean to be insulting. He's just worried about me."

"I know. And he did apologize nicely."

Yeah, Greg had never heard Dad refer to himself as a "socially inept idiot" before. The sight of Mom's serious nod of agreement would keep Greg smiling for days.

Jill stretched the boundaries of her shoulder strap to twist in the seat so she faced him. "Greg, do you think I'm crazy? I mean, really insane?"

"No, I don't." He blurted the reply instantly, but saw disbelief etched on her brow. He took a breath and spoke more slowly. "I don't know what I think about all this, Jill, but I know for sure you're not insane."

She studied him for a moment, then gave a nod. "Thank you. I guess if you don't believe my dream is true, at least you aren't ready to have me committed."

He smiled. "You committed is exactly what I want. Committed to a future with me. To us."

The bad pun failed to elicit a response. "Sometimes I can't imagine why you want to marry me. I don't have anything to offer you. I'm nothing but a broken down has-been-who-never-was."

Her head bowed forward and her eyes lowered to her hands resting in her lap. For a moment he thought she was staring at the engagement ring, but then noticed her right thumb tracing the scar on her left hand.

He reached across the console and gently entwined her fingers in his. "You are not a has-been. You're an amazing woman with incredible intelligence and wit, a tremendous capacity to love, and a talent most people only dream of having." He paused. "I have a confession. For the first year we dated, I was the tiniest bit intimidated by your talent. I'd think, *How could someone with her passion and ability ever fall for a musical dunce like me?*"

That brought the whisper of a grin to her face. "You're not a musical dunce. You have talent, too. Your singing voice is amazing. You just don't use it."

He shook his head. "I don't have your gift."

The grin faded, and her gaze dropped again. "Neither do I. Not anymore."

"Don't say that. You have many gifts." He squeezed her hand. "God doesn't give gifts and then take them back, you know."

Her head jerked up, and she speared him with a startled look. "What did you say?"

"I said God doesn't take gifts back."

She studied his face for what seemed like forever, then spoke slowly. "Someone else told me that last year."

"Well, there you go. You'll find a way to use your gifts. I'm sure of it."

Tears glittered in her eyes. "Thank you, Greg. I love you."

Her words, spoken so softly, lodged in his chest. If he wasn't careful he'd start tearing up himself. "I love you too."

Her smile lingered as she faced forward again. Greg drew in a satisfied breath. They hadn't really resolved anything about this dream business, but at least the atmosphere between them no longer held that uncomfortable icy sharpness. For tonight, that was enough. Time enough to tackle the issue of the yard signs tomorrow.

Chapter 18

Thursday, December 1

As Jill descended the stairs the next morning, the doorbell rang.

"I'll get it," she called down the hallway.

She'd barely opened the front door when Mrs. Tolliver and Mrs. Montgomery pushed their way inside.

"Good morning, dear. How did you sleep?" Mrs. Montgomery peered up at her, as though studying her for signs of sleep deprivation.

"I slept well, thank you." Jill shut the door behind them.

"No more dreams?" Mrs. Tolliver paused in the act of unwinding a long wool scarf from her neck, her expression disappointed.

"No, ma'am. The dream hasn't returned since Monday." Jill didn't know whether to be relieved or not. She definitely felt fit after two good nights' sleep, but now that she was committed to delivering the warning, why had the dream disappeared?

Both ladies paused in the act of hanging their coats.

"Is the fire still coming?" Mrs. Montgomery asked.

Jill didn't hesitate to nod. Even without the dream's return, the weight of its message still lay heavily on her. Her father's letters compelled her to act. "Yes. It's still coming."

Relieved smiles lit both wrinkled faces.

"Look what I have." Mrs. Tolliver opened a shopping bag and extracted two books. "I got them at the library yesterday afternoon."

She held them out for Jill's inspection. Yellow sticky notes stuck out from the pages of both. Jill almost groaned when she read the title of the one on top: *Dream Dictionary for Dummies.*

Mrs. Tolliver opened the second book to a marked page as they walked into the living room. "They both have alphabetized listings of dream symbols, and this one says the time on the clock may have special significance. What time did the clock say in your dream, Jill?"

Jill shuddered. The image was burned into her mind. "Five after ten."

"Ah. Not *exactly* ten, then." The elderly head bobbed up and down, as though that observation explained everything.

Nana bustled into the room. "There you are, girls. Tea's steeping in the pot, so that will be ready in a minute." She rubbed her hands together and looked toward the stack of unpainted signs. "We have a lot to get done today."

Mrs. Mattingly took possession of the Dummy book and seated herself in a wing chair. She opened it and began flipping through the pages. "What does it say about fire?"

"Oh, that's a good one," Mrs. Tolliver answered. "Fire can be several things, but this book says it might mean a change is coming, some sort of transformation. Or it could stand for repressed sexual passion." Sparse gray eyebrows waggled in Jill's direction.

Heat smoldered in Jill's face.

"Don't be foolish, Edna." Though the smaller and more shriveled of the two, Mrs. Montgomery's disapproving frown gave her an air of authority. She snapped the book closed. "Did you ever stop to think the fire might be a *real* fire, and the clock might actually mean something's going to happen at 10:05? Otherwise, what's the point of all this?" She waved a vein-lined hand toward the signs.

Mrs. Tolliver inspected the book doubtfully. "Well, I suppose that's possible." Her expression cleared. "Or it could be both. Maybe a real fire is going to happen, and that'll be the beginning of a transformation for the Cove."

The shrill ringing of the phone rescued Jill from what was proving to be an extremely uncomfortable conversation. She hurried toward Nana's desk and picked up the old-fashioned corded phone there. "Hello?"

"Oh, Jill, it's you." She recognized the breathless voice.

"Mrs. Cramer," she told the others.

Mrs. Cramer rushed on. "I was just getting ready to leave, and I went to turn off the television. Jill, you're going to be on the news right after the commercial break!"

The words didn't immediately register. Then their import struck Jill. She stabbed at the television set in the corner of Nana's living room. "Turn it on. Hurry."

Nana dove for the remote control and pointed it at the old console. After a moment, the picture flared to life. Jill clutched the receiver and waited, breathless, through two commercials before the CBC newscaster's face filled the screen.

"And now we have an interesting story from the harbor community of Seaside Cove, where a local celebrity took over a political meeting Monday night to announce—" a smirk twisted the man's mouth. "—the end of the world."

The man's face disappeared. Jill's head went light when she

saw herself holding a microphone, Greg at her side. She looked awful. No makeup. Dark pouches under her eyes. Why hadn't she taken the time to run a brush through her hair?

"I support everything Greg said, and I think his plan is vital for the future of Seaside Cove. I hope you'll vote for him to represent you on the council. But that's not what I want to say. I want — no, I have *to tell you something that's going to sound really crazy. I've had these dreams. Well, only one dream, but I've had it several times."*

A groan sounded loud in the room. It took a moment for Jill to realize it came from her. Horror crept over her as she watched her own pronouncement of disaster, saw the stunned expression on Greg's face, the rush of people who surrounded her chair. Blindly, she felt for the desk chair behind her, scooted it out, and sank into it.

The television reporter returned to the screen. "That was Jillian Elizabeth King, formerly a professional classical pianist who has now become, apparently, a local prophet of doom." The smirk deepened. "Whether or not the residents of Seaside Cove accept her prediction remains to be seen." The camera angle switched. "In other local news, a Halifax swimmer has announced his decision to — "

The television screen went black. Nana set the remote control on the coffee table. Jill realized she was still holding the telephone receiver, and replaced it without a word. Nobody looked in her direction. Blood roared through her ears as numbness crept over her. Had Greg's father seen that? She gulped against a suddenly dry throat. Had Greg?

"Well," Nana said after the silence stretched on long enough to be embarrassing. "We said we wanted to get the word out. I think we got our wish."

The other two ladies made encouraging sounds, but Jill paid no attention. Her fingers tapped on the phone receiver while thoughts turned over in her mind. One by one they fell into place. The quality of the video the news had just broadcast wasn't professional. More like a home movie. And it had been taken from close range. Like, from the front row of chairs in the gymnasium. The thought ignited a white, hot fury. She slapped her hands on the surface of the desk and propelled herself to her feet.

Nana peered at her anxiously. "What's wrong, dear?"

Jill was pleased that her voice sounded far calmer than she felt. "I'll be back later, after I've taken care of something."

Correction. Some*one.*

~

"His shed is in my yard." Mr. Rice thrust his jaw forward in Greg's direction. "I want you to make him tear it down."

Greg nodded in an understanding manner. "If we can verify that your neighbor's new shed does, indeed, cross the property line, then you're within your rights to ask him to move it."

"I know where the property line is. I've lived there longer than him. It runs smack-dab between the tree in the back and the light pole out front."

"So step one is to get a copy of— "

A tap on the door interrupted. Greg looked up to see the door crack open and Teresa's head peek through.

"I'm sorry to bother you, but I'm afraid this might be important." She held up a pink square of paper, the ones on which she recorded phone messages for him.

Teresa had been with him since he opened his practice, and he'd come to rely on her professionalism and discretion. If this message was important enough to interrupt a client consultation, then it probably required his attention. He extended his hand, and she slipped into the room to bring it to him.

"I'm sorry for the interruption, Mr. Rice," he told the man. "This will only take a ..."

Words evaporated from his mind as he scanned the note. It was from Jill.

"I wrote exactly what she told me," Teresa said.

Tell him I am going to need a lawyer soon, because I'm on my way over to assault my fiancé's girlfriend.

Her fiancé's girlfriend? What did that mean?

Last night's conversation in the car came back to him.

He catapulted out of the chair and rounded the desk toward the door. "I'm sorry, Mr. Rice. An emergency's come up. Teresa will schedule you for another appointment. No charge for today."

He ran out the door, and when he reached the sidewalk remembered that his car keys were in his coat pocket in his office. No time to go back for them now. He could run the five blocks to the café faster.

~

Jill's fiery anger had cooled to a slow burn by the time she marched through the café's front door. Only half the tables were occupied today, but at her entrance, every head turned her way. No fifties music today. Instead, the sound of the CBC newscaster's voice projected from a television screen suspended from the back corner and angled so it could be seen in the entire room. The slimy snake didn't want to miss the results of her handiwork.

The customers' voices fell silent. Some stared openly, but most averted their faces as though afraid she might speak to them. A wave of embarrassment threatened to send heat rushing to her face. She was accustomed to getting attention when she entered a room, but not like this. Usually people were happy to see her.

Behind the counter stood the busty Judas, pretending like she hadn't noticed Jill's arrival. Jill marched through the dining room and made her way to the counter, where old Mr. Towers sat in the chair beside the wall, sipping coffee. She ignored him and stood at the opposite end of the counter, her hands clutching the back of a tall stool.

Rowena glanced up, but her gaze didn't connect with Jill's. "Hi, Jill. Can I pour you a cup of coffee?"

Jill gave a sarcastic blast of laughter. "I don't think so. I'd be afraid to drink it."

Rowena's eyebrows inched up and disappeared beneath fluffy bangs. "What do you mean?"

"Don't try that innocent act on me." Jill put steel in her voice. "At least have the courage to admit what you did."

Rowena's head tilted upward, her nose high in the air. "You're obviously upset about something, though what that has to do with me I have no idea."

"Oh?" Jill pointed toward the television screen. "And I suppose you didn't see the news report a few minutes ago."

The woman's glance circled the room behind Jill. "We saw it. But you can't seriously think I had anything to do with that."

Jill inflated her lungs with an outraged breath, ready to let go with a verbal blast that would knock this Jezebel on her well-padded behind, but the bell mounted on the top of the door jangled, and a shout stopped her.

"Jill!"

She turned to see Greg striding toward her, his face bright

red, his chest heaving to draw in noisy gulps of air. Good. This concerned him, too, so he needed to be here.

"I see you got my message."

He reached her side and stopped for a moment, doubled over with his hands resting on his thighs, and drew in huge breaths. When he could speak, he straightened.

"What is going on here?"

"That double-crossing snake," Jill pointed at Rowena, "sold the video of Monday night's meeting to CBC in order to make me look like a lunatic."

"I did no such thing." The glare Rowena shot at her melted into an endearing plea when she turned toward Greg. "She's obviously not thinking clearly."

"CBC?" Greg raked fingers through his hair, his expression confused. "What video?"

"You didn't see the news about twenty minutes ago?"

"No, I was meeting with a client."

"Well, don't worry. I'm sure you'll be able to catch it again this evening." She folded her arms across her chest with a jerk and glared at Rowena. "Compliments of your campaign manager."

Rowena didn't answer, but her expression shouted denial louder than words.

Not a sound came from anyone else in the room as the women commanded the attention of everyone. The table of fishermen in the far corner actually turned their seats around so they could watch the show without craning their necks.

Jill ignored them and fired an accusation across the counter. "You can't deny that video is the one you took. It was shot from the center of the front row, exactly where you sat in front of Greg in your low-cut blouse, flashing cleavage under his nose."

Someone behind Jill tried to stifle a laugh, and Rowena's eyes opened wide.

Greg put a hand on Jill's back and said in a low voice full of warning. "Jill. Don't do this."

She rounded on him. "Watch the news, Greg. You'll see that video can only be hers."

"It did look like my video." Greg and Jill both jerked their heads toward Rowena, who winced. "It had to be, since I was the only person in the front row filming the meeting." Her chin shot up and she stared directly at Jill. "But I didn't give it to CBC. Someone stole it from me."

"Oh. Right."

Greg ignored Jill's sarcastic comment and asked. "Someone broke into your house?"

Rowena's teeth appeared to clamp down on one corner of her lower lip as she shook her head. "I had the little disk thingy here to give to you. But I forgot when you were here Tuesday night, so I set it on the shelf so I'd remember to give it to you yesterday." She pointed to a curio shelf hanging on the wall beside the register stand. "But you didn't come in yesterday." Her gaze flicked briefly to Jill's face and then returned to Greg's. "When I saw the news, I looked for the disk. It's gone."

"Well, that explains it." Greg heaved a relieved sigh. "Who knew it was there?"

Rowena shook her head. "Could have been anyone from Tuesday to last night. Half of the Cove's been in here, and that shelf is in plain sight." She arranged her features into an expression of pained innoncence. "I'm so sorry, Greg. I would never do anything to embarrass you. You know that, right?"

"I know you wouldn't, Rowe." Greg turned a smile toward Jill.

"See? We'll get to the bottom of this and figure out who did it. Maybe the television station will tell me where they got it."

Jill's mouth dropped open. How could he be so gullible?

"Surely you don't buy that baloney. Someone just *happened* to see a disk lying on a shelf, and they just *happened* to decide to steal it with no idea of what was on it? She's lying, Greg."

Rowena's spine stiffened to the point that her chest stuck out even farther than usual. "It just *happened* to be in an envelope with 'Greg's Video' written clearly on the front. Anyone who went to that meeting Monday night and saw me doing the recording would know what was in the envelope." Her expression hardened. "I think you'd better leave, Jill."

Now it was Jill's turn to stiffen. "Not until I get to the bottom of this."

The weasel spoke to Greg without removing her glare from Jill. "Greg, this is my property, and I can serve whoever I want. I don't want to cause you any more trouble than you already have, but if she's not out of here in thirty seconds, I'm calling William."

Jill gasped. William Akers was the local law enforcement officer. That woman wouldn't *dare* have her arrested.

"Come on, Jill." Greg slipped a hand under her arm and tugged.

"No." She tried to shake him off, but he held fast. "You didn't see — "

"Later," he snapped.

Muscles tensed in his rigid jaw as he pulled her toward the door. Jill had seen Greg angry several times, but never had the full weight of his anger been directed toward her. The sight of his face threw icy water on the smoldering fury that had burned in her since seeing the news broadcast. She shut her mouth and allowed him to lead her outside as every head in the café turned to watch their progress.

On the sidewalk, while traffic zoomed by on Harbor Street, he faced her. "What were you thinking? You called Rowena a liar to her face, in front of a room full of customers."

Okay, probably not the most tactful way to handle the situation, but that didn't make her wrong.

"Greg, she is lying. I know it. Maybe she didn't give that video to CBC, but she knows who did. She probably even put it there by the cash register on purpose, so someone would take it."

He threw his head back toward the sky, fingers raking through his hair. "Why would she do that? She's my number-one supporter. Why would she want to make me look bad?"

"She doesn't. She wants to make *me* look bad. She's after you, Greg. I can't believe you don't see that."

He glanced at the windows, and slipped his arm through hers. "Come on. We'll talk about this later. You can give me a ride back to the office."

The gesture might appear to onlookers like reconciliation, but the stiffness in his arm told Jill he wasn't happy. She followed his gaze and saw at least a dozen faces staring at them through the café windows. Greg was right. They should talk about this later, in private. Then she could convince him that Rowena Mitchell was not the innocent campaign supporter he thought she was.

Chapter 19

Jill dropped Greg off at his office barely in time for his next meeting. He left, after extracting a promise that she wouldn't return to the café. Feeling like a child who had been chastised, she gave her word and left.

A group of people lined the sidewalk in front of Nana's house. Her pulse picked up speed at her first thought that something had happened to Nana and a crowd had gathered to watch her being carried away on a stretcher. But there were no emergency vehicles in sight. When she pulled into the driveway and shifted into Park, the crowd migrated toward her and surrounded her car. At least three cameras flashed in her face through the window.

This was *not* good.

For a moment she considered putting the car in Reverse and leaving. But that would be cowardly. She'd started this snowball rolling downhill when she took the microphone in Greg's meeting. She had to see it through, no matter how gigantic it grew.

Resigned, she twisted the key in the ignition to shut off the engine and dropped the keys into her purse. After a pause to steel herself, she opened the door and stepped outside.

More cameras flashed. People called her name. A woman directly in front shouted her question to be heard above the din of the others.

"Miss King, can you tell us what's going to happen on Tuesday?"

Jill shook her head. "All I know is that we have to evacuate the Cove before ten in the morning." She took a sideways step toward the house.

The woman jumped in front of her. Anxiety carved deep creases in her face. "All of the Cove, or just certain parts of it? I live all the way out on Schooner Circle. Do you think I'll be okay there?"

"I'm sorry. I don't know anything else." She edged past the woman.

"But what about people who can't leave?" Another lady, older than the first, caught her in a frightened gaze. "I don't drive, and my husband is out at sea for another week and a half."

Jill opened her mouth, but closed it again. She had no advice to give. Shaking her head, she pushed between two people and gained a few steps toward the porch.

"You can ride with me," the first lady said. "Just pack light because I'll have two kids in the car too."

"Don't be stupid," shouted someone from the rear of the crowd. "Nothing's going to happen."

A derisive laugh sounded from nearby. "Yeah. She's as loony as Daffy Duck."

When the two women who'd just arranged to evacuate together turned to argue with the crowd, Jill shot between them and dashed up the porch steps. The door handle refused to turn. Locked.

"Don't leave!" someone yelled. "I have more questions."

Heart thudding loudly in her ears, Jill shook her head. How could she answer their questions when she didn't know anything else? She dug in her purse for her keys. Why hadn't she kept them in her hand?

"Loony tunes." The first man's shout was met with laughter.

A high-pitched warbling wail rose mockingly over the laughter. Jill's stomach gave a queasy lurch. She recognized that sound.

The front door opened, and a pair of hands jerked her inside. The door slammed behind her and Nana slid the deadbolt into place.

"Hooligans." Her darkly reddened lips were pursed into an angry kiss. "They'll be gone soon. I've called the police. Are you okay, Jill?"

Jill rubbed her arms with her hands and willed her heartbeat to return to normal. She nodded. "They called me a loony tune, and somebody started making the sound of a loon. It sounded just like Katharine Hepburn in *On Golden Pond.*"

Nana shook her head, her features scrunched with disgust. "At a time like this, we get a kook on our front porch doing bird impressions." She put an arm around Jill and sent her toward the living room with a gentle push. "Go on in and help the girls finish up those signs. I'll get you some hot tea."

Jill glanced at the door. Beyond the frosted glass, dark figures moved in the yard. At least two of the people out there believed her. They were making plans to evacuate even though she couldn't give them any details, while the others would stay in the Cove on Tuesday, gambling their lives on the fact that she was crazy.

With a shudder, she joined the ladies in the living room.

~

Greg pulled his car into Ruth's driveway and parked behind Jill's. Across the street, a small cluster of people stood watching him.

What was going on? The sky was dark, and behind the crowd a cold wind whipped the harbor against the rocky shore. He slid out of the driver's seat and stood, trying to make out their faces. A camera flash went off, followed quickly by a second.

Reporters, or just curious gawkers? He didn't wait around to find out, but dashed across the walkway and up the porch steps. The door was locked again. Now he understood why. He punched the doorbell with a glove-encased finger.

The porch light came on. Inside, a figure topped with fiery red hesitated on the other side of the frosted glass.

"Ruth, it's me." He raised his voice to penetrate the door. "Greg."

The lock clicked, and the door cracked open just enough to let him step through.

"What's all that about?" He waved toward the people outside as she relocked the door.

"They've been there all day, waiting for Jill to come out. There were a bunch more earlier, and on this side of the street. Trampled down the snow and turned my yard into a muddy mess." Ruth frowned. "The police told them they had to get off our property or they'd be arrested, and that made them leave. But as soon as the officers left, they came back." She glared toward the door. "I hope they freeze into Popsicles out there."

Greg arranged his features to appear calm. If he looked less than one hundred percent supportive, she might turn that Medusa stare on him.

"Where's Jill?" He glanced toward the living room.

"She's upstairs in her apartment."

He left Ruth and headed up the narrow stairs. He'd dreaded this conversation all day. Like a coward, he hadn't called Jill even during the few breaks in his busy meeting schedule. What could he say? She was clearly wrong about Rowe. He'd stopped by to apologize on the way over, and was relieved to find the café owner generously willing to accept his explanation that the stress of this dream thing had Jill acting out of character. All afternoon he'd expected a call informing him that Rowe was pulling her support for his campaign. Not that he would blame her.

Soft music reached his ears halfway up the stairs and grew louder as he approached the apartment door. An orchestra played the familiar strains of "Silent Night" on the stereo in Jill's front room. He crossed the kitchen, then stopped in the doorway, his breath momentarily snatched away.

A dozen burning candles filled the room with soft, flickering light. In the corner, multicolored lights twinkled on the Christmas tree, whose branches were covered with glittering ornaments. Jill stooped to rummage inside a box on the floor in front of the tree. She wore jeans and a bright red Christmas sweatshirt with a dancing reindeer on the front. He remembered that sweater from two years ago. The color complemented her dark hair and creamy skin, and made her eyes gleam. She straightened, and he saw what looked like a thick wad of paper in her hand. With slow, careful movements, she peeled back the layers to reveal a delicate glass ornament. She held it up in front of her face to admire it, and caught sight of him.

The smile that lit her face burned brighter than any candle. His throat tightened. She was so beautiful.

"My father gave this to my mother before they were married. He brought it back from overseas." She turned and hung it in a place of honor, on a branch at eye level in the front of the tree. "After reading his letters, it kind of feels more special. He loved her so much."

I love you that much. The words were on the tip of his tongue.

But they sounded stupid, sappy, especially after the scene in the café today when he'd dragged her out. He swallowed and said instead, "You decorated your Christmas tree."

"I decided it was time." She bent over the box and pulled out a gold-and-white angel. "You're just in time to help me put the finishing touch on it. The angel goes on last." She held it toward him. "Would you?"

He crossed the room and took the ornament from her. The gauzy, cone-shaped gown was hollow, allowing the topper to rest securely on the uppermost point of the tree. Greg rose on his tiptoes and set the angel in place.

"There." Jill took a step back, her eyes glowing with candlelight as she admired her tree. "What do you think?"

Greg didn't take his eyes off of Jill. "Breathtaking."

She slipped an arm around his waist and squeezed. "I meant the tree, silly."

"Oh. Yeah, it's nice too."

Grinning, she shoved him toward the sofa. "Have a seat. I'm going to clean up my mess and then I'll get you a bowl of chili. Nana and I made it, and we saved you some."

"Sounds great."

If she'd saved supper for him, that meant she wasn't angry about this afternoon. At least, she wasn't angry with him. And after finding her like this, glowing with beauty and doing something as normal as decorating a Christmas tree, he was having a hard time hanging on to his determination to be stern.

"So, I hear you had some excitement today."

She stooped to pick up several wads of paper and toss them into the box. "You mean besides becoming a television star and marching into a public place to confront the sneaky snake who made me look like a fool to half of Nova Scotia?"

Yeah. Not mad *at him*. "Actually, I was talking about having to call the police to chase the people off your front lawn."

"Oh, that." She dropped the last of the ornament wrappings in the box and folded the flaps closed. When she finished, she leaned over the box for a moment, her head bowed. "Did you see the evening news?"

"Yeah." Teresa kept a small television set in the conference room so she could watch her soap opera while she ate lunch in there. "So did my father."

The phone call had come within seconds of the end of the news story. Dad had been nearly apoplectic. Greg's ears still stung from a couple of his juicier words.

"Greg, I'm sorry." He heard sincerity in her voice. "I hope you know I never intended for that to happen." She picked up the box and headed for the kitchen. "I promise the next time I won't sound like such a nutcase."

Her words sank in as she disappeared through the doorway. Greg leaped off the couch and dashed after her, alarm zinging through his brain.

"Next time? What do you mean by that?"

She removed the access panel to the attic and shoved the box inside before answering. "I'm meeting with the reporter from CBC Saturday afternoon. That way I'll get to present my side."

"What?" Greg didn't mean to shout, but the word blasted out of him. Why couldn't she give up this crazy idea? Was she *trying* to make herself look like a lunatic, and him too? "Jill, you can't do that."

She slid the access panel back in place. "I have to, thanks to Rowena."

He shook his head, unable to follow her logic.

"She sent that video to make me look like a lunatic to CBC.

I hadn't slept for days, I didn't have a bit of makeup on my face, and I looked awful. No wonder everybody thinks I'm a loon. I need a chance to explain what's going on calmly and rationally, so people won't discount this warning as the ramblings of an escapee from an insane asylum."

"Jill, do you hear yourself?" He raked his fingers through his hair. "You don't honestly think people are going to take you seriously because you're dressed nicely and wearing lipstick."

"And speaking rationally? Yes." She nodded. "Some will. And those who don't won't be able to say I didn't do everything I could to warn them."

"But what if nothing happens, Jill? Have you thought of that? What if Tuesday comes and goes, and Seaside Cove isn't destroyed?"

She came to stand in front of him and peered up into his face. "Then I will publicly admit I'm wrong. I hope I am. But Greg, if I'm right and I do nothing, I'll never be able to live with myself. Can you understand that?"

"I ..." Greg's mouth went dry. They were headed for a confrontation. He couldn't deny her sincerity, but how could he agree with her behavior? "I wish you'd think before you act, Jill. Today at the café, for instance. You were out of line to accuse Rowe of lying."

Her face hardened. "I don't think so, and it upsets me when you take her side over mine."

"I'm not taking anyone's side. I understand how you jumped to the conclusion that she leaked the video to the news. But she explained what happened."

"I don't believe her." Her face took on a stubborn set. "She's trying to come between us so she can have you. Just watch. She'll tip her hand eventually."

There was no arguing with her over this. She was determined to believe Rowe had designs on him. He threw both hands in the air. "I give up. You're going to do whatever you want, regardless of my opinion."

"Greg." She spoke softly, and placed a warm hand on his arm. "Don't think that. I value your opinion more than anyone else's. It's just that I don't think you understand how strongly I feel about this. If you did, you'd know I'm only doing what I have to do." She stepped forward and wrapped her arms around his waist. "In five days this will be over, one way or another. After that, I'll be free of this feeling. I know it. Please hang in there for five more days and life can become normal again."

But what if it doesn't? When nothing happens on December 6, what will that do to you?

He bit back his fears and enfolded the woman he loved in his arms.

"Okay," he whispered. "Five more days."

Chapter 20

Friday, December 2

"Can you believe they're already out front?" Nana stood at the front window peeking through the curtains when Jill came downstairs.

"Yes, I saw them from upstairs." Jill popped a last bite of toast into her mouth and took her coat down from the rack. "Just two cars, though. Not as many as yesterday. At least they're across the street. I should have time to run to my car before they stop me."

"If they come into my yard I'll have them thrown in jail." Nana picked up a digital camera from a stand near the door and wielded it like a weapon. "I'll provide photographic proof they trespassed."

"Good idea." Jill wrapped a long scarf around her neck. "What's on the agenda today?"

Nana glanced at her watch. "The girls will be here at nine. Eloise is bringing her SUV, and Myrtle got her son's truck so we can carry the signs. We're going to split into two teams and deliver them around town."

Guilt stabbed at Jill. They were doing all the work. "I have my counseling appointment, and then I need to go see Mom since I didn't make it yesterday. If you wait until this afternoon I'll go with you."

Nana waved the offer away. "Everything's under control. But don't forget you need to work on your notes for the meeting with CBC tomorrow."

"I will. See you this afternoon."

Jill dug her car keys out of her purse and grasped the remote, her finger ready to push the Unlock button. She touched the door handle and paused to gather her nerve. Nana turned on her camera.

"Ready?" Jill asked.

Nana nodded.

Jill opened the door and stepped onto the porch. Across the street, two people got out of a Ford Explorer parked on the side of the road, and two more emerged from a Honda. A man and three women headed across the street toward Jill.

"Stop!" Nana ran down the porch stairs in front of Jill, her hand held up like a traffic cop. "If you come onto my property, I'll have you arrested for trespassing." She brandished her camera to show she meant business.

"We need to know what's going to happen on Tuesday." The man, bundled in a blue ski jacket, stopped at the edge of the street. "Please. You have to tell us."

At least he wasn't shouting derisive names at her. These must be people who believed her. The plaintive plea in his voice struck a chord of sympathy in Jill. She didn't stop advancing toward her car, but she did answer the man. "I'm sorry. I don't know any details, only that it's going to happen a little past ten in the morning. If you want to be safe, be out of town before then."

"How far out of town?" The nose of the woman standing next

to him was apple red. She shivered in the cold wind. "Is Halifax far enough, or should I take the kids to my sister's in Quebec?"

The car locks clicked open when Jill punched the button. "I think Halifax is far enough." She shook her head and gave the woman an apologetic shrug. "I'm sorry. I wish I knew more."

When she opened the door, the man stepped up onto the curb as if he would try to stop her from leaving. Nana erupted into action. She ran toward him, waving her empty hand like she was shooing chickens.

"I won't have people tromping around in my yard. We're meeting with CBC at three o'clock tomorrow. Jill will tell the newspeople everything she knows. You can watch it on television tomorrow night."

"But I warn you," Jill added, "I don't have many answers. I'm just as confused about this whole thing as everyone else."

She slid into her car and started the engine. The people headed back across the street, talking amongst themselves as they got into their vehicles. That wasn't so bad, not nearly as painful as yesterday's encounter. A little awkward, though. In a way, she almost wished the dream would return one more time. Then maybe she would notice more details, so she'd have more to report.

Chuckling at the weird turn her thoughts had taken, Jill pulled out onto the street and headed for Doreen's office.

"You look much better today," Doreen told her when they were seated in her office.

"I feel much better." Jill smiled. "It's amazing what a few nights of good sleep will do for you."

"So the dream hasn't returned? What about the memories of the accident?"

Jill shook her head. "I doubt if I'll ever stop having reminders of the accident, but they haven't been bothersome. And no more dreams. The feelings are still here, though. I'm still certain something terrible is going to happen on Tuesday, and I still want to warn people to leave the Cove." She looked away, not sure how Doreen would react to the next piece of news. "Actually, I've decided to do just that, warn people. I don't see how I can do anything else and live with myself. Here, I want to show you something."

She took her father's letters from her purse and let the counselor read them. The professional mask remained in place as she passed them back to Jill.

"So you believe you've inherited an ability to see the future in dreams?"

Only Doreen could deliver a question like that without a single inflection in her voice. Still, every word sounded saturated with disbelief to Jill's ears.

She leaned forward, elbows resting on her knees. "I don't know what I believe. All I know is I'm not going to have the guilt of death hovering over my head if my dream turns out to be true."

"And if it doesn't?"

"Greg asked the same thing. If it doesn't, then I'll publicly eat crow and be happy about it. It's not like I want to see a disaster happen."

Doreen's head tilted. "What else does Greg say?"

Jill shifted in her chair and examined the carpet between her feet. "He thinks I heard about my father's dreams when I was a kid and my subconscious has built this whole thing up because

I'm suffering from post-traumatic stress disorder and December 6 is so close to the one-year anniversary of the subway accident." She glanced up at Doreen's face. "Do you think that's possible?"

"Certainly it's possible. PTSD can manifest in a lot of different ways."

The counselor's voice held a note of hesitation that snagged Jill's attention. She waited out a long silence where Doreen appeared to be attempting to study the inside of Jill's head by peering through her eyeballs.

Finally, Doreen's rigid posture relaxed. "Frankly, you don't show as many of the classic signs of PTSD as you did six months ago. You're no longer afraid of being in a crowd. You're getting out of your apartment more and more. Our sessions for the past few months have focused on moving forward, not looking back. Except for this recent occurrence, you sleep well. You have had these dreams, yes, but those who suffer from PTSD typically dream of the traumatic event, not future events. I do still have an area of concern, though."

"What is that?" The minute the question left her mouth, Jill knew the answer, but she still winced when she heard it.

"Robert. Your inability to learn details of his life indicates you've not yet faced his death. And since that death is closely related to the loss of your career, I think finding out about him is an important step toward your full recovery."

Jill recognized the truth in the counselor's words. A couple of times she'd actually picked up her laptop with the intention of finding out more about Robert, but so far she hadn't been able to do it.

"What did Dr. Bookman say when you spoke with him?"

"I haven't actually met with him yet." She tried to look innocent. "I do have an appointment, though. Wednesday afternoon."

Doreen's lips twitched. "Wednesday. The day *after* December 6?"

"His schedule was full this week, and I've got a lot going on the first couple of days next week." Jill gave a sheepish grin. "At least, I *think* I do."

The counselor actually chuckled. "I suppose you do." The laughter ended and she became serious. She leaned forward and held Jill's gaze. "If you become anxious, or overwhelmed, or experience any feelings you think are cause for concern, promise you'll call me. No matter what time it is."

"Wow. You're giving me free reign to wake you up in the middle of the night?"

Jill would have laughed, except Doreen's expression made laughing impossible. Apparently, she really was concerned that Jill would have some sort of breakdown and ... what? Kill herself, maybe? Grab a blowtorch and create her own disaster if nothing happened Tuesday morning? Either idea was ludicrous. But if it made Doreen feel better to say it, fine.

"I will," Jill promised.

"Good." Doreen clicked her pen shut and dropped it in the holder. "Then unless you call, I'll see you next Friday."

Jill almost responded, *If we're still here,* but decided against it. Who knew how a therapist would interpret a statement like that?

~

When Greg entered his law office, he found Teresa already seated at her desk, a telephone propped against her ear.

"Yes, Mr. Vickers, I'm sure he's aware of the ordinances concerning owners cleaning up after their animals." She grimaced at Greg. "No, sir, he can't do anything about that. He hasn't been elected yet. Have you tried talking to your neighbor about her cat?"

Greg laughed silently and started toward his office. She waved him to a halt.

"Yes, I will certainly give him the message. Thank you for calling, Mr. Vickers."

She hung up the phone with one hand while the other finished writing on the message pad. "You would not believe the answering machine this morning. Thirteen messages."

"Please tell me they weren't all from people wanting me to clean up after their neighbors' pets."

"Oh, no. Only one of those." Her lips formed a prim bow as she handed him a stack of pink notes. "Most of them are about Jill."

He froze in the act of taking the messages. "Bad?"

"Well, they're not good." She folded her arms across her chest and rocked back in the chair, eyes fixed on him. "What is going on with her, Greg? Is she okay? You know." A pink polished fingernail tapped against her temple.

Greg avoided her gaze under the guise of scanning the stack of messages. "She'll be fine. She's under a lot of strain right now." The excuse was starting to grow thin with overuse.

"Well, you haven't asked for my opinion, but I'm going to give it to you anyway. Her behavior isn't doing your reputation any good." She nodded toward the pink slips. "You'll see when you read those."

Torn between telling her to mind her own business and thanking her for sharing her opinion, Greg chose to do neither. He jerked his head once, and headed for the refuge of his office.

"Someone left you a present on the front porch last night. I put it on your desk."

A present? Christmas was still weeks away, and his birthday

wasn't until May. He stepped into the office, his gaze drawn to the desk.

In the center lay a bunch of bananas. When he approached, he saw they'd each been written on with a black marker. In block letters, five said, "Jillian King." The sixth read, "You, if you stay with her."

The message was clear. Jill was bananas, and if he didn't distance himself from her, so was he.

~

Jill turned onto the street where she and Nana lived. Sunlight glinted off the windshield of a van parked across from the house. For a moment, she was tempted to drive past and come back later. But where would she go? Greg was working, and she'd already spent an hour at the nursing home.

The spark of awareness she'd seen the other day in Mom didn't reappear. Instead, Jill had filled the time with one-way chatter, Mom's dull eyes fixed on a distant object visible only to herself. Of her dream, Jill said only, "Nana and I have made some signs warning people about Tuesday." She felt uncomfortable saying more, because the nursing staff hovered near the door, watching her with surreptitious gazes. After an hour, she kissed her mom and left.

After the nursing home, she'd driven into the city for a visit to the music store. Mariah and Kaylee needed lesson books, and she'd picked up a few extras to have on hand for future students. She had not stepped inside a music store since before the accident, and was pleased to experience not even a twinge of discomfort. She'd left the store smiling.

Eyeing the van across the street from her home, Jill's spirits flagged. The loony tune taunt still rubbed against her feelings like sandpaper. Would she have to run a gauntlet of insults to get into her own house?

At least it was only one van. Resigned, Jill pulled into the driveway and parked her car. While she gathered her purse and music books, she kept an eye on the rearview mirror. The van's side door opened, and she caught a glimpse of movement inside, but nobody immediately emerged.

Curious, Jill got out of her car and watched. A woman hopped out, cast an anxious look her way, and fixed a ramp to the side of the van. Then she climbed back inside and a moment later, appeared again walking backward down the ramp, pulling a wheelchair.

When she reached the ground and turned, Jill saw that the person seated in the chair was a child. A tickle of unease erupted in her stomach. What was that woman doing bringing a disabled child here?

"Are you Jillian King?" Anxious eyes searched her face as the two approached.

"Yes, I am. May I help you?"

The child was bundled against the cold, but the woman wore no coat. Her throat convulsed with a swallow. "I hope so. No one else has been able to."

Jill smiled at the little girl. The child's mouth slacked open, her head held to the wheelchair's high backrest with a strap around the forehead. Jill couldn't see her limbs, but one mittened hand curved sharply inward, and beneath the thick blanket the bulge from one leg twisted at an awkward angle to the other.

"I saw you on television last night, and I know it's a long shot, but I wondered if you could help Rachel."

Jill shook her head, confused. "I don't understand."

"We've tried everything. Doctors. Herbalists. Physical therapy. Everyone says there's no cure."

"I'm sorry. I don't know what help I can be. I'm not a doctor."

"I know, but you had that dream, so there's something special about you." Desperation choked the woman's voice. "I thought maybe you could heal her."

Shock slapped Jill like a lightning bolt. "Excuse me?"

"The last doctor we visited said it would take a miracle, so when I saw you on television I thought you might be able to do a miracle."

The child watched her with a familiar dull gaze. Jill saw that same vacant stare almost every day when she visited Mom. An ache flared in her chest, and she took a backward step. "I — I can't heal anyone."

The woman pushed the chair forward. "Won't you try? We're desperate."

Tears blurred Jill's vision. If she could heal, wouldn't she have healed herself and her own mother a long time ago? When she was fourteen she'd begged God to heal Mom; his answer was no. "I wish I could help, but I can't."

The look of defeat on the mother's face sent a blade of pain knifing through Jill's heart. She couldn't stay there, not another minute.

"I'm sorry."

Tears spilled over her cheeks as she turned and fled to the porch. Her fingers fumbled to get the key in the lock, but she finally did. Inside the house, she managed to get the door closed before she collapsed on the bottom step leading up to her apartment. Her sobs echoed up the stairway.

Chapter 21

Saturday, December 3

"We're renting buses," Nana announced Saturday morning.

Jill stared over her coffee cup, her eyes bleary and burning. Not much sleep again. No dreams, only the haunting memory of vague stares and a drowning feeling of helplessness.

"Buses?"

Nana's red head nodded. She wore a liberal amount of extra-bright blue eye shadow today. "The girls and I were talking last night about that woman out front, the one who didn't have a ride. There are probably lots of people in the Cove in the same position. The residents at Centerside Nursing, for one thing. I checked into the price, and we decided it's well worth the expense."

"I thought we'd just take Mom with us in the car."

"What about the others?" Nana planted her elbows on the table and held her cup in front of her mouth. "They have to have a way out too, don't they?"

"I suppose you're right." The memory of the nurses hovering in the hallway outside Mom's door yesterday made Jill hesitant. What would they say when Nana pulled a bus up to the front door and started ushering their residents out? "Where will we take them?"

"We talked about that." Nana looked slightly uncomfortable. "Do you have any idea how long we'll need to be gone? I mean, is it a matter of hours or days?"

Numbly, Jill shook her head.

"Pity." She reached across the table to pat Jill's hand. "That's all right, though. We figured we'd take everyone to a shopping mall in Halifax for the day. They can get some Christmas shopping done if they want. There are restaurants, so we don't have to worry about feeding them, and we'll be able to return them to the Cove fairly quickly afterward. They'll probably want to get back and check on their homes."

"What if..." Jill hated to say the words. She swallowed. "What if they don't have homes to come back to?"

Nana seemed unconcerned. "In that case, the government will have to step in and do something. They do, you know, if there's a large-scale emergency."

The doorbell rang. Jill closed her eyes, her insides tangling into instantaneous knots. Was it anxious believers, curious gawkers, or insult-lobbing skeptics?

With a determined set to her jaw, Nana rose. "You stay here. I'll handle them."

Feeling like a coward, Jill huddled over her coffee cup and let her grandmother face the music alone.

A moment later, she returned. "Look who I found on the front porch."

Relief washed over Jill in waves at the sight of Greg. She jumped out of her chair and threw herself at him. "Oh, Greg. I'm so glad it's you."

"Now that's the kind of greeting a man loves to get." A quiet laugh lightened his words as he returned her energetic hug.

"Have a seat." Nana pulled out a chair for him. "I'll scramble some eggs."

Greg shook his head. "I didn't come for breakfast. I've got some work I need to get done at the office before a noon meeting."

"On Saturday?" Jill asked. "You're a workaholic."

"I take after my dad. But I do have time for a cup of coffee."

With a final squeeze around his waist, Jill released him. She poured his coffee and refilled Nana's while they settled at the table, then slid into her own chair. Two of the three people she loved most in the world were right here. She searched Nana's face, then Greg's. One believed her dream, and the other didn't. The question that had hounded her in the dark hours of last night had to be addressed, and she couldn't think of anyone whose opinions she valued more than theirs.

"Could I talk to you two about something?"

"Of course," Nana answered instantly.

Greg's eyes widened a fraction, as though wondering what new insanity she was about to spout, but the expression was gone as quickly as it came. He covered her hand with his. "You can talk to me about anything, Jill."

She smiled her thanks for his support, but then fell silent a moment. How to phrase this without sounding crazy? Well, crazier than usual. She stared at the dark liquid in her cup. The overhead light reflected off the glassy surface. Finally, she blurted her question in a rush.

"Do you think this dream comes from God?"

Neither answered immediately. Jill rushed on, her thoughts taking form as the words tumbled out. "I've prayed and asked God to take the dream away, and he didn't. Last night I prayed for him to take away this crazy compulsion. Instead, I feel more strongly than ever that I have to warn people, even if nothing happens. Why would that be, unless ..." She bit her lip, "unless the whole thing was his idea."

She risked an upward glance. Nana's expression was thoughtful, as though weighing her answer. Greg averted his eyes, focused on the vinyl placemat in front of him. Disappointment shafted through her. She knew his answer without hearing it.

"I think your dream is a gift to the people in the Cove." Nana's words were slow, ponderous. "And my personal opinion is that all good gifts come from God." She cocked her head. "So yes, I think so."

Greg's head shot up. "How can you say that? Why would God choose Jill to deliver a message like this?" He cast an apologetic glance her way. "I love you, and I think you're incredible, but why you? Your faith isn't any stronger than most people's."

She couldn't take offense at his words, because they were true. "I know that. In fact, for the past year I feel like any faith I once had has been in shreds. That's what I'm trying to understand. Why me?"

"Because you're willing," Nana said. "That's what God is looking for, isn't it? People who are willing to do as he asks?"

"I wouldn't exactly say I jumped eagerly into this whole thing." Jill waved a hand vaguely toward the front room, which until yesterday had been covered with painting supplies and yard signs.

Nana's shoulders shrugged. "Sometimes we need a good shove."

Greg's struggle showed in the deep lines on his forehead, his frown. "I'm just not convinced. Seems to me if God really wanted to send a warning, he'd send an angel to announce it in the town square or something."

Jill hid a sigh behind her coffee cup. Ripples disturbed the hot surface. If she couldn't convince her own fiancé, how in the world could she expect anyone else in the Cove to believe her?

Nana's stare speared Greg for a moment, then softened when it turned her way. "Jill, listen to me. No one can answer that question for you. Only you know if this warning comes from God. You need to pray about it, and then do what you feel is right. That's all any of us can do."

Greg nodded, though reluctantly. "I guess that's true."

Jill toyed with the handle of her cup. She had prayed last night for hours. Her determination to see this thing through was stronger than ever. Did that mean God was behind the warning? If only she could be sure.

There was one more question she wanted to ask, but she was almost afraid of the answer. "Are you planning to be here when I talk to the reporter this afternoon, Greg?"

He looked startled. "Me?"

"You don't have to say anything, but you *are* my fiancé."

His mouth opened, then closed without a word. He looked like she'd just backed him into a corner and waved a machine gun in his face. She knew he didn't want to be associated with her. He was embarrassed to be seen with the town loon.

"The girls and I will be here." Loyalty rang in Nana's voice.

Greg raised his head, and his brave smile held a touch of resignation. "Me too. If you want me here, I'll be here."

A wave of gratitude washed over her, and left her eyes stinging. He would come, even though he didn't believe in her cause. He'd risk the disapproval of his friends and supporters, even his father, just because she asked him to.

She couldn't do that to him.

She got up from her chair and circled around to stand behind his, then bent over and wrapped her arms around him from behind. "Thank you. I can't tell you what that means to me. But you don't have to. If Nana and the others will be here, I'll have plenty of supporters."

The breath left his chest with a whoosh. "Are you sure?"

"I'm sure." She planted a kiss on his cheek and straightened. Her hand lingered on his shoulder, and he covered it with his own.

"Just do me one favor, will you?" He twisted around to look up at her. "Don't tell the CBC reporter God told you to warn people to evacuate the Cove."

Nana stiffened in her chair, outrage apparent in her rigid posture. "And why not, if it's true?"

Jill had to hand it to Greg. He rarely lost his composure, even in the face of a powerful force like Ruth Parkins.

"Because it won't help her case any if she starts saying she's hearing voices," he replied, his expression calm. "People will start comparing her with Charles Manson or David Koresh."

"Or Joan of Arc," Nana shot back.

As if that was any consolation. Jill's hand dropped to her side. They burned Joan of Arc at the stake for heresy.

"That was terrific, Mariah. Exactly right."

The child's grin broadened under Jill's praise, and she repeated the right-handed finger exercise, chanting the name of each key as she touched it.

"C. D. E." She hesitated while her thumb searched for the F. A smile lit her face when she found the right note. "F. G-A-B-C." The last four notes followed in rapid succession.

"Excellent."

"What about this hand?" Mariah raised her left, her feet swinging beneath the piano bench.

Jill's chest tightened. "It's the same, only in a lower octave, and you use different fingers for the keys."

"Okay." The little girl turned an expectant gaze toward the lower register, awaiting a demonstration.

The time had come. She couldn't expect the child to know how to do an exercise she'd never seen. Jill's fingers twitched as she lifted her left hand from her lap and held it poised over the keyboard. Breath caught in her chest, she lowered her hand to the keys. The smooth ivory touched her fingertips with the gentle kiss of a long-lost lover. Oh, they felt so good. Slowly, but without hesitation, she ran up the scale as expressively as if it were a Beethoven concerto. A muscle twinged when her middle finger crossed over to the B, a mild reminder of the damage that had been done, but not terribly painful. Unable to stop herself, she descended the scale and then raced upward toward middle C again.

A smile took possession of her lips. A simple scale was a long way from real playing, but at least it was a step. Her hand fisted, and she pressed it to her lips to stop a triumphant laugh from bubbling out.

"Like this?" Unaware of the chasm Jill had just leaped across, Mariah placed her fingers where Jill's had been and stumbled through the exercise.

"Exactly like that." Jill beamed at the girl, and Mariah preened. "Don't worry about speed yet. That will come. Instead, focus on tempo. Each note should be held the same length of time as the one before. Let's try it again."

Relishing her own sense of accomplishment, Jill turned her attention to her student.

~

Eleven o'clock came and went with no sign of Kaylee. Jill paced from the piano to the window a dozen times, but no amount of straining her eyes toward the end of the street produced a glimpse of Becky Fontaine's car. At eleven-fifteen, Jill looked up the phone number and called. No answer. She left a message and paced some more.

At eleven thirty, when Kaylee's lesson would have ended, Jill grabbed a piece of notepaper and wrote a quick note. Kaylee had been so excited last week she wouldn't have forgotten about her lesson. Something must have come up, and her mother forgot to call. She paper clipped the note to the front of the new lesson book, slipped it in a bag, and headed for her car. The Fontaine's house was out of her way, but she had time to swing by on her way for a short visit with Mom.

The Fontaine home was a tidy single-story house in a quiet neighborhood. A gigantic inflated Santa Claus riding a motorcycle dominated the front yard, tethered to the ground with cords and stakes. Jill left her car running in the driveway, intending to dash up to the front door and hang the bag on the knob.

The muted sound of piano music from inside the house made her hesitate. She recognized a piece from her CD, only played with less expertise. Kaylee must be home. Maybe she had forgotten about her lesson. Jill pressed the button for the doorbell.

The music didn't stop, but a few seconds later the door opened. The pleasant expression of inquiry on Becky's face faded. "Jill. Uh, hello. What are you doing here?" No sign of the flighty, friendly smile from last week.

"I was in the neighborhood, and I thought I'd stop by to

deliver Kaylee's piano lesson book." She held up the bag. "She missed her lesson this morning."

Becky shot a quick glance over her shoulder before slipping outside. She shut the door, but kept her hand on the knob behind her. "Didn't my mother-in-law tell you?"

She hadn't seen Alice Fontaine since Thursday, when they finished painting the rest of the signs. "Tell me what?"

"We've decided to hold off on the piano lessons for now." An awkward smile flitted across her lips. "We have so much going on already, you know? You have to draw the line somewhere."

Stunned, Jill took a backward step. "You can't let her quit." She pointed toward the closed door, the piano music coming from inside. "Surely you know how talented she is. She has to be encouraged."

"We're not saying she can't play, but lessons aren't going to work out right now." Becky's gaze shifted away.

Realization hit Jill with the strength of a boxer's punch. This wasn't Kaylee's decision. Her parents were forcing her to quit piano lessons, not because of a busy schedule, but because of *Jill.* They didn't want their daughter spending time with the town loon.

"I see." Her mouth felt like someone had stuffed it with cotton balls. "I bought this for her. She might as well have it."

She thrust the bag toward Becky and didn't wait for her to take it. The book fell to the concrete as Jill whirled and made her escape without looking to see if Becky picked it up. She put her car in Reverse and zoomed into the street, wiping tears from her eyes so she could see to drive.

Chapter 22

THE CAFÉ ALWAYS PACKED A good lunchtime crowd on Saturdays, and today was no different. Even at two o'clock, every table was occupied. Greg made for the only empty stool at the high counter, nodding at the diners as he wound through the room. He had avoided his favorite haunt yesterday, not certain of his reception after the confrontation between Jill and Rowena on Thursday. When Rowe turned and caught sight of him, her welcoming smile dismissed any hesitation he might have felt.

"Welcome, Councillor." She swiped at the counter with a wet rag and slapped down a clean paper placemat. "Missed seeing you yesterday."

"Busy day." Greg slid into the chair and smiled an absent greeting at the man seated next to him.

Rowe waved the young waitress away, planted her elbow on the counter in front of him, and rested her chin in her hand. "How about a bowl of my special beef stew to warm you up?"

"Tempting, but I've been thinking about one of your thick, juicy cheeseburgers all day."

She grinned and asked with a saucy southern twang, "Ya want fries with that?"

"Sure. Why not?"

Her eyebrows arched. “Calorie splurge, huh? Not that you need to worry about that.” Her admiring gaze dropped toward his chest and continued down to his waist, then cut back up with a flirtatious twinkle. “Not like me. Everything I eat goes straight to my thighs.”

She turned toward the grill with an exaggerated wiggle of her hips. The man next to Greg laughed. “No evidence of that, Rowe.”

Greg busied himself by peeling a napkin from the dispenser, for the first time uncomfortable with Rowena’s boisterous flirting. Jill’s accusations echoed in his mind. Could there be any truth to them? He didn’t think so. Like he’d explained the other day, that was Rowe’s way. She treated everybody the same.

A hamburger patty hit the grill with a sizzle, and Rowena returned to set a glass of ice water in front of him.

“I’ve been scheming for you, honey.”

Startled, Greg looked up into her face. “Huh?”

“You know. Campaign stuff.”

“Oh.” He gave a weak laugh. “Yeah. The campaign.”

“We need to decide on a slogan and logo pretty soon.”

“You think I need a logo?”

“Definitely. Not a cutesy cartoon picture or anything like that. Just a certain color scheme and font that people will come to associate with your name. And the slogan should be something catchy, but still make a statement about what you stand for.” She sketched in the air with a hand. “*Say Yes to Greg Bradford. Say Yes to the future.*”

The man next to him nodded. “That’s not bad.”

“Not bad?” Greg shook his head admiringly. “It’s good. I like it.”

“I’ve got some more ideas, too. I figured you and I could talk on Monday, when it’s quieter around here. Say around ten in the morning. That work for you?”

"Sure. Thanks, Rowe. Look forward to it."

Dimples creased her cheeks. "Stick with me, darlin', and this election's in the bag."

She winked again before disappearing into the back room. A nagging disquiet made Greg shift in his chair. *Say 'Yes' to the future.*

He picked up his water glass. With all the turmoil of the past week, the future seemed pretty uncertain right about now. Oh, not the future of the Cove. His future. Jill's future. What would happen on Tuesday, and how would that affect their future? She'd asked him to stick with her until Wednesday, when all this mess would be behind them, one way or another. He'd agreed.

So why was he sitting here, when she clearly wanted his support during this interview with CBC?

Because my father will have a heart attack if he sees me on the news, acting like I support this crazy scheme.

Not to mention what it would do to his campaign. The message of the bananas sat like a two-ton anchor in his mind, pulling his thoughts to depths he didn't want to visit.

I could go and stay in the background. Nothing says I have to appear on camera. Just be there for Jill.

Whatever Jill was going through, he couldn't leave her to do it alone. Because when Tuesday came and nothing happened, he wanted her to know he'd still be there. She'd need a strong shoulder to cry on, someone she trusted. Ruth would be no help, because she was too deeply involved in this mess.

Yeah. That's what he'd do. Stay quietly in the background, off camera, and support Jill.

He jumped off the stool. "Hey, Rowe, cancel the cheeseburger. I just realized I've got to be somewhere."

She appeared in the doorway from the back room, holding

a bag of frozen fries. "You want me to wrap it up for you? It'll be done in a minute."

"No time." He dug a ten out of his pocket and tossed it on the counter. "Sorry for the trouble."

His watch read ten minutes past two. If he wanted to get there before the reporter arrived, he needed to hurry.

~

The Sign Brigade, as they'd decided to call themselves, clustered around the kitchen table, laying out their plans for Jill. Mrs. Fontaine had been embarrassed at the fact that her daughter-in-law pulled Kaylee from her piano lessons with Jill, and promised to work on Becky as soon as the dream disaster was over. Her certainty that Kaylee would return did little to soothe Jill's raw feelings, but at least she intended to try. Even if Kaylee studied under another piano teacher, the important thing was for her to continue developing her gift.

"Now, be sure to mention the time and place to load the buses." Nana slid a scrawled note across the table to Jill. "I've written it all down in case you get nervous and forget."

"Nana, I'm not nervous. I've performed on stage in front of thousands, and I've never had a single case of stage fright."

"Don't say that, honey," Mrs. Tolliver warned, her features alarmed. "You'll jinx yourself."

"It's just one reporter." Jill poured confidence into her smile and bestowed it on the ladies around the table. "I'll be fine."

Mrs. Cramer didn't appear convinced. "I've heard people say when the light goes on that television camera, words fly right out of their heads and they end up babbling like idiots."

A comforting thought.

Nana turned a reproving stare on Mrs. Cramer. "Jill is not going to babble like an idiot." She glanced at Jill. "You do have your notes written down, though? Just in case?"

"Nothing formal. Just a few bullet points of things I don't want to forget to mention."

Beside her, old Mrs. Mattingly studied her profile with the intensity of a bird dog eyeing a quail. "I think you need more makeup," she announced. "They say those reporters wear heavy makeup, and if you don't have much on you'll look washed out standing beside them. You were so pale and wan last time you were on the TV."

Five pairs of critical eyes inspected her face.

Mrs. Fontaine agreed. "Definitely a darker shade of lipstick. That one makes you look a tad sickly."

Sickly? A flutter erupted in Jill's stomach. Okay, maybe she was a *little* nervous.

Nana twisted around in the chair to glance at the clock on the microwave. "Shouldn't they be here by now? I thought they'd arrive a few minutes early to set up their camera or something."

A tap sounded on the back door. Oh, no. Who could that be? A reporter would come to the front. The flutter in Jill's stomach became full-blown nausea.

"I'll get it." Nana rose and approached the door with the determination of a barroom bouncer. She cracked open the mini blinds and turned toward Jill with a pleased smile. "Look who's here."

When she opened the door, the last person in the world Jill expected to see stepped into the kitchen. The nausea evaporated as she jumped out of her chair and flew into Greg's arms.

"Hey, beautiful." His whisper tickled the hair above one ear.

"I can't tell you how glad I am to see you." The shoulder of his heavy coat muffled her words.

Strong arms tightened around her. "I couldn't let you face this alone."

"Thank you." The telltale stinging of tears threatened. She stepped away, sniffing, and grabbed for a napkin to stop them before they ruined her mascara.

"You look terrific." His admiring gaze swept her from head to toe.

She stood a little straighter at the obviously heartfelt compliment. Agonizing hours of indecision had gone into selecting her wardrobe for today's interview. Jill finally settled on a dark blue suit with an attractive lime-green blouse that created the professional, competent air she hoped to project.

"She's going to darken her lipstick," Mrs. Tolliver informed him from her chair.

"I think she's perfect." Greg's expression became hesitant. "I want to be here to support you, but I don't think it's a good idea for me to be part of the interview because of the campaign and all. I hope you're okay with that."

In other words, he still didn't believe in her dream, and didn't want to appear as though he did. Jill's pleasure in his presence slipped a notch, but she steeled her expression not to show it. She raised up on her tiptoes and planted a lipstick kiss on his cheek.

"I understand. You can stay here in the kitchen, and you'll probably be able to hear everything."

His forehead wrinkled. "From all the way outside?"

Nana crossed to the sink to rinse her empty coffee cup. "No, from the living room. We thought Jill and the reporter could sit in the wing chairs. The fireplace will make a cozy backdrop. Sort of like a Barbara Walters interview."

Greg's shoulders heaved with a laugh. "You're kidding, right?"

"You don't think that's a good idea?" Jill asked.

"I don't think it's possible." His gaze circled the ladies in the room, and realization cleared his features. "You haven't looked outside, have you?"

An apprehensive chill zipped up Jill's spine and throbbed at the base of her skull. She raced out of the kitchen toward the living room window, the Sign Brigade close on her heels. With trembling hands, she pulled back the drawn curtain.

The front yard was packed with people, and two police officers hovered nearby, anxiously watching the crowd. Parked at the curb in front of the house was not one television truck, but three. The logos on the side panels announced the presence of CBC, Global Maritimes evening news, and CTV Halifax. Several of the people clustered closest to the porch steps were familiar to her from the various news programs, including the newscaster who had run the story on CBC a few days ago. Others jockeyed for position holding microphones and elaborate cameras.

Greg pointed to a woman in jeans and a navy peacoat. "That's Brenda Osborne from the *Metro News*. I met her outside the courthouse when I was defending a case a few months ago. I'm not sure, but I think the guy next to her is from *The Chronicle Herald*."

Stunned, Jill could only stare, slack-jawed, at the mob who overflowed the boundaries of the yard.

"Look at all those cars." Awe made Mrs. Fontaine's voice come out in a whisper. "They're lined up and down the street."

Greg nodded. "That's why I came to the back door. I had to park on the next street over and cut through the yard behind here."

"Look at all those people tromping my lawn into mud." Nana shut her eyes, a grimace twisting her features. "I hope the grass comes up in the spring."

Jill let the curtain fall back into place. Panic churned in the depths of her stomach now. This interview had gotten out of hand. Had all those people come to scoff at her, or were they like the ones yesterday morning who only wanted more information? Either way, this thing had exploded beyond her control.

"It was supposed to be one reporter." She shook her head disbelievingly. "One."

Greg slipped an arm around her waist. "Well, now you have a full-blown press conference, complete with spectators."

Mrs. Montgomery rubbed her hands together, her eyes gleaming. "Think of all the people who will hear your warning."

Nana placed a finger against her lips, thinking. "I wonder if it's too late to hire more buses."

Jill searched Greg's face and saw resignation there. He didn't believe her, didn't want to be associated with her. Was probably embarrassed for her. But at least he was here. Even though he wouldn't be at her side during the interview, just knowing he would be on the other side of the door gave her a strength she hadn't realized she would need until now.

She straightened, gathering that strength around her like donning a mackintosh before a rainstorm. "I think I'll go put on some darker lipstick."

Chapter 23

Jill didn't want to hide the professional image she'd worked so hard to achieve beneath a coat, so at three o'clock she stepped onto the porch in her suit. A frigid harbor breeze ruffled her hair, and she forced herself not to shiver. At least there was no snow falling, and the sky was sunny.

Nana and her friends followed Jill outside and arranged themselves in a line behind her. When they realized that they, too, would appear on television, there had been a rush for Nana's dressing table to refresh their makeup. Mrs. Tolliver had gone a little overboard with the powder and came close to resembling a white-faced mime, but Jill couldn't spare any time worrying about that. She needed all her energy to battle the only case of stage fright she'd ever experienced in her life. Throwing up on camera certainly wouldn't help her cause.

Eight or ten people mounted the porch steps to stand in front of her. Microphones were extended in her direction, and three men carrying large cameras on their shoulders arranged themselves to get a good angle. A familiar newscaster extended his hand.

"Ms. King, I'm Steven Welch with CBC."

Jill shook his hand, but couldn't force any words out. Her throat had become alarmingly tight.

"Belva Rhoades," said the woman next to him. "CTV Halifax."

Jill managed to smile and nod as she shook the hands of reporters from all of the area television stations and newspapers. When she recognized the man who'd written the front-page article in the local newspaper, she was pleased that she didn't scowl.

"Thank you all for coming." Her voice wobbled, and she flashed a nervous smile at them and the crowd gathered behind them. "We really weren't expecting a turnout like this. I guess I'll start out by telling you what's happening, and then see if you have any questions."

The reporters nodded, and as a group, backed down to stand on the second step, giving Jill a clear view of the mob in the front yard. William Akers and another police officer stood off to one side, their watchful stares fixed on the crowd. There had to be at least fifty people there. Some wore curious expressions, some anxious. A few were openly skeptical. Toward the front, she caught sight of the woman who had asked whether Halifax was far enough to take her children to safety. At least that explained how word got out around town. Nana had told them the television reporter would be here at three.

The papers in Jill's hands shook visibly. If she'd suspected this kind of press coverage, she would have written out her speech word for word. As it was, she'd have to improvise.

"Nine days ago, I had a dream. A very vivid dream."

"We can't hear you," someone at the back of the crowd shouted.

From the sidewalk came, "Talk louder!"

Jill projected her voice. "Nine days ago, I had a dream. I didn't see many details, but when I woke I was left with the impression of a coming disaster. I couldn't shake the impression that I needed to warn the people of Seaside Cove." She cleared her throat. "At first, I ignored it. I figured it was just a bad dream.

A nightmare, actually. But it kept coming back, and I saw a few more details each time. Fire, and injured bodies. And death ..."

The crowd remained silent as she recounted the events of the past week, how her certainty of the dream's validity had grown until she knew she couldn't ignore it. The expressions on the reporters' faces directly in front of her ranged from professional courtesy to encouraging smiles. She didn't dare look at the crowd.

As she talked, her confidence grew until finally the papers in her hand stopped trembling. "When I interrupted the meeting last Monday, I had barely slept for days. I realize now I must have looked like a raving fanatic, and I regret that." She glanced at the three television cameras in succession. "I don't regret my warning, though, because I feel more strongly than ever that there will be some sort of disaster in Seaside Cove on Tuesday morning. But I do regret that my erratic behavior may have caused some to discount my message. That's why I wanted to talk to you again, so you can see that I'm rational, and I'm convinced that the warning of my dream is true."

She paused to let her gaze sweep across the crowd. "I know this sounds insane. Like I'm acting on little more than a gut feeling. But I have to ask — how many of you have ever had a feeling you couldn't ignore? A small, still voice urged you to do something. On impulse you made a phone call to a friend, then discovered she was going through a hard time and needed encouragement at exactly that moment. Or it's four days until your next paycheck and your refrigerator is already starting to look empty. You feel the urge to look in the pocket of an old coat, and you find a twenty-dollar bill." The next words clogged her throat for a minute, but she forced them out. "Or you choose a taxi over the subway even though it costs more, and the subway train you would have been on crashes."

Heavy silence met her words. She took a moment to collect her composure before continuing.

"Or maybe you've had a feeling like that, and ignored it. Just imagine this: What if you hadn't? What if you'd acted? Just imagine." She straightened and lifted her head high. "That's what I'm doing. All I can do is what I feel is right. If there is something to my dream, then my warning may help save lives, lives of people I care about in Seaside Cove. If I'm wrong, well, at least I followed my conscience and no harm was done. So you see, I just had to deliver the message. You have to decide for yourselves if you believe me."

That seemed like a perfect place to stop. Jill folded her papers.

"The buses," Nana hissed from behind. "Don't forget the buses."

"Oh, yes." Jill switched to the second note, the one with Nana's expressive scrawl. "The ladies standing behind me have been extremely supportive in helping to get this message out to the residents of the Cove. They've arranged for buses to evacuate those who have no other way to leave. If you'd like a ride out of the Cove, you should be at Harbor Square by seven thirty Tuesday morning. Space will be limited, so only bring what you can carry in your lap."

A rumble rose from the crowd as people commented on that news.

Steven Welch from CBC asked a question, his voice pitched loud enough to be heard by most of the watchers. "Ms. King, have you had any other prophetic dreams?"

Jill shook her head. "Never. There's nothing special about me at all." The memory of the disabled child and her desperate mother surfaced. She looked directly at the CBC camera. "I have no special powers or anything like that."

"Then how do you explain this dream?" The reporter from the *Metro News* asked.

"I can't," Jill answered without hesitation. "It's never happened before, and I sincerely hope it never happens again."

"I have an idea." Mrs. Tolliver stepped up beside Jill, her eyes gleaming in her abnormally white face. The rest of the Sign Brigade buzzed like startled bees.

Jill swallowed a groan. *Please don't pull out the Dream Dictionary for Dummies.*

"I found something interesting on the Internet and haven't had a chance to tell you, dear." The elderly woman smiled up at Jill, then turned her attention to the reporters. "There's evidence that people who've suffered a blow to the head sometimes develop psychic abilities. It has to do with using different parts of the brain that aren't damaged."

Jill struggled to keep her face impassive. Surely Mrs. Tolliver had not just told the reporters she had brain damage. Possible headlines erupted in her mind, none of them good.

"I don't have an explanation," Jill hurried to say before someone could ask Mrs. Tolliver a follow-up question. "All I know is that I believe something is going to happen on Tuesday."

"You're crazy!" The shout came from somewhere near the driveway.

"Yeah. She's a real loon," agreed someone on the opposite side of the yard.

The rumble of the crowd grew loud, with some shouting, "I believe her!" and others saying, "She's a nut case." The high-pitched warbling wail of a loon rose over their voices.

The television cameras swung away from her and swept over the crowd. Voices rose as arguments became heated. The reporters in front of her started shouting their questions to be heard over the noise, but they all spoke at once and Jill couldn't understand them. She cupped a hand around her ear and leaned toward them.

Something hit her shoulder, then landed with a wet splat on the wood in front of her feet. More startled than hurt, Jill looked down at an overripe tomato splattered on the porch. Juice stained her suit jacket, and a couple of seeds clung to the fabric. Another one whizzed by her head. It hit the house with a thud and exploded. Somebody was lobbing rotten fruit at her! The hovering police officers rushed into the crowd as the newspaper photographers' cameras clicked with furious speed.

The front door opened, and Greg charged out of the house.

"That's enough." He didn't shout, but his voice held an air of authority that projected to the back of the crowd. "Ms. King is through here. Leave, all of you."

Greg's arm circled Jill's shoulders. Shaken, she allowed herself to be turned and guided toward the door. Though she had promised to answer questions from the reporters, she had no idea how to maintain a professional image while dodging tomatoes. As she and Greg made their escape, Nana and the other ladies stepped forward to form a barrier between her and the reporters, who rushed up the stairs shouting questions. Greg closed the front door as Nana's angry voice threatened to have everyone thrown in jail for trespassing.

Greg led her into the living room, where she collapsed into one of the wing chairs. A cheery fire snapped in the fireplace, its carefully crafted atmosphere gone to waste.

She bowed her head and covered her face with her hands. "That was terrible. I've made things worse, haven't I?"

Greg dropped onto his haunches beside her chair, a comforting hand on her leg. "Not necessarily. You were calm and articulate. I think you accomplished what you wanted to do."

She peeked at him between her fingers. "But I didn't convince you, did I?"

His gaze dropped away from hers. She bit her disappointment back and leaned forward to wrap him in a hug.

"Thank you for being here, and for rescuing me."

"Always. That's my job."

His breath warmed her ear while his words warmed her heart.

~

Greg stayed with Jill and Ruth all afternoon. Though the bulk of the crowd had wandered away when the media left, a few lingered, apparently in hopes that Jill would make another appearance. Whether they were merely curious or had more hostile intentions, Greg didn't know, but he didn't want to risk leaving the two women alone.

Ruth's phone had begun to ring within minutes of the fiasco with the tomatoes, and Jill's cell phone not long afterward. They fielded a few genuine questions, but when one caller's comments became insulting, Jill looked so distraught that he suggested they stop answering. Ruth unplugged the house line and confiscated Jill's cell. When Greg received a call from a number he didn't recognize, he turned his phone off too.

At five o'clock, they set the television in Jill's apartment to record CBT's *Live at 5* program and gathered downstairs in Ruth's living room to watch CBC. Greg sat next to Jill on the couch. She appeared outwardly calm, but he felt her leg trembling when the show's music began. He reached for her hand and twined his fingers in hers.

A nervous smile flickered on her face. "I feel like we should make popcorn or something."

"I hope Myrtle remembered to turn her recorder on channel seven." Perched on the other side of Jill, Ruth didn't take her eyes off the screen.

The first few stories were about a minor earthquake in Quebec City, and the latest accusations in an ongoing dispute between two high-profile MPs concerning accusations before the ethics commission. Beside Greg, Jill crossed one leg over the other and began to bounce her foot with nervous energy. He started to voice a soothing comment, but the words stuck in his throat. Were Dad and Mom watching too? He knew they were. They never missed the news. He kept his mouth shut so Jill wouldn't hear a hint of rattled nerves in his voice.

Nobody spoke through the commercial break. When the news show returned, Steven Welch's face filled the screen.

"Can people predict the future? That question has sparked heated debate among the residents of the small community of Seaside Cove."

"This is it." Ruth pointed the remote control at the television and cranked up the volume.

Jill took her finger from her mouth where she'd been chewing a nail and leaned forward. Her grip on Greg's hand tightened.

"On Thursday we told you about Jillian Elizabeth King, a former concert pianist who interrupted a local political meeting last week with a prediction of disaster. Today, Ms. King held a press conference in front of her home in Seaside Cove to convince people that she is not, as she put it, a 'raving fanatic.'"

Greg winced. The nearly imperceptible smirk on Welsh's face clearly indicated he thought differently. The scene switched to a shot of Jill standing on the porch, a line of elderly ladies behind her.

Wind buffeted the microphone, but her words rose clearly over the noise. Greg hadn't been able to hear everything from inside the house, so he listened with the trained ear of a trial lawyer hearing a testimony. She spoke calmly and convincingly. The only indication of nerves he saw was the trembling of the paper in her hands, but to an untrained eye that might be attributed to the wind.

When she got to the part where she asked if anyone had ever experienced a feeling they couldn't ignore, she looked directly into the camera. Greg felt as though she were speaking to him. Sincerity rang in her tone, showed in her bearing. The confidence he'd seen her display so many times on the concert stage emerged and gave weight to her message. Her words were so convincing he almost believed them himself.

"Excellent," he murmured, squeezing her hand.

She looked away from the television long enough to flash a smile in his direction. When one of the old ladies on screen stepped to her side and claimed Jill's accident had given her psychic abilities, both she and Ruth groaned.

"That old idiot," Ruth said. "She just wanted to be on the news."

The scene changed again, this time a moving shot of a neighborhood street with hand-painted evacuation signs in almost half the yards.

"They put our signs on there." Ruth nodded with a jerk. "Good."

Welsh's voice sounded over the panning scene. "Some Seaside Cove residents are ready to believe King's warning. They're making plans to evacuate on Tuesday."

A woman's face appeared, a microphone in front of her mouth. "I'm not taking a chance. What if she's right? My family's going out of town on Tuesday, just in case."

Another voice-over by Welsh. "Others aren't convinced."

A red-faced man standing beside a young woman said, "Believe her? Are you kidding? She's crazy."

"I know him." Ruth glared at the screen. "He works at the gas station over on Fourth Street. Just see if I ever go there again."

"That opinion seems to be shared by many," said Welsh's voice.

The scene switched back to Jill. From off-camera came a man's voice calling, "You're crazy!" Voices rose. The camera's lens swung in that direction to pan over the arguing crowd, then returned to Jill, whose face had gone ashen.

Greg tensed. Here it came. This was where things got really ugly.

The camera showed the tomato hitting Jill, her eyes widening in shock, and then another soaring past her head. Behind her, the front door opened and he appeared, his expression fierce as an angry pit bull's. He rushed to Jill's side, shouted toward the mob, and led her away.

Welsh returned to the screen. "The story takes an interesting twist here. That man you saw at the end of that clip is Gregory Bradford, a local attorney who recently kicked off a campaign for a seat on the Halifax Regional Council. Bradford is King's fiancé, and it was at his meeting last Monday where she first went public with her prediction of disaster. We were unable to reach Mr. Bradford for a comment after the press conference, but we did speak with his political opponent, Councilman Richard Samuels."

An angry buzz started in Greg's ears as Samuels appeared in front of the camera standing beside Welsh. The Cove's lighthouse was visible behind him in the distance. From the nearer surroundings, Greg identified his location as the sidewalk in front of Ruth's house.

"Bradford has some interesting ideas." Samuels spoke into

the microphone Welsh held. "He's a little too progressive for my taste, but we'll see whether or not voters agree with him or me during the council election."

"What do you think of Ms. King's dream?" Welsh asked.

Samuels laughed. "Well, let me put it like this. On Tuesday morning I won't be getting on one of those buses with Bradford and Ms. King. I'm staying right here in the Cove, where I belong."

A dull ache throbbed in Greg's temple. After his angry glare at the tomato-throwing crowd, Samuels had appeared calm, pleasant, and competent. The contrast couldn't be missed.

Welsh, once again in the studio, faced the camera to wrap up the story. "And there you have it, folks. The residents of Seaside Cove must decide: Is pianist Jillian Elizabeth King a psychic, or a psycho? I guess we'll have an answer on Tuesday. In other news — "

The screen went black when Ruth jabbed at the button on the remote. "Psychic or psycho, indeed." Her pursed lips displayed outrage. "I'm never watching that station again."

Jill turned on the cushion to face him. "Greg, I'm so sorry. You were only helping me, and they twisted it around to make it look like we're doing this together."

With a sinking feeling, Greg realized she was right. That's exactly what it looked like. A dull ache threatened to throb in his temple.

"It's not your fault," he told her. "You certainly didn't ask them to throw tomatoes at you. And I guess I shouldn't have turned off my cell phone. Then they could have gotten hold of me for a comment."

"What would you have said?"

He fell silent. The truth was, he didn't know. If he publicly professed that he didn't believe Jill's dream, people might interpret that as agreeing with those who thought she was crazy. She would be devastated. On the other hand, if he agreed with her he might as well adopt a bunch of bananas as his campaign logo.

He pressed his fingers against his throbbing temple. "I don't know."

An awkward silence fell between them. He knew she was disappointed in that answer, but what could he say? He loved her, but he just couldn't make himself believe this dream thing.

"Well." Ruth slapped her hands on her knees and stood. "I'm going to get supper cooking. You're welcome to stay, Greg. I've pulled a chicken out of the deep freeze."

Normally, he loved Ruth's chicken, but the news story had killed his appetite. "Thanks, but I need to get going." He squeezed Jill's hand and forced a smile. "I'll pick you up for church tomorrow."

"Okay. Have a good night."

She didn't move from the couch when he rose. Before he left the room, he looked back to find her staring at the darkened television set, deep in thought.

He let himself out of the house. The temperature had dropped with the sun, and his breath froze as it left his lips. On the walkway, he caught sight of Jill's car alone in the driveway and stopped. Why hadn't he pulled his car around? Now he'd have to cut through the neighbor's yard again, and he'd be frozen by the time he got to it.

Oh, well. Maybe the cold would help clear his thoughts. He certainly needed to have his wits about him when he made the inevitable phone call tonight. Hands shoved into his coat pockets, he headed for the backyard. For the first time in his adult life, he dreaded talking to his father.

Chapter 24

Sunday, December 4

Left to her own devices, Jill would have sat on the back pew, but Greg led her down the center aisle of the sanctuary to their customary spot on the fifth row. She did her best to ignore the stares they collected along the way, though her face burned like a Yule log on Christmas morning. Whispers followed in their wake, the collective noise a loud drone in which a few discernable words stood out.

"... television ..."

"Did you hear ..."

"... insane, poor thing."

Greg reached their pew and waited for her to step inside, his expression stoic. Miserable, Jill slid onto the cushioned seat and made a show of studying her bulletin. The minutes crept by at a slug's pace before the organist finally began his prelude, and the congregation's voices receded to an ignorable hum. Only when the choir filed into the loft did she raise her gaze to see Nana's encouraging smile.

The morning hymns were familiar, but neither she nor Greg

joined in. Jill held her half of the hymnal, her eyes fixed on the page. The absence of Greg's melodious voice spoke as loudly as the headline in the *Metro News* this morning. "From Professional Pianist to Doomsday Prophet" had led the local news section. The sweet-looking lady reporter from yesterday used her pen as skillfully as a swordfighter, and didn't fail to mention the relationship between the injured pianist and the political hopeful. No doubt Greg was as humiliated as she, only he was too much a gentleman to admit it.

When Reverend Hollister took his place behind the lectern, Jill settled into her cushion with relief. Now people would have someone else to look at for a half hour or so.

"My message this morning comes from a book that most of us probably haven't thought about since we were children." He paused and looked over the congregation. "It is from the book of Jonah, which tells the story of a prophet who exhibited a great deal of reluctance to obey the Lord."

Jill's head went light. No. Surely the minister wasn't planning to preach about *her* this morning. Eyes bored into the back of her head from all over the sanctuary, and in front of her several people actually turned in their pews to stare. Beside her, Greg became very still. He did not look at her, but kept his eyes fixed on the pulpit.

Reverend Hollister recounted the story of Jonah, who ignored God's direction to prophesy the destruction of the city of Nineveh and was swallowed by a whale as a result. Jill edged down in the pew until she couldn't see him over the head of the person in front of her. Never had she been more humiliated in her life. Swallowed by a whale? What was the man trying to say? He continued to describe how angry Jonah became when he finally obeyed and the disaster didn't happen. Blood roared in her ears, blocking out the rest of the sermon until nearly the end. The room swam, and she closed her eyes. She would *not* faint.

"Does the Lord still give prophecies today?"

An expectant silence rested on the congregation like an invisible cloud during the pause that followed Reverend Hollister's question. Still slouched down, Jill leaned an inch sideways so she could see his face.

After a lengthy pause, he shrugged. "I don't know. But I submit to you, that is not the question we should ask ourselves. Instead, we should each prayerfully examine our own response, as the people of Nineveh did. Instead of pointing a finger of ridicule outward, let us search inwardly. Let us each ask, 'What is the Lord saying to me?' And when you hear from him — " his smile circled the room " — and I know you will, follow his direction. That's all he asks of any of us. In the name of the Father, and the Son, and the Holy Spirit. Amen."

He returned to his chair behind the pulpit. Jill's thoughts whirled as though caught in a twister. Did Reverend Hollister just publicly support her? Or had he simply made the point that everyone must decide for themselves? Greg turned a wide-eyed stare toward her, his lips parted in astonishment.

A movement on the other side of the sanctuary drew her attention. Mr. and Mrs. Herndon stood, their features molded into nearly identical masks of outrage. Mrs. Herndon's gaze connected with Jill's, and her tight-lipped glare breached the distance like a dart. Heads high, the couple marched into the aisle and toward the rear exit. Around the sanctuary, more than two dozen people followed their example. A trio of ladies in the choir loft braved Nana's fierce stare and joined the others.

Horrified, Jill watched them go. This stupid dream had caused a division in her church. If she could have conjured up a crack in the floor, she would have gladly crawled into it.

When there was no more movement, Reverend Hollister spoke from his chair in the front. "Paul, I believe it's time for our closing hymn." Jill was amazed at his calm, even tone.

Paul Nester left his place on the front row of the choir and approached the pulpit, nervousness apparent in his quick, shaky movements. He cleared his throat. "Our last hymn this morning is number three hundred, eighty-five. Please stand as you are able."

While the congregation got to their feet, Greg leaned over and whispered in her ear.

"When they sing 'Amen,' head out that way as fast as you can." He nodded toward the side aisle and the door behind the organ. "We're going out the back exit."

Jill nodded. An escape plan sounded like an excellent idea. In fact, if she could think of a way to escape the next two days, she'd do it in a second.

~

They made it to Greg's car without encountering anyone. When they pulled out of the parking lot, Jill looked back and saw the first members of the congregation exiting the church.

She slid down in the seat and covered her eyes with a hand. "That was horrible. I can't believe Reverend Hollister compared me to Jonah."

"He never said your name," Greg pointed out.

She lifted her hand to give him a sideways look.

"Okay, yeah," he conceded, "no doubt who he was talking about. But at least he supported you."

"Did he? I didn't hear him say he supported me. He just asked people not to ridicule me."

He took his eyes off the road to flick a quick smile her way. "Well, that's something. At least he didn't denounce you as a false prophet."

Jill studied his profile. Beneath the smile he looked uncomfortable. His hands clenched the steering wheel like a vise, and he had barely looked at her all morning. With a suddenness that nearly overwhelmed her, she hated her dream. Why her? Why would God destroy her life?

"I'm sorry, Greg. I didn't ask for this to happen, you know."

His chest inflated. The breath blew out slowly. "I know. It's not your fault. You're just doing what you think is right."

Jill's weight pressed against the safety belt as the car slowed. She looked up to see they had joined a line of traffic approaching the Harbor Street intersection.

She straightened and peered at the road ahead, where a line of cars stretched for several blocks. "What's going on?"

"I don't know. There seems to be a traffic jam. Maybe there's been an accident."

They crept forward, gaining only a small amount of ground in more than fifteen minutes. Finally, the stoplight loomed in the windshield ahead of them. Jill caught sight of a sign waving above the roof of the car ahead of them. Crooked black words on white poster board proclaimed, "Repent, for the End is Near!" Another sign on the other side of the street proclaimed, "Armageddon Will Happen on December 6." In the distance she saw several others but couldn't make out the words.

She covered her mouth with a hand. "No. This can't be happening."

Greg remained silent, though his stony expression shouted

his feelings louder than words. As they approached the intersection, she got a good look at one of the people carrying a sign. He wore multiple layers of tattered clothing, and his unwashed hair hung in dreadlocks past his shoulders. As she watched, another man ran toward the sign-carrier. This one looked familiar and held an elaborate camera in front of his face. One of the newspaper photographers from the press conference yesterday.

The real loons had arrived in the Cove to join the party, and the press was here to see them. Jill closed her eyes, but couldn't block out the image of tomorrow's headlines flashing like neon in her mind. Where would this end?

Chapter 25

A COUPLE OF PICKETERS FOUND THEIR house in the early afternoon. Their homemade signs read, "Evacuate the Crazies from Seaside Cove" and "No! No! We Won't Go!" Jill watched from the window in the front room as Nana chased them out of the yard and pounded a hastily painted sign of her own into the frozen ground. It warned "Trespassers Will Be Prosecuted!" The pair took up stances across the street.

Nana returned to the house and slammed the door behind her. "Are you going to visit Lorna this afternoon?"

Jill let the curtains fall back in place and turned. "I don't think so." She jerked her head toward the front door. "What if they follow me? I don't want them to bother Mom."

"Tell you what. I'll go with you early in the morning. We can make arrangements for the residents' bus on Tuesday." She checked the lock on the door, then headed down the hallway. "I'm going to make a coffee cake to feed the girls tomorrow. Want to help?"

Jill shook her head. "I think I'll relax upstairs for a while."

"That sounds nice. You might even try to take a nap."

She disappeared into the kitchen. The distant sound of Nana humming "A Mighty Fortress," one of the morning hymns, followed Jill up the stairs.

Upstairs, she paused to admire her Christmas tree. Though nowhere near as beautiful as Faye's, the sight of the gently twirling ornaments gave her a warm feeling that almost chased away the chill of unpleasantness caused by the picketers. It still looked a little sad, though, without a single package beneath it. She'd been so focused on painting signs and getting ready for her news interview she still hadn't managed to do any shopping. The thought of venturing into the city made her shudder. What if she were recognized? She might cause a riot in the middle of the mall. And besides, what was the point in shopping before Tuesday? For all she knew, there wouldn't be a house to come back to Tuesday night.

She could at least make her shopping list, though. The stores all had websites that might give her some ideas. That way, she'd be ready to buy everything all at once, after things in the Cove had calmed down.

Glad for something to do, Jill retrieved her laptop and settled on the sofa. An hour slipped away while she surfed and compared, and jotted down notes about the best prices for the gifts she intended to purchase.

Her task complete, she started to close the laptop. She moved the cursor to shut it down, but her finger hesitated over the button. The article in the *Metro News* had included a recap of the subway accident. Not pleasant for her to read, but neither had it been as painful as she'd feared. For the past year she'd avoided learning any details of the accident, a fact that Doreen had mentioned many times. How could she ever put the tragedy behind her if she couldn't even read about it? How could she ever truly mourn Robert's death if she lived in fear of seeing his name, of learning who he was and how he knew so much about classical piano?

Maybe it was time.

She returned to the Internet search page. What keywords to enter? *New York subway accident December 8.* That ought to do it. She clicked the Search button and a list of results displayed, more than she'd expected. The top few links were news reports, and she selected one from the *New York Times'* website dated December 9. The headline read "Subway Accident Claims 97 Lives."

A curious sense of detachment crept over her as she skimmed the article. She knew the bare facts, that the train had derailed while rounding a sharp curve, and that the subway motorman was suspected of being under the influence of illegal drugs. Nearly half of the 196 passengers had not survived the crash, and none of the survivors had escaped without injury. Her hip ached, and the scar on her left hand tingled, unnecessary reminders.

She pressed the Back button and clicked through a few more articles, searching for victims' names, but the only name she found was Stephen Sullivan, the motorman who had been later convicted of manslaughter and sentenced to fifteen years in prison. Then she found a note about a memorial service held in honor of the victims two months after the crash. A memory surfaced. She'd received a couple of letters from someone asking if she would attend. Her third surgery, scheduled for a week before the event, had provided a convenient excuse, but in truth there was nothing that could have compelled her to go.

I should have gone. Robert's family might have been there. I could have told them about his final moments.

A sharp pang of regret brought the sting of tears to her eyes. She had spent so much effort trying not to think of Robert's death that she'd never really considered his family, how they might like to hear from someone who had held his hand at the end. How selfish of her.

The thought took her by surprise. Surely it took a fairly healthy person to recognize their own selfishness. Maybe she was getting better.

She returned to the search page and added the words *memorial service* to her criteria. The article at the top of the list had no picture, only a description of the service held in Central Park in honor of those who'd lost their lives in the crash. As she hoped, a list of the victims was included. She scanned the names.

There was no one on the victim list named Robert.

A swelling hope in her chest threatened to crowd her heart. Had he lived? No. The rescue workers who pulled her from beneath the heavy steel had called her fortunate because, as they said, no one else in that car had survived. Robert had died. She'd witnessed his final moments.

Pulse pounding like a drum in her skull, Jill returned to the search page. A query for *survivors* produced no new articles. The paper wouldn't list the names of the survivors as they did the victims. There had been no service for the survivors. On impulse, she typed in her own name, and wasn't surprised to find several articles mentioning her among the injured. The phrase "brilliant career cut tragically short" brought a tight lump to her throat, and she forced her eyes to skip over that part. A half-dozen other survivors were mentioned or quoted, but no one named Robert, Rob, Robbie, or even Bob. Not one.

Thoughts whirled through her brain. What if the rescue workers and the emergency room doctor were mistaken? If Robert lived, wouldn't he have contacted her? They had supported each other through a horrible time. The public knew she had survived, so if he'd really wanted to find her, he could have. Or maybe he didn't want to contact her. If he lived, he would have sustained severe injuries, as she did. Hadn't she gone to great lengths to avoid anything that would remind her of the crash? It was possible that he wanted to avoid thinking of her the same way she'd avoided thinking of him.

She had to know. Somehow she had to find a list of the survivors. But how?

Her gaze fell on the computer screen, on the headline of the article she'd just read about the memorial service. The lady who organized that event would have a list. Where had she put those letters? She was fairly sure she hadn't thrown them away.

Her bottom desk drawer was a frightful jumble of correspondence. Fan letters from her concert days, get well cards, notices from her college alumni association, newspaper clippings about her performances. She pulled out the pile of papers she hadn't bothered to organize in the past year and began shuffling through them.

A few minutes later, she uncovered a typewritten letter from a woman named Susan Rochester, describing the planned memorial service. Jill scanned the missive and found what she was looking for, phone numbers for calling Ms. Rochester's office or cell phone. She snatched up her phone from the coffee table and, before she could back out, dialed the cell number.

A female voice answered on the second ring. "Hello?"

"Hi, is this Susan Rochester?"

"Yes it is. Who is this?"

"This is Jillian King calling from Nova Scotia."

A second's pause, and the voice became warmer. "Oh, yes. The pianist. How are you? I hope you've recovered from the accident."

"I'm fine, thank you." Jill swallowed. "Listen, I know this is an unusual request, but I'm wondering if you have a list of survivors. I made an acquaintance on the subway that day, and I'm trying to discover what happened to him." She cleared her throat. "Part of the road to recovery, you know."

"I understand completely." Sympathy colored the words in rich hues. "I do have a list. It used to be on my computer, but I cleaned off the drive last month. I'm sure I have a hard copy in my files. I can call you back, or would you like to hold the line?"

"I'll hold, if that's okay."

"All right. Give me a moment."

A clatter sounded in Jill's ears as the phone was set on a hard surface. Seconds ticked away, each one stretching into what seemed like hours. Jill's grip on the phone grew tighter as she watched the numbers on the clock pass. Two minutes. Three. Four.

Finally, a scraping sound and Ms. Rochester's voice returned. "Found it. Now, what is your friend's name?"

Is. Present tense. A ridiculous sense of hope eased a fraction of Jill's tension.

"I don't have his last name, I'm afraid. Only his first. It's Robert."

"Okay, Robert." A moment of silence, and then Jill heard the rustle of paper. "It's in alphabetical order by last name, so I'm just scanning ..." Another rustle of paper. "I don't see a Robert."

Invisible bands constricted Jill's chest. "What about Bob, or Rob, or some other derivative?"

"Hmmm, let me see. No, nothing like that either. Maybe — " Ms. Rochester paused, then continued in a softer tone. "Maybe he didn't make it. Have you checked the victim list?"

"Yes." Jill leaned back against the sofa cushion, her head suddenly light. "There were no Roberts there either."

"Listen, if it would help I could copy this list at the office tomorrow and mail it to you. Maybe one of these names will jar your memory."

A polite way of saying she didn't think Jill's memory of Robert was accurate. Jill closed her eyes and Robert's face loomed before her. She saw him clearly, heard the timbre of his voice as he introduced himself. He rolled his R's slightly, giving his name an aristocratic feel. *Rrroberrt.* She was sure of it.

"That would be very helpful, Mrs. Rochester." She knew with certainty the list would reveal nothing to her. "Thank you."

Ms. Rochester verified her mailing address, and Jill thanked her again before they hung up. She sat on the couch, her feet propped on the edge of the coffee table, and stared at nothing as she tried to make sense of her discovery. Robert was not a victim. He wasn't on the survivor list, either. She was positive he couldn't have walked away from the crash unharmed, so there had to be some record of him. But there wasn't.

She pulled her computer onto her lap and stared at the empty box on the search screen, thoughts spinning through her brain. The man she'd met and talked to exhibited an in-depth knowledge of classical piano music. Surely only someone who played would be so familiar with the spiritual nuances of Liszt. And he'd recognized the brand of her music portfolio.

She typed *classical pianist Robert.*

The statistic at the top of the page indicated over five million results matched that criteria. If she had to, Jill intended to go through every one of them. She settled back in the chair and prepared herself for a long, tedious evening.

The first link took her to an advertisement for a wedding pianist in Massachusetts, but the picture revealed the man to be far younger than her Robert. The second showed her a video of an African man seated behind a piano. Robert's skin had been the almost pearly white of someone who didn't see much of the sun. Mechanically, she clicked the Back button and selected the next link on the list.

When the page opened up, a familiar face stared at her from the screen. Not her Robert, but another one she knew well. She'd studied him, played his music. The screen projected an old-fashioned painting of famed German composer Robert Schumann. She studied his face, and memories of his life that she had learned in music history class slammed her with full force.

The hair on the back of her neck prickled to attention.

Robert Schumann had dreamed of becoming a concert pianist, but had been unable to realize that dream because of an injury to his hand. Instead, he went on to become an extraordinary composer, creating music for others to play. But his life ended tragically. He died in a German mental institution in 1856.

She'd forgotten that. Or maybe in the past year she'd avoided remembering, as she'd avoided thinking about the accident.

His eyes peered at her from the laptop screen. What had driven the brilliant musician crazy? Was it a neurological disorder, or did his insanity have a psychological or physiological cause? Jill raised her left hand from the keyboard, her gaze drawn to the scar. Or did Robert Schumann lose his mind because of the loss of his music?

And was the same thing happening to her?

~

A loud knock pulled Greg out of a light sleep. He jerked upright on the couch, disoriented. The insistent pounding continued, and his groggy mind finally identified the source.

"I'm coming," he hollered in the direction of the apartment door. "Hold your horses."

He punched the power button on the remote control to turn off the boring conversation of a couple of sportscasters and tossed the device on the couch on his way to the door. Jill's image filled the peephole.

He swung it open. "Hey, beautiful. I didn't expect to see you."

In the next moment he was nearly knocked off his feet when she threw herself at him. Hysterical weeping made her words unintelligible, and sent a shaft of alarm through him.

"What's wrong? Has something happened to your mother? Ruth?"

Hair whipped into his face as she shook her head. "N-no. It's me." She drew a shuddering breath. "I think maybe I really am crazy."

"What?" He drew her into the apartment and led her to the couch. When they were seated side by side, his arm around her heaving shoulders, he said, "Tell me what happened."

"I looked up Robert on the Internet. I can't find him! Oh, Greg, he didn't exist. And then there's the other Robert, and he went insane. Just like me."

Her words made no sense. "Hold on. Back up. There were two Roberts on the subway?"

She shook her head. "No, only one. Or maybe not. I can't find him anywhere, not on the victim list or on the survivor list. I think I made him up. But while I was searching for him, I found a website about Robert Schumann, a famous composer. I knew about him before, but I forgot. He hurt his hand, and he went crazy, and he died in an institution more than a hundred years ago. Just like I'm going crazy." Wild sobs made her next words unintelligible.

Greg held her close while she gave herself over to weeping. His mind worked to fit this information into the whole. There had to be a logical explanation. He refused to believe Jill was insane. Traumatized, yes, but not delusional.

Only when her sobs gave way to shuddering breaths did he venture an explanation. "Jill, listen to me. Let's talk about the Robert on the subway. What if you didn't make him up? What if you got his name wrong?"

She shook her head. "No. I remember. He said his name was Robert."

"Did you study Robert Schumann in school?"

"Yes. He's famous." She brought her hands up to press against the sides of her skull. "I've played his pieces millions of times."

He took her left hand in his and caressed the scar with his thumb. "Maybe the man on the subway had the same general features, the same coloring. He might have even had a similar name, like Richard or Roger. And then afterward, when your hand was hurt, your mind put the two together because deep inside you identified with Robert Schumann. You'd been traumatized, Jill. You were in shock. The doctors said it was pretty amazing that you remembered anything."

Tear-filled eyes moved as she searched his face. "You think so?"

"It's possible," he said.

Her stiff posture became even more rigid. "Then that means I've fabricated part of my memories. This is more proof of what you already think about my dream, that I've pieced together this whole elaborate story from repressed childhood memories because I was traumatized during the accident."

He couldn't deny it. She would see the falsehood if he tried. But that was the only explanation that made sense, so he gave no answer.

Her shoulders slumped. "You believe I'm nuts."

"Come here." He pulled her to his side and leaned against the back of the couch. When she snuggled next to him, he dropped a kiss on the top of her head. "You're perfectly sane. I'm not an expert by any stretch of the imagination, but I do know one thing. You've changed in the past week or two."

"No kidding." Her body heaved with a shudder.

"No, really. You have more energy, more drive than I've seen in a year. You're not as depressed. You've got a goal, and you're working hard to accomplish it." He squeezed her tighter. "I'm not happy about the goal, but I like the new Jill."

"You do?"

"No. I *love* her."

"Thank you. That means a lot to me." She relaxed enough to settle deeper in his embrace. "I'm positive something horrible is going to happen on Tuesday, but at the same time I'll be glad when it's over with. I want to put this whole thing behind us."

"You're not the only one." An uneasy feeling settled in his insides. How would Jill react when Tuesday came and went without the disaster she was so sure of? Would she be able to move on, or would her depression return and possibly worsen?

They'd find out in two more days.

He forced the note of uncertainty out of his voice. "The whole town will be glad when this ends."

Chapter 26

Monday, December 5

Jill and Nana arrived at Centerside Nursing just as Mom returned from breakfast in the dining room. They met an aide wheeling her down the hallway when they rounded the corner to her room. The girl looked uncertain when she caught sight of them. She picked up her pace and deposited Mom's wheelchair in her room, then hurried out.

Nana stopped her. "Would you please tell the administrator we'd like to speak with him if he has a moment?"

The wide-eyed girl nodded and left. A twang of regret twisted in Jill. Before this dream business, the staff used to come and chat with her in Mom's room.

"Good morning, Mom." She stooped to kiss the slackened cheek, and received no response.

"Hello, Lorna." Nana patted the frail hand laying on the chair's armrest, her face bearing the pained expression she always wore at the sight of her once-vibrant only child. "How have you been, dear?"

Dull eyes stared with an unfocused gaze at the window.

"Sorry I didn't come yesterday, Mom." Jill lowered herself to the edge of the bed and gestured for Nana to take the visitor's chair. "We had kind of an eventful day."

Nana glanced at the dark television set on top of the dresser. "I wonder if they let her watch you on the news."

A man and woman entered the room, the nurse and Mr. Eldredge, the facility's administrator. Jill's heart sank at the nurse's carefully blank expression. Mr. Eldredge, who didn't smile all that often anyway, looked as mournful as a funeral director. He jerked his head in an unfriendly way toward her, then focused his attention on Nana.

"I understand you'd like a word with me."

"Thank you for giving us a moment of your time." How Nana managed to smile into that solemn face, Jill couldn't imagine. "I expect you've seen my granddaughter on the news."

He inclined his head, but did not glance in Jill's direction. "And read several newspaper accounts."

"Then I won't need to explain. We've arranged for a charter bus to arrive tomorrow morning at seven thirty. I'm afraid there will only be forty-eight seats available, but I assume you can make other arrangements for the rest of the residents."

"I'm afraid that's quite impossible."

Nana glanced at Jill and then addressed Mr. Eldredge. "I could probably manage two buses, if that will be helpful."

A chilly smile lifted the edges of the man's mouth. "You misunderstand. We don't need any buses. The residents of Centerside Nursing will not be going anywhere tomorrow. We will not condone this insanity." He glanced meaningfully at Jill as he uttered the last word.

Inside Jill's ribcage her heart thudded heavily at the insult. She rose from the bed and stepped closer to Mom's side.

Nana seemed to gain three inches when she stiffened. "You would risk the death of the people in your care? Most of them are helpless. They rely on you for safety."

"Our residents are perfectly safe." The nurse couldn't quite filter a touch of disdain from her voice. "We won't have them upset with all this nonsense."

In the hallway, an ancient woman inched past the door, propelling her wheelchair with slow, labored movements. No way that woman could get away on her own. She could barely get herself down the hallway.

"Please." Jill addressed Mr. Eldredge. "It could be like an outing. They won't be upset. If nothing happens, they'll return in the afternoon after a nice, scenic drive in the city."

"Young lady," he said to her, "you are clearly disturbed. I urge you to seek psychiatric help as soon as possible."

Jill reeled back against the bed as if slapped.

Nana stepped forward to form a short, redheaded barrier between them, her shoulders stiff with outrage.

"You can't talk to my granddaughter that way." Her voice rang in the room and echoed down the hallway.

"Madam, lower your voice or I will be forced to have you removed from the premises."

Nana's indignant breath hissed inward. "When disaster strikes, don't say you weren't warned. The deaths of these people will be on your hands." She picked up their coats and handed Jill's to her. "Have my daughter ready to leave in the morning. We'll be by to pick her up at seven."

The nurse protested. "You can't take Lorna."

Jill paused in the act of slipping her arm in her coat sleeve to imitate her grandmother's unyielding air. "Yes, we can, and we are."

"But she'll catch her death." The woman cast a desperate look at the administrator. "This is not in her best interest. She's had a cough."

They all looked at Mom, who neither coughed nor displayed any sign she was aware of the argument taking place in her room.

"You told me several days ago the doctor said she was completely healthy." Jill buttoned her coat and stooped to press her cheek to her mother's. "We're not leaving without her."

Nana lifted her nose into the air. "Lorna is my daughter, and I am within my rights to take her for an outing if I want."

The nurse turned an appeal toward the administrator, who stood indecisive for a moment. Then he gave a slight nod. Jill's breath left her lungs in a rush.

"Seven o'clock," Ruth repeated to the nurse. "Let's go, Jill. We have a busy day planned. We have some new signs to paint."

Jill pressed her lips to Mom's scalp. "We'll be back for you in the morning, Mom."

Together they marched past the outraged nurse, and startled a cluster of aides listening in the hallway just outside the door.

~

Greg pushed through the door of The Wharf Café at a quarter past ten for his meeting to discuss Rowena's campaign ideas. The bell jangled its announcement of his arrival.

"Sorry I'm late, Rowe. I got held up on a phone call."

The restaurant wasn't empty. Four people were seated at a table on one side of the dining room. Mitch Landry and Carl Allen occupied two chairs, their expressions serious. Seated across from Bob, Rowena turned toward him but didn't meet his eye. The identity of the fourth person didn't at first register, because he didn't fit in this setting.

What was his father doing here?

He came to a halt halfway into the room. The door whooshed closed behind him.

"Dad? What's going on?"

Silence.

"I'll get you some coffee, Greg." Rowe rose from her chair and hurried to the counter.

Dad pointed to the chair at the end of the table. "Have a seat, son. We want to talk to you."

A list of possible reasons these three Cove residents had gathered together and then contacted his father formed in his mind. It probably had something to do with the election, since Carl, Mitch, and Rowe were his biggest supporters. Maybe they wanted to brainstorm campaign ideas.

Their serious expressions denied that possibility. There could be only one topic of conversation today.

Jill.

Greg made his way to the chair on Dad's left with a halting step. As he seated himself, Rowe placed a fragrant mug of coffee in front of him and returned to her chair. He downed a swallow of the scalding liquid to buy himself time to gather his composure.

Mitch cupped his hands around his own mug. "Greg, the four of us want you to know that we're behind you all the way."

Dad and Carl nodded, though Rowe still hadn't looked directly at him.

"I'm excited about this plan of yours," Carl said. "It's the right thing to do in Seaside Cove."

"I appreciate your support." Thankfully, his voice betrayed no hint of his whirling thoughts.

Mitch went on. "We think you have a good chance of taking Samuels's seat on the council. But this dream of Jill's is doing some damage." He raised a hand to prevent any interruption, though Greg hadn't opened his mouth to speak. "Now, you know I think a lot of Jill. I've known her from church longer than I've known you. But she's not thinking right just now."

"She's acting crazy, son," Dad said.

Greg jumped to Jill's defense. "She's not crazy. If you'd been in that subway accident and had the only career you'd ever dreamed of ripped away, you might experience some stress yourself."

"I'm sure that's true." Dad held his gaze. "But you're about to have your career ripped away from you, too, and it's going to be her fault."

"Come on, it's not as bad as all that." He looked toward Carl, hoping to find someone to agree with him.

Carl looked uncomfortable. "I think it is, Bradford."

"Especially after Saturday's news conference." Rowe finally spoke. "And Samuels sure made the most of you showing up there. Did you hear him?"

Greg dropped his head forward. "Yeah." He'd watched the interview again on the late news, and noted how Samuels had managed to mention "Bradford," "Ms. King," and "getting on those buses" all in the same sentence. A politically savvy move that had left him cringing.

"The whole town's gone crazy over this thing," Dad said. "When I drove here this morning, I passed a store advertising a fifty-percent-off disaster sale. People with signs were marching up and down Harbor Street, shouting at each other. The police arrived when I went by."

Mitch cleared his throat. "That's why we wanted to talk to you. We think you need to distance yourself from Jill and her dream."

"Publicly," Carl added. "Call a news conference like she did."

Greg shook his head. What would happen to Jill and him if he did that? The memory of her weeping last night still wrenched his heart. He couldn't be the reason for more tears.

"Don't you think that's a little extreme?"

"No, we don't," Dad said. "You've got to let the people know you don't buy into the lunacy."

"The lunacy isn't Jill's fault. She's horrified by all these signs proclaiming the end of the world. Those are the crazy people, not her. This will all blow over tomorrow. When no disaster happens, Jill plans to make a public statement saying she's glad she was wrong and she only did what she felt was right. It'll be fine."

A flash of color drew their attention to the sidewalk outside the café. A short line of people carrying signs paraded past, four gray heads and one bright red. Ruth's sign read, "Evacuation Buses Boarding at 7:30 a.m. Be There or Suffer the Consequences."

An awkward silence descended around the table. Greg closed his eyes and massaged his throbbing temples.

"It's not going to blow over, son," Dad said. "Samuels is going to throw that video in your face every chance he gets between now and the election."

"That's why it's important for you to make a statement today," Rowe said. "Otherwise, he's going to point out that you didn't deny anything until it was all over. He'll use it to make you look indecisive."

Mitch leaned toward him over the table. "If you do it today, then you'll render that weapon ineffective."

Greg rubbed a hand across his mouth, his thoughts jumbled. Their reasoning made sense.

"Son, remember what's at stake here. We've planned this for a long time. If Jill loves you, she'll understand that."

Would she? He'd made no secret of the fact that he didn't believe her dream. Though disappointed, she seemed to deal with that okay. But a public statement?

Suddenly, he needed to get out of there. These four people wanted the best for him, of that he was certain, but their words bored into his brain like a drill. He needed to be alone, to lay out his thoughts and come to his own decision. The chair legs scraped across the floor when he stood.

"Thank you for your advice." The words sounded stilted, tight. He forced a smile and tried again. "Really. I appreciate you wanting to help me. You've given me a lot to think about. But I, uh, need to go."

Nobody said a word when he headed for the door and stepped into the freezing cold outdoors.

Rowe caught up with him halfway across the small parking lot. "Greg, wait a minute."

He shoved his hands in his pockets and stopped.

"I'm sorry I called your father. I thought he'd be able to convince you better than the three of us." The anxious look on her face begged him to understand.

He had to admit, he would have preferred that she talked to him privately before arranging what amounted to an intervention. But what was done was done. He couldn't be mad at her for trying to help.

"You were just looking out for my best interests," he told her. "Don't worry. We're fine."

A cloud of breath blew out of her mouth. "I hope so." With a small wave, she retreated to the warmth of the café.

Greg walked to his car. Thankfully, his schedule was pretty light this afternoon. He had a lot of thinking and praying to do.

Jill spent the day hiding in her apartment. Every time she looked out the window she found people lined across the street like autograph hounds camped in front of a celebrity's house. Only she knew these people didn't want her autograph. A couple carried professional-looking cameras, and once she was pretty sure she spotted the newspaper photographer from the *Metro News.*

When Nana and the rest of the Sign Brigade headed for town armed with their new handiwork, they'd all insisted she stay behind.

"You might cause a riot," Mrs. Tolliver had said.

Relieved, Jill stayed home while they trooped off to join the sign parade on Harbor Street. The idea of marching around the Cove with a sign weakened her knees, though she felt like a coward for allowing a bunch of geriatric picketers to take the heat for her. Still, the excitement they had been barely able to contain assured her that they were enjoying their part in this evacuation effort far more than she.

The front doorbell rang at four that afternoon. Cautiously, she peeked out the upstairs window. Snowflakes fluttered down from dark, heavy clouds. Relief flooded through her at the sight of Greg's car in the driveway. Her step lighter than it had been since the confrontation at Centerside this morning, Jill practically skipped down the stairs and threw the door open.

The sight of Greg's smile warmed the chill in her core. "Hey, beautiful. Can you spare a cup of hot chocolate for a freezing lawyer?"

Laughing, she threw her arms around him. "I think so. I might even be able to find a few marshmallows to throw in." Over his shoulder, three cameras pointed in their direction from the other side of the street. She stepped back and pulled him inside. "You should have come to the back door. Now your picture will be on the front page tomorrow."

He twisted the deadbolt. "You know what they say. Any publicity is good publicity."

Yesterday's headlines loomed large in her mind. "I'm not so sure about that." She preceded him upstairs. "What are you doing here so early, anyway? Shouldn't you be working?"

"That's what I wanted to talk to you about." They entered her apartment. He shrugged out of his coat and spoke over his shoulder while she filled the kettle. "I've got to go out to the orchard to talk to Dad about something."

She turned. "Really? What about?"

Busy pulling out a chair from the small kitchen table, he didn't meet her eye. "Oh, just some campaign stuff."

Prickly bristles of discomfort brushed against her spine. Was he being purposefully evasive? She set the kettle on the fire and rummaged in the cabinet where she kept tea, coffee, and instant hot chocolate. It wasn't like Greg to be vague.

"I wanted to make sure you knew if you need to get hold of me this evening, call Mom and Dad's house phone. My cell service is sketchy out there."

"Okay." She retrieved two mugs from another cabinet and spooned hot chocolate mix into both of them. A question had burned in her mind for days, but she hadn't gathered the nerve to ask him. Tomorrow was the big day. This would be her last chance.

She kept her back turned, her gaze fixed on the first signs of steam that wisped from the kettle's opening. "So, will I see you in the morning?"

A long silence answered her. She closed her eyes, fighting a wave of near panic. She knew she wouldn't see him in the morning. His plan was probably to stay as far away from the fiasco of tomorrow as he could get. If she could do the same, she would too. But what if . . . her heart clutched at the thought of losing him.

A noise from behind told her he had risen from the table. In the next instant, she felt the warmth of his body when he came to stand close behind her.

"That's the other reason I came by this afternoon. I wanted to make sure you save a seat for me on one of those buses."

The meaning of his words didn't register at first. When they did, she turned and peered into his eyes. "You're coming with us?"

"If you have room for me."

She searched his face. What had caused this about-face? "What about your campaign? There's sure to be media crawling all over the place."

A flicker of something crossed his features. Worry? Sorrow? His throat moved as he swallowed. "It'll work out."

She shook her head. "I don't understand. I thought you didn't believe in my dream."

He ducked his head. "I've been thinking about Reverend Hollister's message yesterday. I did what he said. I asked myself, *What is the Lord saying to me?* And you know what?"

Jill hardly dared to breathe. "What?"

"I think he's saying, *Trust me. And trust in the love I've given you for Jill.* So, no, at first I didn't believe in your dream. But now I've made the decision to believe." His gaze softened and his arms came up around her. "And I've always believed in you, Jill."

Her heart soared heavenward. She threw her arms around his neck and pulled him down for a joyful kiss. The truth of his mother's words resonated through her soul. Surely two people who loved each other this much could overcome anything.

Chapter 27

"HAVE YOU GOT EVERYTHING READY to go?" Nana wheeled a gigantic suitcase down the hallway.

"Just about." Jill took the bag from her and carried it outside. What did Nana have in here? The thing weighed a ton, and there were already three full boxes loaded into the SUV.

"Be careful." Warm light framed Nana in the doorway. "That has my mother's cut-glass pitcher and bowl set in it."

Jill stopped at the bottom of the porch stairs and looked at her grandmother through a curtain of falling snow. "I thought we said — never mind." She dragged the heavy suitcase through the thick layer of snow that had accumulated on the walkway.

"As long as we have the room, why not?" Nana called after her. "I'd just hate for anything to happen to it."

Earlier today Jill had removed the rear seats of Nana's SUV so they'd have more room for their valuables. Though Nana and the Sign Brigade had decided to ride in the buses, she insisted that Jill drive her vehicle. Neither hers nor Jill's had four-wheel drive, but at least the SUV would be weighted down with household items, which would make it safer on snowy roads. She glanced up at the dark sky, and fat snowflakes dusted her face. Greg had called earlier to tell her he was staying the night at the orchard because of the weather, but the weather forecasters said this storm would blow itself out soon. By morning the road crews should have the roads in fairly good shape. At least the snow had driven away the gawkers. Their street was empty.

With a grunt, she hefted the suitcase into the back and slid it as far forward as it would go. There was still enough room for her big bag and a little space for anything Greg wanted to bring. Initially they'd planned for Mom to ride with Jill, but now that Greg was coming, Mom would ride on the bus with Nana. Despite the snow, warmth flooded through her at the thought of Greg's visit this afternoon. Smiling, she slammed the rear hatch shut.

"I'm all set." Inside, Nana closed the door behind Jill and raised a hand to brush snow out of her hair. "I'll just throw whatever else I have in my overnight bag and take it with me on the bus."

"I'll get my stuff loaded in a little while. I want to make one more pass through the apartment."

"I'm going to bed." Nana brushed at some snow on Jill's shoulder before heading toward her bedroom. "Don't stay up too late. We have a big day tomorrow."

Jill chuckled as she climbed the stairs. That probably qualified as the understatement of the century. One way or the other, the day was sure to be eventful.

Her suitcase weighed a fraction of Nana's, and still had plenty of empty space. She inspected the contents. Several changes of clothes. A few pieces of jewelry that used to belong to Mom. A photo album with pictures of her childhood before Daddy's death. Her laptop. What else should she take? Her gaze circled the bedroom but fell on nothing of value, sentimental or otherwise.

The living room held even fewer items of importance to her. What did she care about television sets or knickknacks? The special Christmas tree ornaments had already been taken from the tree and packed in one of Nana's boxes. The only thing still in here that had ever meant anything to her was ...

She turned toward the corner where she had spent so many hours. The Schimmel rested in the shadows, its graceful curves somehow expectant. Her piano. She could still remember the thrill of sitting on the bench and playing it for the first time after it had been delivered. How often had this piano accompanied her as she soared into the skies on wings of intricate harmony? How many times had she poured her soul through its ivory keys?

How could she leave it behind without saying good-bye?

Almost without thinking, she slid onto the bench. Would she ever see it again after tomorrow? Deep inside, she suspected that she would not. Her constant companion. Her friend.

Her eyes fluttered closed. *God, I want to play. I know it won't be perfect, but please. Just once more.*

She lifted her hands. Without opening her eyes, her fingers brushed the keys she knew better than she knew her own body. The opening notes of a song seemed to play themselves. Franz Liszt's *Liebestraum*. She didn't stop to consider the selection. Who else would she play but Liszt?

The abused tendons of her left hand protested the unaccustomed activity, but she continued with ruthless determination. She couldn't quite make the stretch, and faltered badly several times. It didn't matter. She was playing, and her soul responded to the music. The harmonics enthralled her, swept her away.

I'm doing it, God. I'm doing it.

Tears leaked between her closed lids to run in rivers down her cheeks. She didn't stop to wipe them away, couldn't take her hands from the keys. The romantic swells of melody pulled her in and urged her forward, then plunged her beneath a thunderous waterfall of pure joy. She welcomed the flood, embraced it, and let it wash away the grime of tragedy she had collected over the past year.

Not until the piece ended did she open her eyes. Her soul vibrated within her, sparkling and clean and refreshed with awe from the gift she'd been given. Robert had been right. God hadn't taken away her music after all. It had been there all along, just waiting for her to have enough faith to touch the piano again.

"Thank you, God." Her whisper caressed the air as moments before her fingers had caressed the Schimmel's keys. "Thank you."

Chapter 28

Tuesday, December 6

At seven fifty-five, Jill parked the SUV on the curb, behind three huge buses that lined the street in front of Harbor Square. Despite her and Nana's request, the nursing home staff did not have Mom ready to leave when she arrived at seven. Though frustrated, Jill had calmly requested the help of an aide to get her mother dressed.

The tight-lipped nurse responded, "We're short staffed today. You'll have to do it yourself."

Jill did, wondering if the aides had all called in sick so they could join the evacuation.

She switched off the vehicle's engine and peered at the woman in the passenger seat. "We're here, Mom."

Mom was having a good day, despite the rocky beginning. She'd enjoyed the short drive over, watching the sights through the window with more attention than Jill had seen her display for days. At the moment, she stared through the windshield at the activity in the small community park. Her expression displayed, if not comprehension, at least interest.

Jill followed her gaze. The scene in Harbor Square was certainly interesting.

A mob double the size of the one at the press conference crowded the small square. An invisible barrier divided them. Signs floated high above the heads of both halves. On one side she spotted, "Evacuate the Crazies from Seaside Cove," and others with similar sentiments. Wincing, she tore her gaze from them. The crowd on the other side of the park included the man with dreadlocks who had made the front page of the *Metro News* this morning. His sign, waving proudly above his head, proclaimed the end of the world at 10:05 this morning. Police officers paced between the two groups. Two white vans sporting the logos from CBC and CTV Halifax, both with satellite-shaped antennae sprouting from the top, had actually pulled up on the sidewalk, and she caught a glimpse of a giant video camera weaving its way through the crowd. Apparently, the news had decided to go for live coverage of the event.

A small group separated themselves from the supporters and approached the SUV, Nana's shining red head among them.

"Here's Nana, Mom."

Jill stepped out of the vehicle and the Sign Brigade rushed to circle her, their excited chatter a jumble of words.

"Guess what?" Mrs. Fontaine elbowed Mrs. Cramer out of the way and planted herself in front of Jill. "My son and daughter-in-law took the kids out of school for the day and went to Halifax."

"You mean they finally came around?" Considering Becky's abrupt removal of Kaylee from piano lessons, Jill could hardly believe the woman had changed her mind.

Mrs. Fontaine clasped her hands, eyes gleaming. "No, of course not. They tried to tell me they'd planned this day as a family outing for weeks, but I know better. They're not willing to risk us being right, but they don't want to admit it."

"I suspect a lot of people have done the same," Mrs. Montgomery said. "They believed us, but they don't want to become targets. The cowards."

A smirk settled on Mrs. Cramer's face. "My family is all here." She waved a hand behind her, toward the crowd.

"How did it go at the nursing home?" Nana peered through the window, where Mom sat in the passenger seat watching them.

Jill grimaced. "Don't ask."

She got the wheelchair out of the back and wheeled it around to the door while Nana helped Mom out of the car. When she was seated, Jill straightened and scanned the crowd.

"Where's Greg?" She'd expected him to be here already.

"I haven't seen him." Nana busied herself tucking a warm blanket around Mom's legs. None of the other ladies would meet her gaze.

Worry nibbled at her mind like a mouse on a piece of cheese. Had something happened to him? An accident, maybe? Or what if he changed his mind? A sick feeling settled in her stomach.

"I'd better call him."

She leaned into the SUV and grabbed her purse, then fished out her cell phone. The screen informed her that she'd missed a call from Greg. He must have called while she was inside the nursing home. With trembling fingers, she punched in the numbers to listen to his message.

"Hey, beautiful." At the sound of his voice, some of the tension left her knotted muscles. "The roads are awful out near the orchard. I'm going to be later than I thought. It'll probably be nine thirty before I get there, and then I need to take care of something quick. But don't worry. I'll meet you at Harbor Square into time to get out … own … by ten." Static interrupted, and broke up the rest of the message. " … charger at home … battery … then …" The message ended.

"Greg's going to be a little late." She slipped the phone back into her purse.

Concern drew deep creases in Nana's forehead. "We can't hold up the buses. Call him back and tell him you'll meet him in Halifax."

"I can't. I think his battery died at the end of the message." She poured confidence into her smile. "Don't worry. We'll follow you as soon as he gets here. Now let's get Mom on the bus before she gets chilled."

Nana didn't look convinced, but she wheeled her daughter toward the front bus, which had been fitted with a ramp. The driver wheeled her inside and helped Jill secure the chair in a special section on the front row designed for wheelchairs. When she was settled, Jill arranged the blanket snugly around her legs, then squatted down on her haunches so she could look into Mom's face.

"There. You're all set. I'll see you at the mall in a couple of hours. You can help me pick out Nana's Christmas present."

She started to rise, but Mom's right hand shot out toward her. It waved erratically for a few seconds before coming to rest on Jill's arm. Fingers clutched at her coat sleeve.

Startled, Jill looked into her mother's face. "What is it, Mom?"

Her lips moved, but no sound came out. The eyes closed for a second, then opened again. Intensity gleamed in their brown depths as she tried again.

"Tthhhhhaaaank ooo."

The whisper came out harsh, and it was the most beautiful music Jill had ever heard. Emotion clogged her throat as tears rushed to her eyes. She knew. The moments of clarity may be few, but Jill was grateful that this was one. She gathered her mother into a hug.

"I love you, Mom."

If only she could stay and prolong this moment. But the minutes were ticking away, and there weren't that many left. She wiped away tears as she descended the bus steps to the street.

"All right, everybody!" Nana's bellow projected over the noise of the crowd and echoed off the side of the brick building at the far end of Harbor Square. "We're ready to load."

A cheer went up from the evacuees, and was matched by jeers and boos from the protesters' side of the park. Photographers rushed to the buses ahead of the others and positioned their cameras to broadcast the sight of people boarding. The Sign Brigade divided themselves into three pairs and took up sentry duty by each bus.

Mrs. Tolliver beamed like a gray-headed lighthouse and waved her hands above her head. "Over here to my bus, everyone! I brought games to play on the road."

Mrs. Mattingly rolled her eyes heavenward.

"Ms. King!"

A child's shout drew Jill's attention to the line of people ready to board the bus on the end. She picked out Mariah standing beside her mother and a man who bore a startling resemblance to Mrs. Cramer. She returned the child's wave.

A few people ahead of the Cramers, another familiar face looked her way. Jill's mouth fell open when her gaze connected with Doreen's. The therapist gave a sheepish smile and a slight shrug, then hefted a small suitcase and climbed on board.

"Jill, look who's here." Nana's voice drew her attention to the line nearest her.

She stood beside Reverend and Mrs. Hollister.

Jill went to shake their hands. "Reverend, don't you have a car?"

"Yep." His eyes twinkled. "I just wanted to join in the fun."

Jill's delighted laughter rang in the cold morning air. "Well, we're glad to have you along. We sure could use your prayers today."

"Already done, my dear." He patted her hand before releasing it. "Already done."

With a wide smile for the hovering television camera, Reverend Hollister disappeared into the bus.

Loading took longer than expected. Nana marched between the buses barking like a drillmaster, to the delight of the media. Judging by the way she paused every so often to turn a broad smile toward the cameras, she didn't mind one bit. Jill did her best to ignore them. Though they prodded her with questions and thrust cameras in her face, she remained tight-lipped. She'd already said everything she needed to say. Eventually they gave up.

By the time every evacuee found a seat and got their belongings settled, the clock read almost nine o'clock. Nana, wearing a worried frown, hurried across the street to where Jill stood beside the loaded SUV.

"Are you sure it's wise to wait for Greg? What if he doesn't come?"

The same thought had occurred to Jill several times. She'd listened to his message a second time, just to reassure herself, but worry nagged at her. What if he had car trouble and couldn't get word to her?

"He'll come." She poured more confidence into her voice than she felt. "I'll meet you at the mall."

With obvious reluctance, Nana hugged her and climbed onto

the front bus. Jill waved as the buses pulled away, leaving the air full of exhaust fumes. Hands waved back from dozens of windows.

When they were lost from view, the media cameras turned toward her. Jill ducked into the SUV and locked the doors before they could approach. Greg wouldn't arrive for half an hour, but she couldn't wait here or they'd plague her the entire time. As she pulled away from the curb, the crowd of protesters began to wander away in twos and threes.

She followed the bus route to the main intersection of Harbor and Elm. There she sat at a stoplight and watched the progress as they curved around the wide bay that marked the south end of town. A heavy wind off the main harbor whipped the waters against the giant black rocks that lined the semicircular shore. Spray rose in the air like a thousand fountains. When the buses turned away from the bay at the far end, it looked as if they were disappearing behind a moving wall of mist.

The traffic light changed, but Jill didn't take her foot off the brake. What to do for half an hour? She didn't want to go home. She'd said her good-byes there. Either she'd see Nana's house tonight, or she wouldn't.

A car behind her honked. She made a snap decision and took her foot off the brake. The lighthouse stood sentinel over the northern edge of town. Before the accident she used to go there and sit on the rocks, watching the ships go by on their way to and from Halifax Harbor. She'd never learned to swim. While all the other kids her age had been swimming and fishing and otherwise enjoying the benefit of living near the ocean, she'd devoted her time to practicing her piano. But that didn't stop her from losing herself in the mesmerizing motion of the constantly moving water. That's what she'd do. The lighthouse was a great place to think.

Greg parked his car outside the café and gathered the papers he'd gotten from his office on the way into town. Icy roads had taken much longer to navigate than he thought, and he was late. If he hadn't called Rowe and the others last night to arrange this meeting, he would have left without following through with his plan. But it was important that he do it today, now, before he left town. It was the statement he wanted to make.

As he jogged toward the door, he passed what he at first thought was an empty car. At the same moment he recognized Pat Allen in the passenger seat, Carl rounded the corner from the front of the building.

The B&B owner stopped short. "Greg. We'd decided you weren't coming."

"Sorry. I got held up. Roads are awful." He pointed in the direction Carl had just come. "Do you have a minute? I have something important to say."

The man glanced at his watch. "Uh, not really. We're late as it is. The others are still in there, though. Why don't you give me a call tomorrow?"

"All right."

Carl took a step toward his car, then hesitated. "I want to tell you something. Probably should have told you before." He glanced over his shoulder. "I know how Samuels got his hands on that video he sent to the news."

That pricked Greg's attention. "Oh, yeah?"

He nodded. "Rowena gave it to him."

"Rowe?" Greg felt as if he'd been delivered a blow to the head.

"Yeah. Not directly, but I was there when it happened. Samuels was in the café and she made a big show of saying how you hadn't been by to pick up the video she made of your meeting. Everybody saw her write your name on that envelope and put it up on the shelf by the register. When Samuels left, he slipped that envelope in his pocket when he thought nobody was looking. But I saw. And so did Rowena. I saw her watching, and then she turned her back and ignored it. I knew she'd put it there on purpose. Practically handed it to him with a bow on it."

Greg's mind worked to process that information. He'd been betrayed. Sabotaged.

Correction. Not him. Rowe wouldn't betray him personally, because she liked him. Too much, in fact. She'd been trying to sabotage his relationship with Jill.

A bitter laugh forced its way out of his lungs. "Turns out Jill was right after all."

"Speaking of that," Carl glanced at his watch. "Me and the missus have got to get going. You too, don't you think?"

The reason for Pat's presence in the car became clear. This time Greg's laugh was genuine. "You're evacuating."

A dark red flush stained the man's cheeks. "Yeah, well. Never hurts to be cautious, you know?"

"Go." Greg waved him toward the car. "I'm right behind you."

"You'd better hurry," Carl said as he rounded the front bumper. "You don't have much time."

Greg entered the restaurant at a jog.

Chapter 29

Jill cranked the SUV's heater as far as it would go. Her time on the rocks by the lighthouse had left her cold and wet with salty spray, but at the same time refreshed, even energized. The December wind gathered a frigid chill from the Atlantic Ocean and blew it into the harbor, clearing the rocks of snow and whipping the water into a furious dance. Watching was exhilarating in a way nothing else could be. She'd forgotten.

She shifted into reverse and the vehicle started to roll backward. The rear end lifted as though the tires had climbed a short ridge of some sort. A rock, maybe? Jill stepped on the brakes, but not quick enough. The vehicle bounced as the tires rolled over a bump.

Gingerly, she pressed on the gas pedal. The engine revved, but the SUV did not move. She shifted into drive and gave it a little gas. Nothing. She pressed the pedal farther and the back end slid sideways, but the tires merely spun. She was stuck.

Ignoring a tickle of alarm that brushed at the base of her skull, she put the vehicle in park and got out to inspect the tires. The ridge she'd driven over proved to be a long railroad tie that marked the end of the parking space. It lay buried in snow.

Behind it, her spinning tires had cut deep gashes through the snowy slush, all the way down to the soft mud beneath. The more she spun the tires, the deeper they would sink in the mud.

Maybe she could move the railroad tie. She bent and tugged, but it was too heavy, and frozen into the ground besides. With a gloved hand on the SUV to steady herself, she made her way to the rear of the vehicle to inspect the other tire. When she did, her foot sank in slushy snow up to her calf.

Rising panic threatened to clog her throat. What if she couldn't get out in time? How stupid she'd been to come to the lighthouse. Nobody knew where she was. Would Greg come looking for her, or would he assume she'd already left and go on without her?

Fighting desperation, she fished her cell phone out of her jacket pocket. Maybe he'd turned his phone back on.

Thick gloves made her fingers clumsy. The phone tumbled out of her hand and landed in the wet snow. With a gasp, she bent to retrieve it. Her foot slid and she tumbled forward, landing on her knee with a painful jolt. Her cell phone! Her knee had driven it down into the watery slush. She ripped off a glove and scrambled to retrieve the phone, a sob caught in her throat.

The screen was blank.

"No." The word came out in a long, thin wail.

I'll dry it off. Maybe that will help.

The only piece of dry clothing she wore was her sweater. She unzipped her jacket and rubbed the phone with quick, frenzied gestures. Fingers nearly frozen, she stabbed at the power button. The screen remained blank.

She lifted her face toward the cloud-covered sky. "God, please help me."

Her shout was muffled by the sound of the waves crashing against the rocky shore.

I've got to stay calm. She closed her eyes and drew in a deep breath. *Maybe if I wedge something flat beneath the tires, they'll have something to grip. But what?*

She opened her eyes and scanned the area for a board, or anything flat. Nothing. What about small rocks? If she dug beneath the packed snow that covered the parking lot, she could fill the ruts behind her tires with gravel.

A glance at her watch clenched her stomach muscles into knots with a sense of urgency. After nine thirty. No, gravel would take too long. She needed a quicker solution.

Her gaze fell on the SUV's rear window. The boxes containing their belongings filled the rear compartment.

Cardboard! I can wedge flat pieces of cardboard beneath the tires.

Desperate hope swelled in her chest as she struggled to her feet. She opened the hatch and began pulling items out, tossing them into the snow. When she uncovered a large enough box, she turned it on its side and dumped the contents. The towels that wrapped Nana's precious dishes went to pack the muddy gouges beneath the tires. Nana would understand. Then she ripped the box in two equal pieces and wedged them as far beneath the tires as she could manage. If she could roll backward, she'd fill the gap with more stuff from yet another box, and drive right over the top of the railroad tie.

When her makeshift ramp was as sturdy as she could make it, she returned to the driver's seat. She closed her eyes. "Please, God. Let this work." Breath caught in her chest, she shifted into reverse and pressed gently on the gas pedal.

The tires rolled backward, freed from their ruts.

Five precious minutes later, Jill pulled away from the lighthouse parking lot. Her muscles clenched into knots when she saw the clock on the vehicle's dashboard. Almost a quarter till ten. Greg would probably be frantic with worry. Either that or he'd assume she had left him behind. She turned left onto Harbor Street and pressed the gas pedal.

As she feared, there was no sign of him or anyone else at Harbor Square. She pulled alongside the curb where the buses had been earlier, her hands tightly gripping the steering wheel. Did Greg leave? Or had he changed his mind?

No, ridiculous. That was a paranoid thought. She'd seen love shining in his eyes yesterday, had heard it in his voice when he left the message this morning. *Hey, beautiful.* His greeting sent a thrill through her every time she heard it.

I must have just missed him. He knew where the buses were going. I'll find him waiting for me with Nana and Mom at the shopping mall.

With a whispered prayer that Greg had, indeed, gone on ahead, she took her foot off the brake and stomped on the gas pedal. The tires skidded across a patch of ice, but then found purchase and the SUV shot forward.

Traffic was lighter than normal today. She didn't encounter many cars as she sped along Harbor Street. How many of the Cove residents heeded her warning and evacuated quietly on their own? Her lips curved into a smile.

The next moment, it faded. How many residents hadn't?

Thrusting that thought behind her as she reached the far side of town, she turned onto the road that bordered the bay.

"Glad you finally decided to show up, Bradford." Richard Samuels, seated in the same chair where Dad had been yesterday, made a point of looking at his watch. "We'd just about decided we'd been the victims of a juvenile prank, waiting here for you to show up while you left town with the lunatics."

"Sorry I'm late." Greg ground out the words through gritted teeth. He couldn't force himself to look at Rowe, and Samuels's smirk made him feel sick. Instead, he directed his apology toward Mitch.

"What's going on, Greg?" Mitch turned in the chair to face him.

"Let me get you some coffee." Rowe started to stand, but Greg waved her down.

"I don't have time. I've got to meet Jill and get out of town before 10:05."

Samuels leaned back in his chair, his arms folded across his chest. "So you're going through with this farce. I thought you were smarter than that."

Mitch pushed his coffee mug away, shaking his head. "When you didn't hold a press conference last night, I knew you'd made a decision. I hope you know what you're doing, Greg."

"Oh, I do." Greg set the folder full of papers he carried on the table, then rested both hands on top of it and leaned forward. "Actually, when I finally thought about it, there wasn't really a decision to be made. I've had political goals for a long time, but that's just a job. In the long run it doesn't matter. What matters is my fiancée. Jill needs my support today, and she's going to need it even more in the days to come, no matter what happens." He smiled and looked directly at Rowe. "I love her."

Understanding dawned in Rowena's eyes. She lowered her head to stare at her hands folded in her lap.

Mitch heaved a sigh. "I think it's a mistake, but if that's what you want to do, we'll have to deal with it." His gaze slid across the table toward Samuels.

"No, actually, we don't have anything to deal with." Greg straightened. "I'm pulling out."

"What?" Rowena's head jerked up.

"That's right. I'm withdrawing from the election."

"What— " Mitch appeared to grasp for words. "What does your father think of that?"

"Oh, he wasn't crazy about the decision." A gross understatement. Dad had kept him up most of the night, trying to talk him out of withdrawing his candidacy. "He'll get over it."

Samuels studied him carefully. "What about your tourism plan?"

Greg slid the folder across the table toward him. "It's yours. I strongly believe it's the right thing to do, whether I'm at the helm or not."

Samuels's eyebrows crept up his forehead. "I have to admit, it's a good plan. I think it has merit." He placed a hand on the folder and drew it toward him.

Greg glanced at the clock on the wall. He'd intended to take only a minute here, but it was already nearly ten o'clock. Jill was probably long gone. Well, he'd go after her. He'd made his statement here, and he'd done it *before* 10:05. Hopefully, Jill would accept his explanation.

"Gotta run. See you around." He let his grin circle the table. "Maybe."

He exited the café at a run. The wind battered against him

on the way to the car. It sure was strong today. Must be getting ready to blow in a storm. As he opened his car door, he glanced out at the dark clouds blowing inland across the choppy harbor waters.

Just in time to see the two ships collide.

Chapter 30

Jill aimed the SUV's heater vents at her frozen hands as she navigated the gentle curve of the road. A gigantic *crack* echoed over the bay's churning waters. Startled, she turned around to glance over her shoulder. There, in the harbor just beyond the mouth of the bay. Two ships, one huge and the other smaller. She pulled to the side of the road and rolled to a stop, then unfastened her seatbelt and stuck her head out the window to get a better view. The ships had crashed into each other. The front of the smaller ship was embedded in the bow of the bigger one. Sailors scurried around, looking from this distance like specks being blown by the wind. As she watched, flames erupted on the damaged deck of the large ship.

Flames.

Flames, voracious and vicious, roared in the cold air, whipped into a fury by a morning breeze that drew its strength from the icy Atlantic.

Her dream! This was it. She pulled her head back inside the car and looked at the dashboard clock. But it was only ten o'clock. It wasn't supposed to happen for five more minutes.

And that was *it*? A collision in the harbor, a burning ship? That was the major disaster? They'd evacuated Seaside Cove for this?

How utterly embarrassing.

Her laughter filled the SUV. What a relief! There had been an incident, which validated her dream, though nothing that even came close to the scale she predicted. No doubt she'd be the butt of many jokes and finger-pointing in the weeks to come, but so what? In this case she'd rather be wrong than right. Isn't that what she'd told Greg?

She started the engine and stomped on the accelerator, one eye on the rearview mirror to watch the ships. The SUV shot forward. The road curved around the bay, and the flames leaping into the sky from the deck of the burning ship disappeared from her rearview mirror. She reached up to adjust the angle.

The tires skidded on a wide patch of ice. The back end of the vehicle slid sideways. Her heart slammed a panicked rhythm against her ribcage. Without thinking, she hit the brake pedal.

Wrong move.

Release the brake! Turn the wheel into the spin!

Before she could follow the thought with action, the SUV flipped.

~

When Greg drove down Harbor Street, his eyes were drawn again and again to the two ships in the harbor. Jill had been right after all. This was the disaster she'd dreamed of. She'd been saying fire all along, and also cold. The fire was there for everyone to see, and the strong winds were as cold as an arctic storm.

He approached the center of town, where the wooden docks ran alongside the road on the harbor side, and a short line of cars in front of him slowed his progress to a crawl. Drivers inched forward, their heads hanging out their windows to watch the burning ship, which was slowly drifting from the center of the narrow water passageway toward the shore. To his left, a crowd had gathered on the docks. People lined the old wooden slats, pointing. A couple of television vans had parked in the small lot at the far end of the dock, their cameramen busy filming the "disaster." It was a pretty spectacular sight, actually. Fingers of flames punched at the clouds and belched black smoke into the sky.

"Oh, come on," Greg muttered at the car in front of him. "Pull off the road if you want to gawk."

He smacked the horn, which resulted in a rude gesture from the driver. The car accelerated, though only by inches. It crept toward the south end of the dock and drew alongside the television vans, then stopped again.

With a frustrated grunt, Greg jerked backward against the seat. The clock read 10:02. Jill's timing was a little off, and she certainly overestimated the effect of the disaster, but she had the date right. December 6. A soft snort escaped when he remembered telling her she'd dreamed up the date because of the historical significance of the Halifax Explosion. Funny, that had been caused by a collision in the harbor too.

A chill marched across his skin and raised the hair along his arms. His gaze snapped toward the harbor. The smaller one was a cargo vessel, headed away from Halifax out to sea. The large one faced the opposite direction, toward the city. She sat low in the water, weighed down with a full load of cargo. A huge tanker.

Moisture evaporated from his mouth. What cargo did a tanker carry?

Fuel.

He jerked the gearshift lever into Park and leaped out of the car in the middle of the street.

"Get out of here!" His shout bellowed toward the people on

the dock. A few heads turned his way as he ran toward them, arms waving above his head. "Don't you see what that ship is? She's a tanker! It's not safe here."

A few people backed slowly away, but most didn't move. The television cameras swung around toward him.

"Hey!" Greg ran in their direction. "You've got to warn them. She's going to blow!"

Movement in the distance drew his gaze. A lone vehicle on the road that rounded the wide bay sped out of town. He knew that SUV. It belonged to Ruth. That was Jill. She'd waited for him. But now she was leaving. Good. At least she'd be at a safe distance when —

The rear of the vehicle skidded sideways. Horror bludgeoned his brain as the SUV spun in a full three-sixty, then flipped. It rolled side-over-side not once, but three times. Off the road. Across the giant, jagged rocks that formed the shore. Into the bay.

"Jill!"

The scream ripped from somewhere deep in his chest as he ran for his car. He twisted the wheel and stomped on the gas. The car shot into the center of the street, around the left of the traffic that blocked him, that kept him from Jill. Horns blasted as oncoming cars swerved out of his way. He ignored them, his thoughts fixed on Jill.

She can't swim.

He punched the pedal all the way to the floor. The road sped beneath his tires. The five kilometer drive seemed to take hours, but he didn't waste time looking at the clock. He had to get to Jill.

When he reached the place, he jerked the car onto the grassy side of the road. The transmission protested with a loud clank when he jerked the gearshift into Park long before the tires had stopped moving. He didn't care, but leaped from the car and ran across the road.

The SUV was almost completely submerged upside down in the water. Waves washed over the mangled metal underside. Tires pointed toward the sky like a grotesque bug, belly-up in death.

A choked sob squeezed through Greg's fear-swollen throat. He had to get her out of there.

He was moving toward the water when the tanker exploded.

The blast shook the ground beneath his feet with the force of an earthquake. A blinding white flash burned into his eyes. He blinked to clear his vision, and when he looked again, a gigantic black mushroom erupted into the sky over the harbor. A powerful nausea almost dropped him to his knees at the certain fate of the people on the dock, for probably a good distance inland.

He choked down the rising acid in his throat and climbed across the jagged black rocks toward the water, unzipping his jacket so it wouldn't weigh him down. Jill needed him.

A roar reached his ears when he shed his jacket on the rocks. He glanced up to see a monstrous wall of water thundering toward him.

He dove seconds before the tsunami struck.

Chapter 31

No air. Couldn't breathe. Her lungs were going to burst.

Panic gripped Jill with an icy claw and pulled her downward. Ferocious waves buffeted her body back and forth, sweeping her along in a whirlwind of motion.

Her head broke the surface long enough to gasp air into ravaged lungs. Then she was sucked beneath the churning waters again.

Her floundering hands brushed against something hard. Moving with an instinct she didn't know she possessed, she kicked her legs with every ounce of strength she could muster, grappling for purchase on the rock. Her head surfaced again, and one foot found a hold. She wedged her shoe in place and hugged the boulder with all her might, the waves pounding against her back, until she could catch her breath and gather the strength to climb.

Cold, so cold she could barely move. A cold so deep it sapped her energy. She couldn't shiver, could barely feel the granite beneath her hands as she labored to pull herself out of the water. A smoky chemical smell choked her as she climbed, one laborious centimeter at a time, over the ragged shoreline and onto the sparse grassy hillside beyond.

She rolled onto her back and collapsed.

~

Moments later, or maybe hours later, she awoke. The sulfurous stench still filled her nostrils. She sat up and took stock of her surroundings. She'd crossed the entire width of the bay and come up on the opposite shore, tossed by the waves that churned the water to foam. Beyond the mouth of the bay, the narrow harbor channel was empty. There was no sign of the two ships that had collided. They must have exploded, hence the chemical smell.

My dream was true. There was a disaster.

The knowledge brought no satisfaction, but churned in her stomach. She didn't want to be right.

Smoke billowed into the sky from dozens of sources in the direction of Seaside Cove. Her home. She covered her mouth with a hand, her eyes straining to see the buildings beyond a swell in the land.

The hillside behind her sloped steeply upward. From the top, she might be able to see the town. She struggled to her feet and climbed, using her hands to balance herself on the loose bare soil. The wind at her back deposited a wet, soggy dust on her clothing. After a moment she realized it was ash. At the top of the hill, she stood upright and turned.

The shoreline of Seaside Cove lay in ruins. The buildings that lined Harbor Street had been reduced to charred remains. Structures on the street behind them hadn't fared much better. Black smoke rose from smoldering ruins, and active flames roared from some unseen source. From a distance the faint wail of sirens carried to her across the water. She should be able to see the southern edge of the dock from here. Instead, she saw nothing but debris cluttering the rocky shore.

Her heart twisted. How many people died? The protesters at Harbor Square this morning? The newspeople? Mr. and Mrs. Herndon from church? Rowena?

And what about Greg?

Painful sobs drove her to her knees. *Oh, Greg. Please be all right. If you waited for me ...*

A noise behind her told of someone's approach. Another survivor? She scrubbed tears on her sleeve and squinted to see.

A man strode up the hill with no visible effort, his erect form upright. As he neared she glimpsed silver-streaked dark hair that fell in a swoop across his forehead above piercing dark eyes. A deep cleft punctuated his chin.

Robert?

Numb, Jill couldn't move. Had she lost her mind? He looked flesh-and-blood real. Solid. But that was impossible. She'd made Robert up, hadn't she?

Sensitive lips curved into a wide smile as he approached. "Hello, Jill."

He clasped her hands in the greeting of friends, and his long, artistic fingers pressed hers firmly. He *was* real.

"Oh, Robert." She squeezed his hands. "I didn't make you up, did I? You really were in New York."

His smile deepened. "I was."

"First, the subway crash and then this." She unclasped one of her hands and gestured in the direction of Seaside Cove.

Wait. Why is Robert in Seaside Cove? Confused, she shook her head in an attempt to clear her whirling thoughts. "When did you get into town?"

"I wasn't in town, dear." The eyes that looked into hers softened. "I just arrived. I came to speak with you."

She whirled around to scan the direction from which he came. There were no cars. How did he get here, then? It was as though he just appeared.

A shiver marched across her flesh. Was this yet another crazy nightmare? A new one? "Are you some kind of … angel?"

His answer was a warm smile.

Shock waves zipped down her spine. "Then … I'm dead? You're coming to take me to heaven?"

Joyful laughter rolled down the hillside and echoed back from the water below. "No, dear. The first time I came to you, my mission was to give you comfort, and to encourage you to be strong for the trial that was to come. That's why I called myself Robert."

"But …" Jill shook her head. "Robert Schumann's dream was taken from him. He went insane."

"You only know what the history books have told you. I know his heart, and his mind." His voice became as tender as his smile. "He suffered an injury like yours, but continued to use his gift, even though the outcome was different than he planned. He blessed so many more people as a composer than he would have as a pianist. I thought you'd be encouraged by the reminder that someone else who shared your dream overcame a hand injury and went on to accomplish marvelous things." He touched her lightly on the shoulder. "I'm sorry you were frightened. That wasn't my intention."

The truth of his words pierced Jill's soul, and left a resonating peace as their echo faded away. Robert Schumann hadn't lost his gift after all. And neither had she.

Robert lifted his face to the sky, and then lowered it to catch her in a joyful gaze. "I've been sent to deliver a message." He raised a hand and placed it on her head. Soothing warmth spread through her at the contact, calming her fears. "One day, when your time here is finished, you'll hear these words from the Master himself. For now, I carry his message to you: *Well done.*"

The words fell on her ears with the softness of a caress. Jill's heart leaped in her chest at the sound of them. "I did the right thing?"

Tears sprang to Jill's eyes at the tenderness in his answer. "You did the right thing. Your Father is most happy with you. He loves you. And one day he will delight in hearing you play in the most glorious concert of all eternity. There's music to be played that only you can play, for the most important Audience of all."

Joy illuminated his face. Seeing it, sunshine flooded Jill's soul. "An eternal concert." Awe reduced her voice to a whisper.

Robert's smile deepened. "But not yet, child. Your song here hasn't ended. There are many stanzas yet to play."

He lifted a hand in a blessing, and a delicious serenity washed through her body. She closed her eyes in the moment before his finger touched her forehead—

—and gasped at the searing pain of breath flooding her air-starved lungs. She choked and coughed, and drew another breath. She was cold, colder than she'd ever been, as cold as a frozen grave. Sharp pebbles pressed through snow into her back, and the sound of the surf pounding on a rocky shore filled her ears. In the distance, sirens wailed. An uncontrollable shiver took possession of her body as she drew in a third life-giving breath.

"Thank you, God." Sobs constricted a familiar voice nearby. "She's alive."

Lifting her eyelids took every ounce of strength she possessed. When she did, a beloved face loomed inches above hers. Greg. Her lips still tingled with the touch of his, when he'd breathed life back into her.

"You're alive." She coughed, inhaled, and tried again. "You made it."

Tears streamed down his cheeks as he gathered her in his arms. "So did you. Thank God, so did you."

Drawing a deep breath, she focused on his eyes, eyes that held more love than she could process. "I did the right thing, Greg. He said I did the right thing."

"Who said? No, don't get up. Help is on its way."

"He said," she murmured and then she fell silent. She could share the glorious message later. For now, it was enough to draw warmth from Greg's arms around her, supporting her as he had done throughout this entire ordeal. Whether Robert was an angel or a myth didn't matter. The truth of his message resonated in her soul. *Well done.*

Epilogue

Sunday, December 11

Sunday, a much smaller crowd gathered in the sanctuary. When Reverend Hollister made his way down the center aisle toward the exit, the organist played the opening chords of the closing hymn. *Joyful, joyful all ye nations* — the music reverberated through the church. Jill scanned the congregation as she gathered her purse and coat from the pew. The absence of so many familiar faces caused a throbbing ache in her chest.

"Seems there are a lot of visitors today." Greg's whisper tickled her ear as he helped her into her coat.

"That's a good sign." Jill made eye contact with a stranger a few rows back and returned the woman's shy smile. "They know the church is where they'll find hope and purpose again."

From the choir loft, Nana flapped her hands in the air to attract Jill's attention. When Jill looked at her, she pointed toward the parking lot and mouthed *I'll meet you at the car.* Jill nodded. The three of them were going to visit Mom in her new nursing care center. The nursing staff had welcomed her, and she was settling in nicely. Tonight they were going to Greg's parents' house for dinner. Jill indulged in a smile at the memory of Harold's blustering apologies yesterday. *I'm an old fool. But I had no idea! How could you have known?*

She followed Greg into the center aisle and they moved with the crowd toward the sanctuary exit. The line inched forward as folks stopped to exchange brief words with Reverend Hollister before leaving the church. When they were almost there, a hand clapped onto Greg's shoulder.

"There you are. We wanted to catch you before you left."

They turned to find Carl Allen and Mitch Landry behind them. Mitch leaned heavily on a crutch. His bruised and bandaged face bore evidence of his narrow escape from the fire that claimed two lives in the café. Both men gave an awkward nod of greeting to Jill, but barely met her gaze. She suppressed a sigh. Though many of the townspeople had treated her with varying degrees of awe since the explosion, some appeared embarrassed when they encountered her, as though ashamed of their disbelief. Jill wasn't sure which reaction she disliked more — the stares or the whispered awe.

"We'd like to meet with you tomorrow," Mitch told Greg. "Are you free around nine in the morning?"

Greg cocked his head, studying the pair. "Care to say what we'll be discussing?"

Clearing his throat, Carl admitted, "We're hoping to convince you to withdraw your withdrawal." The lines in his face deepened. "Now that Samuels isn't ..." Silence ensued at the mention of the councilman's passing. Carl cleared his throat. "We need a strong leader."

Mitch nodded, his expression solemn. "You're that leader, Greg. I hope you'll reconsider. The town is going to need you."

Jill watched Greg's face. She knew he wanted more than

ever to see his plan carried out. The task would be bigger now, since the Cove must first rebuild and renew before it could move forward. Jill was confident these men were correct. Greg was uniquely qualified to meet the challenge.

His gaze locked onto hers, and they exchanged a private smile before he addressed the men. "I'm not due in court until one tomorrow, so a morning meeting works for me. I'll be at the café at— " His eyes closed, an expression of pain crossed his features. When he opened them again, sad creases framed his eyes. "Just tell me where and I'll be there at nine."

"My house," Mitch said. "My wife will have the coffee ready."

Another wave of sorrow washed over Jill. Mitch's house wasn't far from the church, far enough away from the dock that the devastation hadn't reached there. Nana's house remained intact, but damaged. Her beloved Schimmel had survived, but Carl's inn had been destroyed by the fire that swept through town after the explosion, as had most of the businesses and homes along the harbor. The café was gone, and its owner with it. Regardless of their past conflicts, Jill mourned Rowena's passing.

Could she have done more to convince those who stayed? The question would never be answered this side of heaven.

Well done. Robert's message echoed in her mind. *One day you'll hear these words from the Master himself.* Had the vision been real, or merely another dream as she lay lifeless on the frozen ground while Greg tried to resuscitate her? It didn't matter. Jill felt the truth of the message deep in her soul.

"Your house at nine, then." Greg placed a hand at the small of Jill's back and they stepped forward to greet Reverend Hollister.

The minister's voice boomed as he took Jill's hand. "Here's our Jonah."

Heads turned her way.

Her face hot, Jill stammered a joke. "I don't know about that, but I'm planning to steer clear of whales for a while."

Reverend Hollister pressed her hand. "No need, my dear. I think you're in the clear now."

"I sure hope so, Reverend." Greg pulled her close with an arm around her waist. "We still have a lot of living to do."

Jill pressed close to him as they said good-bye and moved toward the doors. Robert had said much the same thing. Her song hadn't ended yet. There were too many stanzas yet to play. She tilted her head sideways to look up at Greg. Too much life yet to live.

Greg's hand slid down her arm and entwined her fingers with his as he pushed open the door. A lemony-yellow sun bathed the Cove in bright light today, and sparkled on the snow-covered trees. Jill inhaled the crisp, salt-scented air and whispered a prayer of thanks for life, and for love, and especially for God's music that provided the perfect accompaniment to both. Reaching for Greg's hand, she stepped outside, and into her future.

A Note from Lori and Virginia

The story we've created in *Lost Melody* is entirely fictional, but it was inspired by an actual historical event. In 1917 a catastrophe of unimaginable proportions struck Halifax, Nova Scotia. At that time, World War I raged in Europe, and Halifax Harbour became a crowded hub of activity. On December 6, a French ship named the *Mont-Blanc*, carrying 2300 tons of picric acid, 200 tons of TNT, 10 tons of gun cotton, and 35 tons of a highly explosive mixture called benzol, left the mouth of the harbor and was struck by a Norwegian vessel named the *Imo*. Fire broke out on the *Mont-Blanc*, and she drifted toward the Halifax shore where unwary spectators gathered to watch her burn. When the *Mont-Blanc* exploded, not one piece of the ship remained. Entire city blocks were flattened in the blast that was felt nearly 200 miles away. The biggest manmade explosion before the nuclear age triggered a tsunami, which crashed into the battered city. Reports of fatalities vary, but at least 1600 people lost their lives immediately, and as many as 200 within a few months. Nine thousand people were injured, most of them seriously.

Though unspeakably devastating, the legacy of the Halifax explosion is inspiring in some respects. The world responded, and assistance from many nations flooded the survivors. Halifax rebounded and rebuilt, and today is a thriving metropolis. A memorial was erected to remember those who perished, and every December 6 at 9:06 a.m., a bell rings to commemorate their loss.

Lori read an article about the Halifax explosion, and that article provided the seed for the story you've just read. Our agent brought Ginny into the picture and suggested that we might enjoy working together on a book. She was right. We got together for a weekend of brainstorming, and the story of *Lost Melody* sprouted and grew, as seeds have a tendency to do.

We spent a lot of time discussing the role of Robert in the story. Scripture is full of instances where angels are sent by God to deliver a message, and in the book of Hebrews, we're told that angels are ministering spirits sent to serve those who will inherit salvation. We hope you'll indulge us in the fictional application of those Scriptures. You might be interested to know that the ending you just read wasn't our first. If you'd like to read the original ending, we invite you to visit www.LoriCopelandandVirginiaSmith.com. We would love to hear your opinion about both endings.

We hope you enjoyed reading *Lost Melody* as much as we enjoyed writing it. Please take a moment to let us know what you thought. You can contact us through our website above, or separately at www.loricopeland.com and www.virginiasmith.org.

Acknowledgments

In writing *Lost Melody*, we called on several people who generously shared their time and expertise in various areas. In doing so, they enabled this book to exist. We are extremely grateful to Dr. Patricia Tackett, whose expertise in the area of PTSD helped define Jill's actions and feelings regarding the loss of her musical dream, and the beginning of a different kind of dream. For research on the Halifax area of Nova Scotia, we relied heavily on Janet Sketchley, who took the time to answer dozens of emailed questions and made the setting come alive to us. Huge thanks also to Gail Sattler for her insights on teaching piano lessons to kids. And thanks to Anna Zogg for proofreading at the drop of a hat. If there are any mistakes in this book regarding those areas, the fault lies entirely with the authors, and not with these four wonderful ladies.

We would also like to thank our mutual agent, Wendy Lawton, for introducing us and arranging this co-authored project. Thanks also to Sue Brower, Alicia Mey, Becky Philpott, and all the good folks at Zondervan for working so hard to make this book a success.

Lori and Ginny

Want more?
For bonus material, including an alternate ending
for Lost Melody, *please visit*
www.LoriCopelandAndVirginiaSmith.com

Share Your Thoughts

With the Author: Your comments will be forwarded to the author when you send them to *zauthor@zondervan.com.*

With Zondervan: Submit your review of this book by writing to *zreview@zondervan.com.*

Free Online Resources at www.zondervan.com

Zondervan AuthorTracker: Be notified whenever your favorite authors publish new books, go on tour, or post an update about what's happening in their lives at www.zondervan.com/authortracker.

Daily Bible Verses and Devotions: Enrich your life with daily Bible verses or devotions that help you start every morning focused on God. Visit www.zondervan.com/newsletters.

Free Email Publications: Sign up for newsletters on Christian living, academic resources, church ministry, fiction, children's resources, and more. Visit www.zondervan.com/newsletters.

Zondervan Bible Search: Find and compare Bible passages in a variety of translations at www.zondervanbiblesearch.com.

Other Benefits: Register yourself to receive online benefits like coupons and special offers, or to participate in research.